A MIND TO KILL

SIMON STANTON

A Mind To Kill

Betrayal is personal, revenge is business

Simon Stanton

Copyright © Simon Stanton 2019

Published by Simon Stanton

The right of Simon Stanton to be identified as the author of this work has been asserted by him in accordance with the Copyright, Designs and Patents Act 1988.

All characters and events in this publication are fictitious and any resemblance to real persons, living or dead, is purely coincidental.

No part of this book may be reproduced or transmitted in any form or by any means, electronic or mechanical, including photocopying, recording, or by any information storage and retrieval system, without permission in writing from the publisher.

First published, 2015

www.simonstanton.com

ONE

AFGHANISTAN - THREE YEARS BEFORE

The ground was freezing cold, the soldier could feel it through his boots, stinging his toes. The night air was colder, stinging his eyes and lips. He made a conscious effort to control his shivering, right now it was more important to remain completely still. He crouched down low, close to the freezing ground, in the partial seclusion of hard and dry bushes. He cradled his submachine gun and listened, straining to hear any sound of movement ahead.

He tried to keep his breathing under control, to lessen the mist from his nostrils and make him less visible, and to avoid misting up his night vision goggles. He looked through them into an eerie sparkling green world, penetrating the almost complete blackness of the moonless Afghan night. He adjusted the zoom and peered deeper into the village a hundred metres ahead of him, just beyond the sparse bushes which gave him a small measure of cover. His curiosity deepened and started to border on concern. There were no lights in the village, none. Even in a ramshackle collection of mud huts like this, people still had lights, even the occasional fire. But here there was just blackness and complete stillness. He scanned across the village, hut by hut, each as dark and still as the next. Somewhere there should be movement, some sign of life. The stillness whispered to him that something was very wrong. He knew that no-one lived in the surrounding area, there were only the villagers and their goats and ten million poppy plants. They'd spent a day getting here, all four of them spread out, approaching the village from different directions, inching their way along. They'd seen no-one during their approach, and no-one had seen them, but there should have been people in the village, the intelligence had shown a small population, maybe a few dozen. It was like the inhabitants had been spirited away.

Michael Sanders crouched in the darkness and thought about the situation. The intelligence had been solid, Taliban forces were using the village as an arms cache, storing rocket launchers somewhere close by. Michael and his team had a simple mission; stay invisible, get into the village, and place hidden cameras to keep it under close surveillance. For a Special Forces unit the mission was not their most challenging, but being deep in enemy territory made it dangerous enough.

A movement caught his eye, and he scanned left. He had to wait and focus before he could see the figure, but there he was. On the far side of the village, crouched by the side of hut, almost invisible even in the green glow of the image intensifier, one of his colleagues. The man was in the right location to plant another of the miniature covert surveillance cameras. The figure was completely still.

The voice came into his mind. He couldn't hear it, not like a physical voice, telepathic communication wasn't like that, but the voice was just as real as a spoken voice. 'This place is dead,' came the voice in his mind. 'There's no-one here.' He didn't need to reply.

It was an understatement to say that Michael was still only just getting used to being telepathic. He still had to remind himself every time that it was real, that he and his three colleagues really could use direct mind-to-mind communication. It was bizarre, difficult to believe, but very useful, a silent communication, completely secure against any kind of eavesdropping. With this unique ability, the four of them were a formidable fighting force.

He watched as the figure stood up and walked forwards, a deliberate act of breaking cover, a bold test of the man's belief that the village was deserted. For the first time in a long time, Michael Sanders felt a stab of anxiety, his usual unshakable confidence wobbled for a moment. If anything was going to happen, it was going to happen now, as his colleague made himself deliberately visible. He waited, and waited. Each second stretched into the next, magnifying the silence. But nothing came, no disaster, no shooting, no shouting, no-one rushing out at the appearance of an armed and obviously foreign soldier in their village.

Michael reset the zoom on his goggles and stood up. He took a moment and settled his thoughts, holding in mind the idea of his three colleagues. He spoke without speaking, being aware of the words but without vocalising them.

'The village is abandoned,' he thought/said. 'RV, position one.' His colleagues would know to rendezvous at the position chosen for the first covert camera.

Step by cautious step, he began to make his way towards his edge of the village. The single dirt track stretched from one end of the village to the other. "Village" was being generous; this was just a loose collection of mud huts and wooden shacks and goat pens. With each step his boots crunched on the cold and stony ground and he listened for any reaction from inside the huts, but none came. He reached his comrade.

'What's the point putting out the cameras? There's no-one here to watch,' said his comrade in his normal spoken voice.

From under his helmet a wisp of blond hair stuck out, he never could keep it under control, and the man's concern leaked out just as noticeably. Evan Bullock was six-foot, lean and athletic.

Michael heard something from behind and turned to see the movement in the dark of their remaining two teammates walking towards them. One of them was a big man, tall and broad-shouldered, the other was shorter and a slimmer build. The four of them stood by the side of a mud hut, black-suited figures, image intensifier goggles attached to their helmets, submachine guns cradled in their arms. They couldn't have looked more out of place, if there had been anyone to see them.

'This is like walking into a surprise party and finding there's no party, I'm really disappointed,' said the tall one, his voice deep but still whispering. Vince Marshall was an imposing figure, even in the dark.

The shorter of the four spoke. Julian Singh had a softer voice, well-spoken. 'There's no weapons cache here, this is a bullshit mission.' No-one disagreed.

'Did I miss something?' said Bullock, 'but I'm sure the briefing said there were people here.' The sarcasm in his voice was clear.

'Intel' was wrong,' said Marshall.

'No,' said Singh, 'something else is going on. This place looks like it's lived in, it's just all the people have left.'

'Why? There's nowhere to go,' said Bullock.

Michael turned to Singh. 'Find something and get a sense of what happened.'

The man moved to one of the huts, he pushed through the crude curtain covering the doorway and emerged a few moments later, carrying a blanket. He turned it over in his hands, eyes half-closed, kneading the rough material with his fingers. He half closed his eyes, as though remembering something, or trying to.

Of all their psychic abilities this was the strangest, Julian Singh's ability to connect to a physical object, and through that connect to the people who had handled it. Only two of them had that ability.

'They were sent away, all of them, ordered out,' said Singh. 'Men with guns, soldiers, like us.'

'Why?' asked Marshall.

'Can't tell,' said Singh, turning the blanket over in his hands. 'All I can sense is they were ordered out.'

'This is wrong, very wrong,' said Bullock.

Singh spoke again, 'but one stayed, he's still here.'

In a single movement the four had their weapons in hand and raised ready to fire, fingers flicking off safety catches, crouching, moving away from each other, spreading out. Singh used his right hand to motion towards one of the huts on the other side of the dirt track. They inched their way across the track to the hut, Marshall and Bullock on each side of the hanging blanket covering the opening to the hut, Michael and Singh in front. Singh's voice came into Michael's mind, and he knew into the minds of the others as well.

'He's in the hut,' said the voice, 'just inside. He's listening to us.'

With almost frightening swiftness Bullock pulled open the blanket covering the door and Marshall reached in and pulled the man bodily out onto the dirt track, the man letting out an involuntary yelp.

The man was shaking with fear his hands clasped in prayer then open towards them in prayer again, chattering away in some dialect of Pashto. The meaning of his words was unknown to the soldiers, but their intention was clear, the fear was written all over the man's face, fear they were going to kill him.

Michael looked back at Singh. 'Why's he still here?'

'Don't know, all I saw was the villagers being ordered out by the soldiers.'

'I'll find out' said Marshall, and before Michael could react, the man had his gloves off and reached for the begging villager. The man put his hands up in defence, but the soldier just slapped them out of the way and grabbed the man's head, a hand on each temple.

'Marshall, no,' Michael hissed, too late. The man on the floor stopped jabbering, his voice dropped to an occasional moan, his hands sank to his sides, and his blank eyes stared up at the man gripping his head.

The big soldier leaned over the man on the floor. 'Four of them came here, boss,' said Marshall. 'One of them spoke Pashto. Ordered the villagers to leave.'

'Why?' asked Singh.

'He said others would come, to hurt the villagers, but the soldiers would stop them, kill them, there'd be lots of shooting. This one was to tell them when the others came.'

'What is going on here?' said Bullock.

'So soldiers are coming here,' said Singh, 'and we must be the "others" he was warned about.'

'Who's coming?' asked Bullock, 'who else knows we're here.'

Marshall focused harder on the man, who let out a whimper as he succumbed to the psychic onslaught of Marshall's mental interrogation.

'He doesn't know who the soldiers are, but he is clear they're coming to kill us,' he said.

'Bastards, this isn't a surveillance mission it's a fucking ambush,' said Singh.

'How? How was he to tell them?' asked Michael.

Almost in response the man on the floor took something out from under his jacket, a small black device, sleek and modern, a single red button set in the centre of it.

'Bastard,' said Bullock. 'Radio beacon, they know we're here.'

'We need to get ready,' said Michael, 'Surprise them before they surprise us.'

'What about him?' said Bullock, motioning to the man on the floor. The man on the floor looked up, the fear shining in his eyes, the look of a man who knows his life could end at any moment.

'We take him with us,' said Michael.

There was an unpleasant wet crack as Marshall twisted the man's head violently. The man crumpled in a heap, motionless.

'Problem solved,' said Marshall.

TWO

LONDON - PRESENT DAY (2015) - MONDAY MORNING

The grey, overcast morning had settled over London and looked set to stay, making Finchley as dull as every other part of the capital. Charville Way was just another road, going from Regents Park Road down to Finchley Central Station, a stop on the Northern Line of the London Underground, although here trains ran overground. Occasional commuters walked up or down Charville Way, coming from or going to the railway station. On one side of the road, a chain-link fence and thick bushes separated the road from the railway lines, on the other side was a row of parked cars.

Michael Sanders sat in the passenger seat of the grey Audi A5 and watched, his driver sitting next to him. The car was plain, nothing to attract attention. Sanders was just as plain; average build, average brown hair, jeans and a plain, dark sweatshirt, he could have passed for an accountant on a day off. The front of the station's tired brick building was visible behind him in the car's wing mirror. He watched the commuters, one after another, some ambled down the road to the station, an occasional one hurried, no doubt late for some engagement or other. The morning rush hour had finished, the mad dash of commuters had, for the moment, subsided. Michael had no interest in these people. His target hadn't arrived yet. He glanced at the clock, another few minutes. From within the car he looked up the road towards the traffic lights where Charville Way met Regents Park Road. He looked at the cars parked at the side of the road. Even he couldn't tell which were MI5 assets and which were ordinary Londoners. The ordinary folk would have no idea who they might be standing next to, and that's exactly how it needed to be. Covert surveillance wasn't much good unless it was unseen. Michael could see one CCTV camera, on the side of a lamp-post at the far side of the traffic lights at the top of the road. He couldn't see the surveillance and communications vehicle, nicknamed the Battle Bus, but knew it was somewhere nearby.

'ETA two minutes,' crackled a man's voice from the miniature radio transceiver in his ear. Michael felt himself tense, he was ready.

Two minutes later he heard the train arrive, its brakes squealing as the train came to a halt at the station platform. Another minute and the occupants of the train started leaving the station and walking up the hill. Michael saw his target, just a glimpse in the mirror, then he focused forward, his line of sight not betraying his interest.

'Have visual,' he said, the transceiver in his ear picking up his words and transmitting them. 'Target is wearing a dark grey business suit, dark blue overcoat, carrying a black document case.' The group of commuters, having left the station building, started walking up the road, past the line of parked cars.

Michael watched as the individual walked among the commuters who made their collective way up the hill towards the traffic lights. The man he watched was very obviously the wrong side of fifty, more than slightly overweight, his remaining tufts of hair were grey and wispy. Michael waited until the group was far enough ahead.

'I'm following on foot,' said Michael as he opened the car door and got out. He started walking up the hill. In his jeans, trainers and casual sweatshirt he looked like any other civilian, blending in. Michael walked up the hill keeping a sensible distance, the group ahead had already reached the traffic lights, people going in different directions.

'Target has turned south-west on Regents Park Road,' came the voice in his ear. Spotters would watch the target and report his movement, each staying in a location or even walking in the opposite direction to the target, letting him go past them. Then they'd move and take back-streets to get ahead, always keeping the mark inside a box made of four, five, six or more spotters. They'd change tops, wigs and glasses as they went, the target would never pick them out from the crowds, but it allowed Michael to follow on foot without being seen by the target. Other security service assets (he always thought it was disrespectful to call people assets) would also keep pace, their transceivers boosting the signal from Michael's ear-piece and relaying it to the Battle Bus for onward transmission to the MI5/GCHQ network.

Michael reached the traffic lights and turned left, his target was already almost out of sight, becoming one of the many Londoners walking one way or another along the road. The other exit from the railway station would have been a more obvious choice for anyone going this way down Regents Park Road, unless you wanted time to assess if someone were following you before setting off to your true destination. Was the target practising "fieldcraft", or simply taking the long way around for no good reason? There were more people on Regents Park Road, a main road which ran into the centre of London. His target was now lost in the crowd, but Michael trusted the team, and he carried on walking.

'Do we know where he's heading?' Michael asked.

'Mr Gerald Crossley works for a printing supplies company, there are two printing companies within twenty minutes walking distance,' came the reply. The team in the Operations Centre at GCHQ in Cheltenham would be continually monitoring his location and assessing possible destinations, which "persons of interest" might live locally or be known to be in the vicinity. Computer programs would be running real-time simulations to predict possible outcomes or risks. Gerald Crossley would have no idea of the amount and power of human and technical resources the combined security services were employing to track his location and possible intentions.

Michael looked ahead. Branching off to the right was Hendon Lane. At the moment Michael was one of many walking up or down past shops, offices, cafes, restaurants, dog grooming parlours, banks and other assorted retail premises. But if they had to cross the main road it could be slow, he and his colleagues ran the risk of being more exposed. Michael realised he had been speeding up, so he slowed down, it would be unfortunate to run straight into the back of his target.

'Target has gone into Pedro's cafe, fifty metres ahead,' said the voice in his ear. All positions were relative to Michael's. He stopped. Crossley wasn't going to cross the main road. Michael had the thought that someone skilled in fieldcraft would have crossed the road, an obvious way of checking for anyone following. It was tempting to go and see what Mr Crossley was doing in the cafe, but that risked breaking cover. He'd have to wait and let the spotters do their jobs and relay the details to him. Michael had stopped next to a bench, and after checking for any chewing gum, used condoms or worse, he sat down and waited.

The spotters would walk past the cafe and each get into a location from which they could watch.

'Target has taken a seat and is talking to someone. No audio. ID pending.' One of the team would have used a covert camera to video the pair, maybe even having gone into the cafe and ordered a coffee, walking out and never looking at the pair. The picture of the other person would already be with the analysts in GCHQ, scanning their databases of facial images, cross-referencing. The result was back in moments.

'Crossley is talking to Marcus Berman, known far-right activist, multiple accounts of violent behaviour and breaches of the peace. Berman's on a level two watch list.' Michael struggled to hear some of the updates over the noise of the traffic, but he got the most important parts.

So, dear old Mr Gerald Crossley, printing supplies manager, suspected of being the leader of a secretive far-right group, was having morning coffee with a known thug and violent activist.

A new voice came in his ear. Female. He recognised it, of course, the MI5 Head of Operations. 'If Crossley and friends are planning any firebomb attacks, we need to know sooner rather than later. I suggest you have a quiet word with Crossley as soon as Berman has left.'

'Just what I was thinking,' said Michael. 'Find me somewhere quiet.'

After a few moments' pause the man's voice was back in his ear. 'Three hundred metres, left into The Avenue, two hundred metres there's a footpath goes behind bushes, limited foot traffic, it's not overlooked.'

Michael waited. This would take as long as it needed to. The spotters would tell him when Crossley or his contact moved. Surveillance would be easier if they left separately. They did.

After ten minutes came the man's voice in Michael's ear. 'Berman has left, crossing the road towards Hendon Lane,

Crossley is paying. Now Crossley's leaving, continuing southwest.' Good, he was already heading in the direction Michael needed, and the other man, Berman, was heading away and out of sight. Michael stood up and marched in Crossley's direction. He passed the blue and white front of Pedro's Cafe, an instantly forgettable purveyor of weak tea and cheap coffee. He could see Crossley ahead, walking about as quickly as any mid-fifty-year-old businessman walked.

'Sanders, going quiet,' said Michael. He pressed his finger into his ear, and there was a dull beep telling him that his earpiece had gone on mute. There were some things he didn't want others to overhear.

Michael caught up with Crossley and as he walked past the man he glanced across.

'Gerald,' Michael said with delight, a big smile across his face. 'Lovely to see you again,' and held out his hand for a handshake.

As intended this surprised Crossley who raised his hand to accept the handshake as an almost automatic reflex. Michael took Crossley's hand and let a pulse of psychic energy flow through the hand-to-hand connection. The smile faded from Crossley's face, and he stared into Michael's eyes. Crossley seemed to relax, his eyelids fluttered as his face relaxed. Then, for a moment, he tugged, trying to pull his hand back.

'It's okay Gerald, we're friends,' said Michael. He moved his hand up and down to give any curious passers-by the impression that they were shaking hands and talking, not just frozen like statues. The growing strength of Michael's psychic control was invisible to any observer, but Michael could feel it, a flow of his intention to dominate and control rushing from his mind and into Crossley's, into it and through it.

'I need to talk to you, Gerald, walk with me.' Keeping hold of Crossley's hand Michael walked him further down the road, the man complied without protest, looking a little bemused as though someone had just asked him a bizarre question. They reached The Avenue, a narrow tree-lined road, conveniently quiet. Crossley jerked his hand, surprising Michael, trying to free himself from the handshake. Michael slowed and focused his mind. He reached further with his mind through the linking hands, and felt something push back, like greeting someone and being rebuffed. Michael let the feeling approach his mind, and then he swept it away with a powerful and dominating thought. Crossley stopped pulling.

They walked down The Avenue away from the noise, distraction, and possible intrusion, away from the main road, and away from the MI5 spotters. They reached a wider part of the road and, as expected, on the right was the opening to a footpath which led off the road and around a corner, turning behind a large bush. Michael led Crossley off the road and around the corner, and now they were alone.

He kept hold of Crossley's hand. He let his mind extend out through the handshake. He felt the outer limits of Crossley's mind. It was like looking at someone from the other side of a crowded room, someone who was almost familiar. This was unexpected, there should be no distance, no separation of minds. He must tread carefully, to push too hard against a vulnerable mind could damage that mind.

'Who are you? What do you want?' asked Crossley. Michael was now annoyed, Crossley should be subdued, compliant, not arguing.

'I'm a police officer,' Michael lied. Crossley would never remember the encounter so the lie wouldn't matter, he reasoned.

'No you're not, what do you want with me?' This was becoming irritating, and Michael was considering using more mental force.

The blow to Michael's head was as violent as it was unexpected. For an overweight printing supplies manager, Gerald Crossley had a horribly strong punch. Michael collapsed into the bush, the world spinning around him, aware only vaguely of Crossley running around the corner and back onto The Avenue and out of sight.

MICHAEL STAGGERED TO HIS FEET, his head pounding. He lurched back onto The Avenue, looking left and right. Crossley had gone. With no warning that he was on the move, the spotters might miss him, especially if he'd headed away from the main road. Michael took a moment and calmed himself as best he could. He opened himself to the thoughts and feelings around him, and there it was. Crossley's panic and confusion hung in the air like a cheap perfume. The man had run away from the main road, hoping to find safety in the opposite direction. Michael could tune into Crossley's mind, like focusing on a single conversation in a crowded room. Having made physical contact with Crossley, Michael now had a persisting psychic connection, but something was different this time. The connection felt distant, weak. Between the strange quality of this connection and the banging headache, Michael was unable to reach out to Crossley's mind and exert control at a distance.

And where had that punch come from? No-one had warned him that Crossley presented any physical danger, and worse he'd missed any warning sign. He'd had a direct mind-to-mind connection with the man but got no sense that Crossley was violent. How could he have missed that?

Michael ran in the direction of the panic-sense. The Avenue ran past the backs of office blocks and their car parks, fences bordering residential properties, but the sense was always forwards. Crossley was still out of sight, he must have got a good head start. Michael had a thought that sometime soon he was going to make the man pay for that punch. He kept running. The Avenue turned to the left, and ahead it became a footpath, a canopy of trees hiding it from sight. He thought he saw a figure further down the path, running. Michael stayed in pursuit.

The easiest thing would be to call for support, to have the Battle Bus and the Audi rock up, to have GCHQ access every CCTV camera in the area, but somehow admitting that a man called Gerald had outwitted and outrun him just didn't seem the best thing to do.

'Michael, what's happening?' the female voice asked. Oh shit, this was just the one person he really didn't want to speak to right now. The figure ahead had disappeared in the shadows and the panic-sense had faded. If Crossley was beginning to think he was safe, he'd feel less afraid, and he'd be harder to track. The only way Michael could explain it to himself was that confidence just sort of didn't smell as strong as fear, not physically and not mentally.

Finally, Michael reached the end of the path, and emerged onto a residential street. Suburbia stretched out to the left and right, lines of parked vehicles, semi-detached houses, a young woman and a child standing next to a bus shelter, but no Crossley.

'Shit,' he said, rather more vocally than he meant to. The young woman glowered at him and pulled the child closer to him. He thought about asking her if she'd seen Crossley, but wasn't convinced it was worth the effort.

Left or right? Toss a coin. He stuck his finger in his ear, and the beep let him know his ear-piece was active again.

'I've lost him,' Michael said. There was a pause, not what he wanted.

'What do you mean "lost him"?' the female voice asked.

'I'll give you the details later, for the moment I'm on Manor View and Crossley is out of sight.'

Silence.

'We need to find him. If this man is planning firebomb attacks against soft targets, we need to find him now.' Michael hoped his forceful tone would dissuade anyone from coming back with the reply that it was he who lost the target. No-one did.

'Got him,' came the male voice. 'He's heading up Gravel Hill, the A504. Your quickest way is through the houses to your right and across the sports field.'

'Good. Keep the Audi close but for the moment let Crossley think he's got away.' Oh it was so tempting to call in the car and just set off in pursuit, but wrong-footing the target was more important. He knew, though, that now Eric would be on the move in the Audi, keeping it far enough away to be unobtrusive yet close enough to be on hand within moments.

Michael looked at the houses on his right. Going through a house would be difficult, occupants might object, but gardens were a different matter. He walked up the drive of the nearest house, trying to catch sight of anyone through the front windows. A wooden gate guarded the path to the side of the house, he vaulted the gate with ease and jogged down the path to the garden at the rear. He was keen to run faster, but surprising residents could be awkward, physically running into them at speed would be a significant delay. As he'd hoped, the occupants were either out working or shopping. He sprinted down the garden, clearing the ornamental pond in a single stride and then scaling the wooden fence at the end.

On the other side was the green expanse of the sports fields, several football pitches marked in faded white paint on tired grass. He sprinted across the grass, heading for the buildings on the far side. He guessed they were changing rooms, club room, offices and the like, and he hoped they had clear access out on to the main road. Breathing heavily, he skipped the low wall separating the sports field from the car park, dashed across the asphalt car park and through the gate onto the main road. He looked left and right, no sign of Crossley.

'Where is he?' he asked.

After a pause, the man's voice said, 'We lost him.'

THREE

Anna Hendrickson still sometimes had to pinch herself to remind herself that she did actually work in her dream job. She looked up over the partition between her desk and the man opposite and looked across the office. Most of this part of the building was open plan, "pods" of desks arranged to make team based work areas, though most people focused on their own computer screens. Concealed strip lights lit the office space, but most of the light came from computer screens and desk lamps. This area was in the outer part of The Doughnut, the "secret" headquarters of GCHQ, the UK Government Communications Headquarters. The building itself wasn't secret, no building that big could be secret. The Doughnut was a circular building (hence the name) in a suburb of Cheltenham, South West England. More than one hundred and eighty metres in diameter, it was home to over five thousand intelligence analysts, IT specialists and more. It was hi-tech in every respect.

Almost all the work done inside was secret. Anna had read a newspaper piece recently speculating on what surveillance work was carried out there, and she couldn't help a wry smile at how much the journalist had underestimated the work. This was the heart of the UK's electronic surveillance and intelligence gathering, and Anna was loving every minute of it. Olive skinned, black-haired, too elegant to be called a geek but she was proud of her intelligence and how she used it.

She adjusted the headset and checked the display on her communications panel. She couldn't call it a phone, it was far more than that. Her phone and workstation connected her to one of the Command & Control Centres, a room somewhere in Thames House, the MI5 headquarters building in central London. From the Command and Control room, MI5 personnel were directing a field mission, and Anna was providing communications, analysis and intelligence support. She focused back on the three large flat-panel displays in front of her. On one display multiple windows showed feeds from a selection of CCTV cameras. She noted the train on one screen and checked against the Transport for London information screen in another. She was sure TFL didn't know that GCHQ had direct access to their systems, but then that was true for most systems she was currently monitoring.

'Train on schedule into Finchley in two minutes,' she said. She tried to keep any trace of excitement out of her voice. She needed to be calm and focused and professional.

She heard in her ear a man's voice from the Command & Control Centre relay the "two minutes" notice to whoever they were supporting in the field. Anna was sometimes curious about what the mission might be, who they were supporting, what they were doing. But then this was part of the "secret" service, so she didn't ask.

Anna heard the man next to hear typing into his keyboard and then dialling into another call. Kingston, like Anna, was a senior analyst. Anna was never sure of Kingston's cultural background. His skin was dark, darker than Anna's olive, almost Mediterranean skin, his hair was thick and black and straight, and his features were distinctly not-from-around-here. Anna had never worked up the courage to ask where his family were from (he'd probably say Gloucester) or if Smith really was his family name. Kingston was part of the same team as Anna, but today working on a different activity. Their work was usually sifting through transcripts of intercepted telephone calls or emails or texts, cross-referencing with a vast assortment of other harvested data, working out who was talking to whom, and writing summaries of what might be happening or about to happen. Sometimes, and these were the good days, they got involved in more "interesting" activities. This was a really good day. She'd heard Kingston preparing for his call, running a penetration test of the Bank of England's firewalls, something Anna definitely thought was "interesting".

Anna focused on her headset, she heard a man's voice, it must be the "man in the field". The man they were tracking was wearing a dark grey business suit, dark blue overcoat and carrying a black document case. Anna scanned the feed from a CCTV camera, looking down the road towards the exit from Finchley Central Station. She saw the group of commuters walking up the road, the image was grainy and indistinct. With a couple of clicks of the mouse, she engaged a program which sharpened the image. It still wouldn't show faces, the camera was low quality and no computer program could add in detail the camera couldn't see. As the group of people started to spread out the man in question became clear, he was the only one of the group in a business suit and carrying a document case. She pointed her cursor at the man's image and clicked. This engaged an array of computer programs to capture the man's image and to track it from one CCTV feed to the next. Along with the data from the people in the field they would maintain a location for this individual for as long as they needed.

Other programs were already identifying his mobile phone

signature and cross-referencing all this data to look for connections with any other "persons of interest". Every face that came into view of the selected CCTV cameras would be analysed and searched for in vast databases and on social media sites, looking for (and speculating about) any connection between the individual and the man they were tracking. She felt some sympathy for the civil liberties campaigners; democracy was based on freedom, and freedom required privacy, but to protect that freedom the awesome computing power of GCHQ had all but negated those privacies. Few civilians could know just how little privacy they had left.

She brought her attention back to the matter at hand. Information scrolled on one of the screens. Another window on another screen gave Anna a continual feed of possible destinations or activities. Two items caught her eye.

'There are two printing supplies companies within twenty minutes' walk of current position, flagged as possible destinations,' she said into her microphone.

Kingston's voice caught her attention. 'Mr Mason, are we good to go?' Kingston asked, his voice a nice clear English accent, still no clue as to his origins. Kingston began tapping at keys. Anna was keen to lean over and ask how it was going, but she had to focus on her own tasks. She didn't know who "Mr Mason" was, but she knew that Kingston was using GCHQ's formidable computing power to attack the Bank of England's computer system, to identify any vulnerabilities, any weak spots that a hostile force might exploit.

Anna listened to the conversation on her own headset. The target was in a cafe. She brought up a window showing a live video feed. From the jerky movement it was a body camera, the wearer was walking and the camera was looking sideways as the person walked forwards (perhaps the camera was on the strap of a bag the person was carrying). The wearer walked past a cafe and the screen showed the image through the window of the cafe. In a moment the system highlighted the target's face with a red square, picking the man out from the other customers. Anna clicked on the man sitting next to him, almost immediately another window opened with relevant details. She clicked a button to share the information. At the same time other automated programs captured the images of all the faces visible to the camera and set about identifying them and tagging them for future, more detailed investigation.

'Target is meeting Marcus Berman, details on Command screen.' Everyone in the Command & Control Centre were now seeing the details of Marcus Berman.

Anna heard a new voice, a female voice. 'Suggest you have a quiet word with Mr Crossley as soon as Berman has left.'

"Quiet word" sounded odd, not something she'd heard before in the context of a surveillance exercise.

She heard someone ask for "somewhere quiet" and a moment later someone else gave directions to The Avenue, it sounded like one of the Command & Control team who would have interactive maps of the area and probably knew the area. Computers were good, but human knowledge was still valuable.

'Oh sneaky,' said Kingston. Anna looked over. Kingston was flicking between various windows on his screen, typing furiously then watching the result. No doubt he was trying various viruses and worms, IP attacks, packet hijacks and more to try to get past the Bank of England's outer defences and connect with a system inside their network. It was the kind of work that fascinated Anna, and she couldn't help but watch.

She recognised the program Kingston had opened. It repeatedly mimicked the login page of a Bank of England secure website and simultaneously monitored the time the various messages took to get back and forth. From this it would calculate which Internet servers along the way were passing the messages, and which of these they knew had weaknesses.

'It won't work,' she said.

Kingston looked over and almost scowled. 'You do your job, and I'll do mine,' he said.

'I am doing my job,' said Anna, almost defensively. 'But that won't work, we tried it before.'

Kingston stared at the screen, but then turned to Anna. 'Okay, why won't it work?'

'Their server is configured to mistime the packets, we could never accurately tell which servers were on route.' She suppressed a big grin, but on the inside was smiling all the way back to her screen.

'Anna,' came the voice from the other side of the partition, 'you need to focus on the mission in hand.' That was a slap on the wrist from Wayne, their Section Leader. Anna put her head down and scanned the various windows open on her screens. Wayne could be friendly enough, but he could also be serious, and today Wayne seemed to have his serious head on.

She heard "going quiet" on the headset. Nothing was happening on her screens. Someone was having a "quiet word" with someone else in a "quiet place".

'Bugger,' Kingston muttered.

Anna sneaked a look sideways at Kingston's screen, and realised that his latest attempt wasn't going to work either. It was a good try, but she knew that the Bank's firewalls were proof to that kind of attack, but it did give her an idea. Anna pulled a sticky note from the pad and scribbled a quick note on it, she pressed it down on Kingston's desk, firmly enough that he'd notice. He read the note and frowned and looked across at her. She looked up at him, briefly, and smiled. He read the note again, and frowned again. Almost with a sigh, he put the note down and started typing.

A quick scan of her own screens, just to make sure she wasn't missing anything, and she turned to Kingston's screens. The program she'd suggested he run was currently battering the Bank's systems with a blistering array of attacks, all focused on one single opening, and measuring changes in the response time. Any drop in response would show that the Bank's computer was becoming overloaded with data and that the attack had found a potential weakness. Another idea popped into her head, this really was a very good day.

'Hit the login screen with buffer over-run attacks as well,' she said, half whispering, trying not let Wayne hear her.

'As well?' asked Kingston.

'Yes, the port attack and the buffer attack can sometimes overwhelm the message queue, if it does you've got a way in.'

Anna heard something in her headset and her heart leapt, the male field agent said "lost him".

Anna's heart felt like it missed a beat, she clicked as fast as she could at various controls and windows on her various screens, sending the target's image to various tracking systems. The systems pulled feeds from CCTV cameras in the surrounding areas, scanning faces, searching for Crossley's likeness. An image opened to full view on her screen and the system highlighted a man's face with a thick red circle.

'Target located, heading up the A504,' Anna said into her headset. She heard the information relayed to the man in the field.

That was close. Losing a target in the middle of an operation could be seriously bad news. Anna watched the man on the screen, following his every move as he walked strode up the main road. He didn't stand out from the crowd, except to the ceaseless analysis by the GCHQ computers.

A grunt from beside her interrupted her, Kingston had run into a problem, he was almost clenching his fists at the screen.

Anna couldn't resist peering at his screen, she looked at the information scrolling in one window, the results of the assault on the Bank's login system. She saw that the timings were going up and down, the Bank's server couldn't handle the combined attack, Kingston was nearly there.

She pulled her headset to one side and leaned closer to Kingston. 'Spoof the security certificate of your login packets,' she suggested. Kingston tapped like a manic at the keyboard. The information on the screen went red and stopped scrolling. Kingston smiled and leaned back in his chair. He grinned at Anna.

'You're brilliant,' he said, 'one bank computer well and truly hacked.'

Anna slipped her headset back on just in time to hear the man in the field demanding to know "where is he?"

She scanned all the screens, willing Crossley to appear. She checked the logs from the surveillance programs, there was no sign of Crossley, he'd simply disappeared. In desperation she clicked from one CCTV feed to another, making sure the facial recognition programs were running on all feeds. Her eyes darted from one window to another, from one screen to another, hoping that Crossley would appear in plain sight, saving her from admitting the worst possible outcome. But as someone had once pointed out to her, hope is not a strategy.

'Target has been lost,' she said, trying to keep her voice down, as if such a report would go unnoticed.

She looked up and saw Wayne stand up at his desk, glowering down at her.

ANNA STARED AT HER SCREEN, scanning the text of the email. The email was written in broken and almost nonsensical English, but she highlighted the few keywords she thought were important and clicked the button on the screen to add them to the analysis program.

Wayne had taken her to one side and had been withering in his criticism of her lack of focus on her work and her apparent unwillingness to let other people do their own job. He had left her in no doubt there would be serious repercussions from this, that she could look forward to some very interesting conversations trying to explain why she had chosen to jeopardise an ongoing field operation. She thought about the agent in the field and whether she'd actually left him in danger.

Having screwed up in so spectacular fashion, and in such a public forum (as public as the secret service ever got), Wayne had consigned Anna to the most menial data analysis task he could find for her. He had given her a list of several hundred emails to analyse, and her only task was to pick out potential keywords and log the emails for some sort of further analysis. It required no brain power, offered no challenge and gave absolutely no satisfaction, and that was the point. Anna scanned the second email slowly, very slowly, as slowly as she could, not because she was being careful (she was always careful and could be careful at high speed) but because she had no intention of finishing the task and discovering what Wayne could find next for her. It also gave her chance to imagine new and even more inventive ways of dealing with Wayne. This had started with imagining strangling him with his own telephone cord, progressed to battering him with his chair and had now advanced to imagining the field agent bursting into the heart of GCHQ and gunning down Wayne because he'd kept the best analyst tied up with menial work.

Wayne Browning was Anna's Team Leader. He was a couple of years younger than Anna. She could never work out how he'd risen to his rank so soon. He was good, but he was no Alan

Turing. Browning was tall, lanky, he tried to act more confident than Anna thought he felt. She suspected Browning was one of those who was good at "managing upwards", pushing his subordinates to work hard and then always able to tell his superiors the story they wanted to hear, appearing to be the deliverer of exceptional results but without ever actually claiming to have done the work.

Anna of course didn't actually blame Wayne and knew full well the fault was hers, she just hadn't been able to resist the temptation of beating the Bank of England at a hacking contest, and she'd won. Except that she'd also lost, dramatically. She thought she'd like to ring her friend Amanda and offload all her frustration. Amanda was good at listening, letting Anna just rant about nothing at all, because of course, Anna couldn't rant about any of the details of her job. But using a personal mobile phone inside the operational areas of the Doughnut was strictly prohibited, and Anna had broken enough rules for one day.

She stared back at the email, and some thought irritated her. She couldn't think what it was, an idea was trying to come through. It couldn't be Amanda, she worked in an insurance company and had no idea about communications and surveillance. It couldn't be calling Amanda. It couldn't be the email on the screen in front of her.

Ah, and then it came to her, in a flash, like "getting" a joke, the thought marched centre stage of her brain. The mobile phone.

Anna minimised the window of emails and brought up several new windows running various surveillance programs. She retrieved the logs from the start of the operation, when Crossley had first left Finchley Central railway station. She logged the identifying numbers of all the mobile phones carried by the group who had walked up the road from the station. At the top of the road the group had split up as people went their separate ways, all she had to do was isolate Crossley's phone from the crowd.

More clicks of the mouse, typing on the keyboard, and she was getting close. Looking for one mobile phone was like looking for a needle in a field of haystacks, but she could easily filter out the unwanted haystacks, the other mobiles. Once the group had split up and people travelled far enough their phones would register with other mobile phone transmitters, outside the search area, so they couldn't be Crossley. That immediately ruled out five of the nine. Two of the remaining phones had their Wi-Fi switched on. One had connected to a Wi-Fi point in an office block a mile from Crossley's last position and was still there, the other could be located in a public library. That left just two mobile phones to locate. Both were still active and inside the search perimeter.

More clicks and keys, the third phone had its locate-me function turned on and had just announced to the owner's favourite social media site that she'd arrived at Barnet County Court. The court was on Regents Park Road, and quick review of CCTV coverage of the area showed that Crossley definitely hadn't made it to the court building. So now by elimination, she had the ID of Crossley's phone, and she checked, it was still active. All she had to do was find it.

She picked up her headset and put it on. She looked up to check on Wayne, he was several desks away talking to someone else. She dialled in to the Command and Control line, the operation was still going on. She heard the man, the field agent, talking about needing an Audi, he sounded like he was running. The woman was emphasising, again, the need to find Crossley. But how? Wherever he was, he wasn't in the view of any accessible CCTV camera.

And then the idea came to her. Crossley wasn't in sight of any public CCTV camera, but there were plenty of private

CCTV cameras in the area, the kind people bought in gadget shops and connected to their home Wi-Fi so they could look at the images on their mobile phone. "Look Bill, I can keep an eye on my house with this," people would say, showing anyone who'd look, how techno-savvy they were. But the majority weren't that savvy, because most left the cameras' security settings at the factory defaults, which made them a doddle to hack, and just in case it should prove useful GCHQ had a directory of them.

The downside was there was no real-time capturing of images from these cameras, so it was simply pot luck as to whether Crossley was in sight of any of these, and that was a long shot. There was no way to check each camera one by one, so Anna brought on line a program which swept the current feeds from all the available cameras and scanned them for Crossley's image.

Within moments a flashing red square picked out the familiar face in one of the video feeds, it showed the real-time video image of Gerald Crossley walking along the pavement as though nothing was wrong.

'Target located,' Anna said into her microphone, trying not to sound in any way triumphant, 'heading East on the A504, back towards the sports ground entrance.'

There was a flurry of chatter and orders over the headset as Anna listened to the surveillance operation shift up a gear, and she breathed a very small sigh of relief.

FOUR

Michael had retraced his steps along Manor View and then back along The Avenue, but there was no sign of Crossley. The fifteen minutes it took to achieve nothing at all had passed quickly. Michael reached the top of the road and was back at Regents Park Road. Crossley could have been anywhere by now. He looked over the road and saw the Audi sitting there, the driver ready to bring the car to him at a moment's notice. But where to go? Where to look? Heads would roll for this. How could a middle-aged printing manager outwit MI5 and GCHQ? Even if the man was, as they suspected, the leader of a far-right group. Even if he and his accomplices really were planning firebomb attacks against synagogues and mosques, he still shouldn't have been skilled enough to evade them. Something about all this didn't quite fit. He should have been able to subdue Crossley when he first took the man's hand. Michael had powerful psychic abilities, and Crossley should have been no match for him. But Crossley had been a match, he'd resisted Michael's attempt at invading his mind, and had punched Michael without a second thought, literally. When Crossley threw that punch, there had been no thought in his mind about it. None of this made sense.

'Got him,' came the announcement in his ear-piece, 'Heading back down the A504 towards the sports ground.'

Michael turned and ran. Crossley had somehow let Michael go past and had then doubled back. Someone in GCHQ had done some nice work to find Crossley again, maybe heads could be stuck back on. He slowed to a jog, he didn't want to run into the back of Crossley, nor look too suspicious to passers-by. He couldn't see them, but he knew the spotters were working hard to get back into place, to secure the box of surveillance around Crossley.

'He's gone into the sports ground,' Michael heard. He slowed to a walk as he approached the entrance to the sports ground. As he reached the gates he could see into the car park, and on the far side was the pavilion building with tables and chairs outside and the cricket pitches beyond. The road continued down to the left towards the tennis club. Several cars were in the car park, and a coach, perhaps a school party was here to play on the cricket pitch. He preferred to keep any close contact with Crossley out of public view, especially if things turned ugly again. Michael walked through the gates, looking all around, keeping space around him to avoid any surprises from behind, and trying to walk in as casual a manner as he could. There was no sign of Crossley on the pitch as far as he could see, so the man had to be in the car park or inside the building.

'Get the Audi ready to block the entrance, but hold off for now,' Michael said, keeping his voice down, hoping that if Crossley was close by he hadn't heard the order.

Michael picked up his pace and walked towards the pavilion building. Only moments later he heard the footsteps and turned to see Crossley come out from behind the parked coach and march towards the entrance, hoping to get back onto the main road.

'Block the entrance, now!' shouted Michael, and only moments later the Audi roared into the open gateway, headlights blazing. Crossley was startled and was motionless for a moment, but only a moment, and then ran towards the open space of the cricket pitch.

Crossley might have been surprising, but he was also middle-aged, overweight and unfit, and was no match this time for Michael's running speed. Michael caught up with him with ease and grabbed the man's wrist and threw his other arm around Crossley's throat, bringing them both to a halt. Michael was relieved to see there was no-one on the cricket pitch. People were on the tennis courts, but they were far enough away not to be able to see what was happening.

'Mr Crossley,' said Michael, 'I really would like a quiet word with you, if it's no trouble.'

Michael extended his mind out through his hold on Crossley's wrist. Having made physical contact with Crossley once before he now had a stronger connection with the man, and this time Michael let loose a surge of mental energy, enough to overwhelm Crossley, who staggered for a moment and stopped resisting. Michael led him back to the tables and chairs outside the pavilion building and sat him down. He kept hold of Crossley's wrist. With a strong psychic connection Michael expected to be able to maintain control over someone at this range, but with Crossley he didn't feel like taking any chances, his head still pounded from that punch.

Michael felt his way through the mental connection, trying to establish a firm hold over Crossley's thoughts, but it was like trying to grasp a bar of soap, it just kept slipping away, this was not normal, there was no way Crossley should be able to evade him like this.

'Gerald,' said Michael, trying to sound soothing, 'I need to talk to you about your associates and what you're planning.'

Gerald's face was blank, he said nothing.

'We know you're planning some kind of attack, we know you've been meeting people who are violent, we need to know what they're going to do.'

'Sanders,' came the female voice in his ear-piece, 'I think a little more force is called for. Stop pussy-footing around.'

Michael Sanders summoned his mental energy and let it surge through the connection with Crossley. Crossley stiffened and looked at Michael as though he'd decided to pay attention. He looked at Michael with an almost defiant look in his eyes.

'You've no idea what's coming,' Crossley said.

Michael was uncertain what this meant, and in his moment's pondering Crossley snatched his hand away and turned and ran.

Michael was on his feet but Crossley had a few feet head start. Michael stopped and shouted, 'Stop or I'll shoot.' A bluff, but it worked, Crossley stopped running, he stretched out his arms enough to keep his hands in view. Michael put his right hand under the left side of his sweatshirt just over the waistband, as though his hand were on the grip of a pistol. He wasn't armed, MI5 agents weren't normally authorised to carry firearms in public, only if there was a clear and present danger of facing an armed opponent.

Slowly Crossley turned round to face Michael.

It all happened in an instant.

Michael heard the sharp crack of the gunshot at almost the exact moment blood exploded from the back of Crossley's head and Crossley crumpled to the ground, dead before he hit it.

Michael crouched, scanning the surrounding area trying to see where the shot might have come from. Then he was on his feet running, back towards the pavilion, weaving left and right, not giving the shooter a clear target. If the shooter was on the far side of pitch, Michael now had his back to him.

Michael reached the building and stopped just around the corner. There were voices in his ear, they must have heard the gunshot through his ear-piece.

'Houston,' he said, 'We have a problem, a very very big problem.'

MICHAEL CROUCHED and peered around the corner, looking out across the sports pitch. Crossley's body lay lifeless where he had fallen. Nothing seemed to have changed; there was no shouting, no panic, in fact, no-one around to witness Crossley's last moment alive, apart from Michael, and whoever had shot him. Michael knew that the Audi had already disappeared, as had the spotters, melting away into whichever crowd surrounded them. The surveillance vehicle would be heading for a convenient location, right at the edge of reception range for his ear-piece. MI5 generally didn't want its people involved in police investigations.

'Sanders, leave the area,' came the female order in his ear.

'In a moment,' Michael said, and sprinted back across the field towards the body. It was a risk, whoever had shot Crossley could shoot again, but Michael reasoned they would have shot again already if he had been a target. More likely the shooter had already slipped away.

'Sanders, get out of there, we have to notify the police, we can't wait any longer.'

'In just a moment.' Michael reached the body. If this had been a random mugging, or if Crossley had been careless and walked under a bus then Michael would have walked away and never given it a second look. But this had been a targeted killing.

Nothing about Crossley made sense, this least of all. He slipped out a pair of neoprene gloves and put them on, you never know when a pair of rubber gloves are going to come in handy, fingerprints can be such a nuisance. He rummaged through the pockets of Crossley's suit, looking up frequently, checking. If anyone saw him, it could be difficult to explain.

He avoided touching the pool of blood surrounding Crossley's head. In the inside jacket pocket he felt something plastic. He pulled it out, a plastic wallet containing what looked like a piece of folded paper and a USB memory stick. Michael stuck the wallet into his trouser pocket and stood up, walking back towards the car park. No doubt the civilian police were on their way. Just in case the mission logs were ever to appear in court MI5 couldn't be seen to delay between the murder occurring and them reporting it to the police, they'd probably already given Michael more time than was prudent. CCTV would be the problem. No doubt there were cameras somewhere, he hadn't looked for them when he came in, and he dared not look up into a camera now.

'I'm out of the premises,' he said. He walked down the road back towards the more residential area, walking just like any normal person would walk, not hurrying, not looking around. At least he'd not seen any CCTV cameras on his way through the residential area, he could walk a couple of miles before he called for the car to meet him. Time to think. He could already hear the sirens of the police cars as they tore down Regents Park Road. He was around the corner and out of sight before they arrived. It was, of course, possible that the killer had headed this way too, but the killer had used a long-range rifle, it was unlikely he (or she?) was walking around with a sniper rifle in plain view, that really would arouse suspicion.

He heard the update in his ear-piece, the civilian police arriving on scene, establishing a perimeter, all the usual. The helicopter was on its way, but Michael would be outside their initial search area by the time it arrived, and no doubt so would the killer. So who was the killer? Why kill Crossley? Who was Crossley?

'Control, give me a review of Crossley's profile,' he said.

The female voice came on. 'Anything at the scene?'

'Not much, a memory stick.' He couldn't do anything with the memory stick without GCHQ's support, so no point in hiding it. He wanted to see what the paper was before deciding what to do with it. A reminder of the intelligence on Crossley would give him time to look.

The male voice relayed a summary of the information on Crossley. Email chatter and phone calls to and from known far-right activists, some with histories of violence. Access from his computer to similarly unsavoury websites. Meetings with individuals known to be in favour of acts of violence against non-white and non-Christian soft targets, meaning schools and synagogues and mosques and temples. Nothing conclusive, but enough for Mr Crossley to warrant much closer surveillance. The frequency of the email and phone chatter had increased, messages getting shorter, replies coming quicker, a typical pattern indicating that something was about to go from planning to acting. The sudden stop in all chatter the previous evening had set alarm bells ringing that today was the day when something was going to happen.

So if Mr Crossley—a middle-class, middle-aged manager for a printing supplies company—was planning to throw petrol bombs at a synagogue, who would want to shoot him in the head with a sniper rifle? Yes he probably had enemies, but a long-range headshot from a covered location, that didn't fit, and nor did Crossley's ability to resist Michael's "special" touch.

Judging he was far enough away from the crime scene, Michael pulled the plastic wallet from his pocket. He left the memory stick in the wallet and pulled out the paper. As he unfolded it, the world started to change. It was like the paper was hot and cold at the same time, that it screamed at him in the most awful voice. It screamed of death and destruction, of hatred, and the coldest, darkest longing for revenge. Michael staggered and moaned as the psychic impulse from the paper enveloped him, blotting out the world. The paper had been infused with a powerful psychic charge, someone was sending a message to Michael.

'Sanders, what's happening?' asked the female voice in his ear.

Michael dropped the paper, his vision blurred, his head pounding harder as though Crossley had punched him again.

'Sanders?' The voice had a touch of concern in it, but Michael doubted that was anything personal.

'I'm okay, just walked into a lamp post.' He was sure he heard someone in the control room swear.

Michael breathed deeply and the pounding in his head started to subside. The world came back to him and the storm of furious emotion faded.

'I'm coming back to Thames House,' he said, 'we need to pull together everything we've got, see if we can identify the shooter.'

Standing up and breathing deeply he looked around, the breeze had started to blow the paper into the road. He walked after it and slipped the neoprene gloves back out of his pocket and put them on. Wearing the gloves he picked up the paper, the neoprene separating his skin from the paper. He unfolded the paper. A photograph, of a cyclone, a twister, reaching down from dark clouds and whipping up the dust on the ground below. Scrawled on the paper were words that gave meaning to the psychic message:

"Coming for you."

FIVE

MONDAY - AFTERNOON

Jason Mason was the Bank of England's IT manager, and he was proud of that. His office was modern, a Spartan workspace with desk and computer and phone, all the latest models, he employed modern management methodologies, his mobile phone was always the latest model. He took his responsibilities seriously, he was the man who made sure that the Bank had all the IT resources it needed to keep the country running. He was also the man who made sure that no-one was able to compromise those resources. He didn't like GCHQ interfering in his management, there was no need for their "experts" to try to prove anything or to have fun and games at his expense. Mason had not been a supporter of the idea of a penetration test, that someone from GCHQ would try to breach the Bank's IT defences. Consequently, he'd been furious when the "expert" had managed to breach the security and gain direct access to one of the Bank's servers. Not one expert, as agreed, but two. Mason didn't want to accuse anyone of cheating, but that was the thought in his mind.

Mason felt he had no choice but to demand a call with the head of the team which had led the test. Mason sat in his office staring at his computer screen, waiting for the video call to connect. The video call window opened, he recognised Wayne Browning. Mason didn't like Browning. Typical spook, Mason thought. Good at prying into other peoples' business but no bloody good at doing his own job.

'Good afternoon, Mr Mason,' Browning said with an attempt at a smile, trying to be polite.

'Mr Browning,' said Mason, putting on his best let's-keep-this-professional voice. 'I'm disappointed that your team didn't keep to the parameters of this morning's exercise.' Get in there first, that was Mason's motto. Throw the first punch and then keep them on the ropes, that's how he boxed, every time he imagined what it might be like to actually fight with fists.

'I'm sorry Mr Mason, I...' Browning began, the smile fading. Mason had no intention of letting Browning make any kind of excuse.

'The exercise was for one of your people to attempt to circumvent our firewall within a one hour exercise. They failed.'

'I disagree, in fact,' said Browning, the smile now gone, but again Mason interrupted.

'Two of your operatives took part in the exercise according to your preliminary briefing on the matter.'

Browning hesitated, thinking how best to answer. Mason took advantage of the hesitation.

'Two of your operatives,' Mason repeated. 'Not one, it took two of them. That is not operating within the parameters we agreed.'

'But they did circumvent your firewall,' said Browning, trying to get back some measure of control of the conversation.

'That is not the point, this other operative,' Mason paused as he looked up Anna's name in his notes. 'Hendricks,' he said.

'Hendrickson,' Browning corrected him, annoyance creeping into his voice. 'Anna Hendrickson. She gave some "coaching" from the side-lines, but it was Mister Smith who ran the exercise.'

Mason was having none of it, the tone of his voice sharpened. 'I don't care if Smith had God whispering in his ear, we agreed that it would be one of your operatives and in fact two of them participated, and that was not...' Now it was Browning's turn to interrupt.

'But they did defeat your defences, and no genuine attacker is going to play by any set of rules or agreements.'

'Your person Hendrickson interfered. I believe she was supposed to be engaged in some other operation, that sounds like very sloppy working practices.'

There was some measure of bullshit that Browning was prepared to put up with, that was part of the job. But Mason had crossed a line. It was Browning's turn to sharpen the tone of his voice.

'Mr Mason, I will be submitting a formal report stating that we breached your firewall and that Anna Hendrickson showed some remarkable creativity in finding a weakness in your system and that the Bank of England should be grateful that we found it before anyone else did.'

Mason paused. This wasn't how he had imagined the conversation developing.

'And what of the operation Hendrickson was supposed to be on? She could hardly have been paying attention.'

Browning wasn't sure how much Mason knew about the other operation, or how much he knew about Anna's mistake and recovery. He took a gamble that Mason was simply shooting in the dark.

'I've already submitted a report to the MI5 Head of Operations, saying that not only did Miss Hendrickson track an elusive target but at the same time she also played a significant part in breaching your security.'

Mason said nothing, so Browning continued. 'Miss Hendrickson is one of our most capable analysts, a most valuable asset to my team and to the Service, and it's a good job she works for us and not for some terrorist organisation who might want to compromise your systems.'

Mason suspected he might lose this one on points. Browning ended the call and Mason made no attempt to call back, but he was determined that this would not be the end of the matter.

SIX

Commander Gavin Halbern stood by the pavilion building and watched the activity of the numerous police officers and forensic technicians. Halbern had a solid presence, calm and measured he was often the calm at the centre of the storm. As a Commander with SO15, the Metropolitan Police Counter Terrorism Command he often found his orbit crossing that of MI5. He was responsible for the criminal investigation of crimes involving terrorism. He was a man who knew what he needed to do, and he focused on doing it. Except in cases like this. He didn't like jobs like this one, a jigsaw puzzle with too many pieces missing. He'd received the coded call through an MI5 channel that the police were attending a crime scene and that one of their offices might have been near the vicinity. He stood and watched for a few minutes as Metropolitan Police officers worked to control the crime scene. They had to keep the media at bay—not easy on a sports field—reassure the public who were reading ever more sensational stories from social media on their phones, and establish what had actually happened.

Halbern wasn't sure what, if any, role his team had in this

particular event. But if MI5 had an interest in the dead man, then there was the serious possibility of a link to terrorist activity, and that certainly interested him. So far the regular police had identified the dead man and established that there was nothing remarkable about him, except that there was no obvious reason for him to be here and no reason for a sniper to blow the back of his head off.

Detective Inspector Grace Allen was the officer in charge of the police operation. For her, a crime was a crime and anyone involved was a witness or a suspect, and there should be no shadows to hide in. What she lacked in height she made up for in assertiveness.

DI Allen's voice jerked Halbern out of his speculations.

'So what has this sordid little affair got to do with your lot?' Allen asked.

'I sincerely hope nothing at all,' said Halbern, 'but it's not exactly your usual mugging, is it?'

Allen huffed. 'No it bloody isn't, but the fact you're here probably means this is an ugly affair.' She liked this particular job even less than Halbern. She was used to handling muggings and assaults and robberies and rapes, but a sniper killing was something different. Everyone present made an effort to avoid voicing the shared fear, that the gunman might still be watching them, ready to fire again.

Halbern looked up at the helicopter hovering not far away, no doubt using its thermal imaging cameras looking for anyone hiding under the cover of the trees. Not that anyone really thought that the gunman was still around, he had almost certainly made his escape long before the police had arrived on the scene.

'SOCO found anything useful?' asked Halbern, referring to the Scenes of Crime Officers dressed in their white suits and face masks, fussing around the dead body.

'You mean apart from an ordinary citizen lying dead on a public sports field with his head blown off? No, nothing out of the ordinary,' said Allen. 'Ground's soft, so we've got a couple of decent sets of footprints, one from the victim and one unknown.'

Halbern imagined that the "unknown" footprints were from the MI5 officer, but he didn't say anything. Had MI5 shot someone dead in broad daylight? On a school sports field? It seemed unlikely. He avoided the temptation to imagine what might have been going on between the dead man and the MI5 agent.

At that moment, the white-suited figures walked away from the body, their work done. The "baggers" entered the scene, carrying a body bag and a stretcher. Halbern had seen dead bodies before but had never relished the idea of having to pick one up and wrap it in the body bag and take it away.

'When's the autopsy?' Halbern asked.

'I've had them get ready to do it as soon as the body arrives.'

'I'd like to be there,' said Halbern, thinking that watching an autopsy was the last thing he wanted to do this afternoon.

'I thought you might,' said Allen.

HALBERN WAS glad to be in the viewing gallery and not in the autopsy room itself. It was the smell he didn't like, and the sounds. He and Allen looked through the viewing window down into the autopsy room. Three autopsy tables occupied the centre of the room, workbenches ran around the outside. One body lay on the middle table, naked, a tray of surgical instruments sitting next to it and the overhead lights shining on it. The doctor stood next to the table, ready to perform the autopsy. He was tall, fair-haired, and dressed in surgical scrubs, gloves and splash guard.

The two police officers watched as the doctor walked around the body and examined it, photographed it, fingerprinted it and then carried out a meticulous external examination. Technicians took notes and measurements, they took hair samples and photographs. Too soon it came to the surgical part of the procedure, and the body was lying on the table with its chest and abdomen splayed open. Halbern and Allen both wished the doctor would skip to the important bit, the very obvious bullet wound in the back of the man's head.

Soon enough the doctor turned his attention to the body's head. The doctor sawed off the top of the head and removed the remains of the brain, placing it into a dish for further examination. The doctor used a torch to peer into the now empty brain cavity while one of the technicians took the brain over to a workbench and started to dissect it. Before long, they got together and started talking amongst themselves.

Allen was the first to the intercom button. 'Well, doctor. Anything you can tell us?'

The doctor's voice came through the small speaker set into the wall. 'No surprises for guessing the cause of death.'

Allen and Halbern looked at each other. The doctor continued. 'No other sign of injury so we can rule out any form of struggle or fight before he was killed. Other than that, there's just the usual health issues you'd expect in a middle-aged man who doesn't eat well or exercise enough.'

'Did you get anything from the bullet?' asked Halbern.

'Nothing that you'd find useful I'm afraid. Your ballistics people will need to do a proper analysis, but first look under the microscope suggests a standard 7.62-millimetre cartridge.'

Allen looked at Halbern, expecting some sort of clarification. She lifted her finger from the intercom button.

'Standard ammunition,' said Halbern. 'Used in various NATO weapons, long and medium range. It's nothing exotic.'

Allen pressed the button. 'Thank you doctor, I'll arrange for the ballistics team to look at the bullet. Bag it up.'

'We'll be investigating this as a homicide, unless there's anything else about this case I should know?' she said, half asking.

'As far as I can see it's got nothing to do with us,' said Halbern, telling almost the whole truth.

Allen left, not waiting to make any small talk.

As Halbern walked to the exit from the autopsy suite, his mobile phone rang. He looked at the display, number withheld.

'Commander Halbern,' he said into the phone.

'Good afternoon, Commander,' the voice was unfamiliar. 'This is Mr Smith from Thames House, case ID nine eight five one.'

The case identification was a number referring to each instance of co-operation between MI5 and SO15. It also confirmed the authenticity of the mystery caller.

'Good afternoon Mr Smith,' said Halbern, not for a moment believing the man's name was actually Smith.

'Did anything useful come out of the autopsy on Crossley?'

Halbern found it creepy. He hadn't even left the autopsy suite and MI5 already knew that the autopsy was finished. He didn't really believe that they were watching him at that moment, but it felt like it.

'I'm afraid not. The ammunition was common, nothing to point to any group or individual, no sign of a struggle or that anyone else was involved in the man's death. Is there anything that I should know about this case?' It was worth asking.

'Not at the moment, but I'll keep in touch.' The line went dead.

SEVEN

As soon as he felt he was a safe distance from the police activity, Michael called for the car. Within a minute the Audi rushed to a halt beside him. Michael got in the passenger side, and the driver accelerated away. The driver, Eric, was special forces trained and kept the car within the speed limit, never drawing attention, but managing to find gaps in the traffic that made their journey back to Thames House a lot quicker. Along the way Michael kept listening to the updates from the MI5 Command and Control room into the police investigations into Crossley's murder. He also ordered extreme surveillance of the scene. He knew that by now GCHQ was accessing every CCTV camera in the area, every mobile phone signature, checking the location of all suspects who could carry out such a kill. They would monitor all traffic cameras, checking every car registration plate and confirming every driver's identity. Everyone in the area would by now have had their home and mobile phone records analysed, bank accounts accessed and profiled. Michael suspected that their efforts would be in vain, that this was a professional killing, very professional. But for now, certain suspicions were best kept private.

Eric delivered Michael to the front door of Thames House and then disappeared into the afternoon London traffic. Thames House, the head office of MI5, was an imposing building. On his induction training, Michael had learned that the building's design was of the 'Imperial Neoclassical' tradition, but he had never been quite sure what that meant, nor interested enough to look it up. Today his mind was on other things. He was quickly into the building and to the Operations Directorate on the first floor. He wanted to debrief all the personnel involved while memories were still fresh, and before excuses could be agreed.

The Operations Directorate occupied almost the whole of the first floor and was a mix of small offices and meeting rooms, two large open-plan areas with rows of modern desks equipped with multi-screen computers and communications points ("telephones" to the older members of staff), and several large Command and Control rooms. The Command and Control rooms were every bit as hi-tech as its name suggested, and it was from these rooms that MI5 controlled its various active field missions.

By the time Michael got into the room, the field operation had already been closed down. The Battle Bus was on its way back to its London base, the spotters were already on their way back to The Office (the Service's nickname for Thames House), and GCHQ was clearing up any digital footprints it might have left as it had tramped through system after system keeping its cyber-eye on Crossley. The MI5 analysts and operations team were still in the room, directing the final activities, and preparing for the debrief.

The debrief was a long and tense affair. The suspect had been lost, but had been found again. Some reprimands would be in order later. Michael was at a loss to explain Crossley's unexpected assault and managed to avoid going into too much detail about why it was so surprising that Crossley had escaped from his custody. Michael was keen that good work should be recognised, and someone had found Crossley again. That, of course, brought the focus to the shooting, and there the discussion ended. No leads, no evidence, no surveillance data. No-one had uncovered any reason why Crossley should be the target of a professional shooter.

'Anything from his meeting with Berman?' Michael asked.

One of the MI5 analysts answered. 'We didn't get any audio from their meeting.' Michael struggled to suppress a sigh. 'But lip-reading analysis from one of the spotter's video suggests they were talking about needing more planning and not being ready, but no specifics.'

'Where did Berman go after the meeting?'

'Home, he didn't speak to anyone.'

Michael looked around the room. 'Anything from the wider surveillance?'

The analysts shook their heads. The first analyst spoke again. 'There was no-one else in the area who we suspect of any involvement, we drew a complete blank.'

'Anything yet from the memory stick?' Michael asked.

'It's gone to GCHQ for analysis, we'll see what they turn up,' said the Head of Operations.

The Head of Operations was an imposing woman. Medium height, grey hair, slim build, she had the stare of a championship boxer. Never referred to by name, most couldn't since they didn't know her name, she was responsible for directing all field operations carried out by her section. Her response signalled the end of discussions about the memory stick and the beginning of someone's late-night shift in Cheltenham to recover its contents.

Michael left the Command and Control room and headed for an open plan office area, hoping to find a free desk, he had work to do.

'Michael,' said a hard-edged voice from behind him, the Head of Operations. 'A word.' It wasn't a request. The Head wanting "a word" was uncomfortably close to her description of Michael's psychic interrogation technique. The Head was career MI5. Michael knew little of her history or background, though their paths had crossed. As far as he knew, she was the only one in MI5 who knew about his psychic abilities.

She beckoned him into a vacant meeting room, and she closed the door. No invitation to sit. There was an uncomfortable silence, and Michael was determined to let the Head be the one to break it.

'You had a hold of him?' said the Head of Operations, more as a statement than question. Check.

'Yes,' said Michael.

'So how is it possible that he escaped?' Checkmate. Michael had no answer to this.

'What's going on, Michael?'

'I don't know. Whatever Crossley was into is something off our radar, or...' his voice trailed off.

'Or what?'

'Or he was simply set up.'

'Why?'

'To deliver the memory stick to us.'

'An expensive delivery route, Royal Mail is cheaper, and slightly more reliable.' The Head of Operations was big on sarcasm, but in Michael's experience she'd never really got the hang of humour.

'We'll know once GCHQ has unlocked it.'

'Is there anything else I should know about Crossley?' she asked.

Michael took only the briefest moment to consider what he should, and should not tell her.

'You've seen and heard everything about Crossley,' Michael said.

'I want surveillance on all Crossley's connections, make sure there are no attacks tonight,' the Head ordered. 'I don't want to wake up and hear about any firebombings or muggings.'

Michael was going to say 'There won't be,' but the Head was already on her way out of the room. Michael found a desk in the open-plan office area and logged on to the MI5 network. From there he issued a low-level alert to the Metropolitan Police requesting positive surveillance on premises of religious significance; churches, mosques, temples and the like. During the night uniformed police patrols would deliberately check on possible targets and maintain low-profile yet positive monitoring of vulnerable individuals. He also organised real-time monitoring of the email and phone activity of the three neo-Nazi sympathisers they had believed were Crossley's associates and who were still in the capital (two others were in Birmingham.)

With that organised Michael sat back and pondered the situation, letting the facts and events swim around his brain. He found that often something would come to him, almost as a random thought, but not this time. He kept coming back to the memory stick and the picture. He'd have to wait for the memory stick, GCHQ would retrieve its contents sooner or later. The picture was the problem. It was a message, a warning, but for the moment this was not something he wanted to share, with anyone. It was also something he wished he could put in a drawer and forget about. The phrase ran around his imagination, "we're coming for you." He decided it was too vague, there was nothing specific enough to base action on, so he put the thought in a mental drawer and closed it.

The only solid lead was Crossley, or rather the intelligence they had gathered on him before he was killed. Michael pulled up the logs of the day's mission, found the contact details for the GCHQ team leader and picked up the phone.

It rang a few times before a man answered.

'Browning, Analysis and Op's,' said the man.

'Mr Browning, my name is Michael Sanders, I was in the field for today's operation,' said Michael. He knew that the man on the other end would see the internal caller ID and know that the line was secure, and the caller was genuine, no need for theatrics with code words and the like.

'I was just leaving,' said Browning, 'Can I help?'

'I'm following up on the target we had under surveillance, I need to review the recent surveillance data,' said Michael.

'We've no review scheduled, has the Head of Operations sent an approval?'

Michael almost sighed. With this kind of bureaucracy, how did we win two World Wars, and more? 'Not yet, I'll need to complete the formalities tomorrow.'

'Sorry sir,' said Browning, 'But I can't do anything without her authorisation, and as I said I'm just leaving.'

'Then can I talk to the member of your team who was running surveillance today?'

'Anna Hendrickson, she's...' there was a pause. 'She's away from her desk.'

'Okay, no problem, we'll pick it up tomorrow,' said Michael, and hung up.

Michael went to the bank of vending machines on the far side of the office, selected a cup of the least revolting imitation of coffee it offered and wandered back to the desk. He rang Wayne Browning's extension again. A woman answered.

'Wayne Browning's phone, Analysis and Op's,' she said.

'This is Michael Sanders, I was just speaking to Mr Browning, is he there?'

'No you've missed him, he just left.'

Oh dear thought Michael, how unfortunate.

'Never mind, is that Miss Hendrickson?'

'Yes,' said the woman, with a note of surprise.

'Good, this is Michael Sanders. I was in the field for today's operation.'

'Oh God,' Anna said, 'I'm so sorry about losing the target, I...'

'It's okay, you found him again, that was good work. Now, I need to ask you for a favour. I need to review the surveillance data we had on Crossley.'

'Did Wayne authorise this?' asked Anna.

'Of course,' said Michael. Although Anna couldn't see it, Michael was smiling from ear to ear.

EIGHT

CHELTENHAM - MONDAY, LATE AFTERNOON

Wayne's commute to and from The Doughnut took about an hour, one bus from the Doughnut to the centre of Gloucester then another bus to the outskirts. From there, it was a fifteen-minute walk to his studio apartment. The late afternoon was cool but at least the rain had held off. The walk took Wayne past a school, the gates opening out onto a car park and beyond the car park was the wide green expanse of a football field. Wayne couldn't help but think of Gerald Crossley. On most days Wayne found it easy to leave work at work. He usually found it no problem to switch off and think about meeting friends, playing squash, or whatever else he had planned for the evening. But most days didn't involve someone being shot in the head. It reminded him of the vast difference between fictional secret agents and the real world, his world. Most of his days were analysing data, or supervising other people analysing data, or carrying out security exercises, or even keeping tabs on someone. But this was the first time he, or his team, had been involved in an operation where someone had been killed.

He wasn't sure how to feel about it. He didn't feel sorrow for the man, after all they suspected him of planning firebomb attacks against mosques and synagogues, nasty and brutal attacks against innocent and vulnerable people. But the man had family, and whatever the man might have done, it was obvious that someone far more violent had entered the picture.

As he walked past the larger detached houses, he reached the school and he glanced back at the school buildings. A hundred metres or so behind him another figure ambled along, umbrella in one hand, mobile phone in the other, obviously trying to read the screen while walking. Wayne didn't recognise the character, he recognised most of the people he saw on his morning and evening walk to and from the main road. Everyone else was like him, residents on their way to or from work, or dropping kids off at the school. Something about this man stood out. Big, dark-skinned, and big. Wayne carried on walking and resisted the temptation to look back again. He put a hand in his coat pocket and fingered his mobile phone. The panic-line was on his speed dial list, just in case.

Wayne reached the junction with the road which led into the housing estate where he lived. The houses in the estate were smaller, most were new-builds. Some were separate houses, some, like Wayne's had apartments on each floor. It wasn't far to the next turning, a left into a short road with houses on all sides. Wayne glanced back and the man was still behind him, but closer. How had he closed up so quickly? Wayne looked ahead and there was another unknown man walking towards him from further down the road. Asian looking, much slimmer build than the man behind.

Wayne turned left into his road and walked more quickly towards the far end of the road where his house was. This time he glanced behind, both men were walking obviously together, walking more quickly, and walking straight for him.

His apartment was in a building at the end of a short drive.

He had always liked the bushes that partly obscured his front door, but now the bushes looked threatening. As he approached the bushes, Wayne pulled out his phone. With his thumb he swiped the unlock graphic and in a practised movement tapped the four-digit unlock code.

He reached the bushes.

Before he could react a blond-haired man stepped out from behind the bushes and grabbed Wayne's hand. It wasn't a hard grasp, but it prevented Wayne from pressing any more keys on the phone.

'Wayne,' said the man, in a soft and almost friendly voice. 'We just need a quiet word. It's okay, it's all going to be okay.'

Wayne felt a wave of warmth come over him, for a moment he felt light-headed, it was almost like being drunk, but a nice drunk. The blond-haired man smiled, and Wayne smiled back.

'Shake my hand and smile,' said the man. Wayne moved his hand up and down, despite holding his phone he was shaking hands, he realised he was smiling at the man. Why shouldn't he smile? Why shouldn't he shake the man's hand? There was a reason why not, he just couldn't remember it. Whatever the reason, it wasn't important, everything was okay.

'Shake my friends' hands, we're all friends, it's all going to be okay,' said the blond man.

Wayne turned around, slowly, and there were the other two men he'd seen, also smiling. Wayne shook each of them by the hand and smiled.

A voice came from behind him, a friendly voice, a voice he thought he knew. His new friend.

'Why don't you invite us in, Wayne?'

Wayne heard a voice just like his own inviting his new friends into his house. He watched as his hands pulled his door key out of his pocket and opened the door.

He led them inside, and closed the door.

The front door led straight into the living room. He didn't know why, but he sat down in one of the lounge chairs. He realised that the blond man had pulled up one of the chairs from the kitchen and was sitting opposite him. He wasn't sure what the other two were doing, it was like the blond man filled his entire field of vision.

'Wayne,' said the blond man. 'I need you to do something for me, something very important. It's going to take some time to explain, and everything is going to be okay.'

The man reached forward and put his hands on Wayne's head. Wayne felt like the most comfortable warm blanket had been thrown over him, the comfort flowing through him, filling his mind, and he started to see the most obvious and wonderful things.

Cheltenham - Tuesday morning

ANNA OFTEN LOOKED FORWARD to going to work. She found it strange that most of her friends moaned about going to work, about how they dreaded Monday morning. Even more than usual, Anna was looking forward to going to work. She even got the earlier bus and was at her desk by 7.30am. She'd been on the call with Michael until nearly mid-night reviewing what surveillance they had on Gerald Crossley. When she logged on to her computer, she found the authorisation to work officially on the review of the Crossley case. She was glad, the killing had been shocking but had shown that something very unwelcome was going on, she relished the chance to find out what.

She checked the news feeds and felt a sense of relief when she saw there had been no spike in hate crimes overnight, nothing to suggest that Crossley's believed accomplices had got up to anything unpleasant.

Anna put on her headset and waited for Michael to call. Soon enough the phone rang and the caller ID identified an extension from Thames House.

'Anna Hendrickson, Analysis and Op's,' she said, answering the call.

'Good morning Anna,' said Michael. They'd progressed to first name terms on the previous evening's call.

'So where do we begin today?' she asked, trying not to sound too enthusiastic.

There was a pause, she assumed Michael was thinking. She'd not been able to think about anything else all night.

'I need to trace the route of the shooter, so we need to find where the shot came from.'

Even before Michael had finished speaking, Anna was typing furiously and clicking away with the mouse. Windows of information opened on her screens, data being pulled from various police sources, CCTV systems, GCHQ's own reference databases.

'The police logs so far haven't established a location for the shooter, they say they can't tell from how Crossley fell which direction he was facing, so the shot could have come from any direction.'

'Okay,' said Michael. 'I know something they don't, I had my back to the car park entrance and Crossley was facing me.'

More typing and clicking.

'So the shooter must have been in the cover of the trees of The Avenue.'

'Did the police sweep that area?' Michael asked.

'Yes, nothing found.' It was too much to hope that a professional killer would have been obliging and left the casing from the spent shot just lying around. Anna went on, 'They did house-to-house in the area, most houses were empty at the time, minimal CCTV coverage of the area.'

'Can we get images from any of the CCTV in the houses?' Michael asked.

'Yes, but only live feeds, there are no recordings we can access. I can show you the gardens as they are now, but nothing from yesterday.'

'The shooter could have walked through someone's back garden, onto the road and disappeared into traffic?' Michael sounded a touch exasperated.

'Very possibly, by the time traffic cameras picked him up he'd have been one of many vehicles.'

'Can we...' Michael began, but Anna was in there first.

'Yes, we're profiling all vehicle registrations logged in the area.'

'Anything from the memory stick?' Michael asked.

More typing and tapping. Anna looked up and smiled at Wayne as he sauntered in, his customary cup of coffee in hand. Anna looked back at her screens.

'It was sent down to Technical Services apparently, they wanted to look at it before releasing it to us for analysis.' She paused. 'Oh,' she said with a note of surprise. 'That's not very friendly.'

'What?'

'It's a good job I didn't just plug it into my PC for a look.'

'Why not?'

'As well as the less common components, like circuits that wipe the contents if it's not plugged into the right kind of device, it had a small explosive charge built into the shell. If it was plugged into anything other than a specific adapter, it would have blown the fingers off the user.'

'That's not the sort of thing you buy in your local computer shop,' said Michael. 'That sounds like a military-grade of memory device.'

'It is, the analysis is that it's of Russian design, the device itself probably made in China. No physical evidence was recovered to indicate any kind of ownership, except Crossley's fingerprints.'

'Pity, it would have helped if they'd signed their name on it,' Michael said, jesting. Anna giggled, but stopped abruptly when she saw Wayne frowning at her. Not big on having fun at work was Wayne.

Michael thought for a moment. 'So Crossley was either carrying it with instructions not to try and use it, or he had a device that could read the stick safely.'

'True, but the police didn't find anything like that at Crossley's house. Usual domestic computing equipment, all seized and analysed, nothing out of the ordinary.'

'What about the contents of the memory stick.'

Typing and clicking.

'They've uploaded the contents into the shared folders. I wish they'd tell me when they've done things, it's like working for the secret service sometimes.' Anna's turn to jest.

'Of course the files are encrypted?' said Michael, daring to hope that the owner had reckoned on the physical security alone being enough.

'Oh yes, this might take some time,' said Anna. 'I'm not even sure what they've done to encrypt the files. I don't suppose you've got any suggestions?'

'No, but I'm beginning to doubt that this is a home-grown gang who like straight arm salutes and shouting "Heil Hitler" while they goose-step around the living room.'

'So where did Crossley get this stuff?' asked Anna.

'That's what you're supposed to find out,' said Michael.

Anna paused, not sure whether she should ask the next question which had occurred.

'When you had that "quiet word" with Crossley, what happened?'

'Sorry,' said Michael. 'There are some things I can't tell you.'

'I know, but I've never heard the Head of Operations suggest that someone has a "quiet word".'

'It's just a thing I do,' said Michael. 'But it didn't work this time, Crossley chose not to say anything.'

'We're supposed to be a team, you know?' said Anna. 'If there's anything you can tell me that might help?'

'There's nothing about Crossley I can tell you. But I suggest that if the memory stick was military-grade then so's the encryption on the files.'

'I'll start running some analysis on the files, see if I can figure out how they're encrypted,' said Anna.

'Anna,' Michael said, 'just an idea, but start by looking at British military encryption methods.' He put the phone down.

Anna looked up, Wayne was always a fund of useful information on obscure forms of encryption. She was surprised to see Wayne staring at his screen in a kind of eyes half-closed daydream. She decided to ask him later.

NINE

The sign at the end of the road read "Industrial Estate". That might have been how the estate agent described it, and perhaps once there had been industry here, but not now. The estate, such as it was, comprised several cramped streets of mainly empty commercial lockups. Dirt and grime characterised the place, a light breeze blew litter against the rusting shutters of the empty units.

The fifteen-year-old Ford Transit, just as rusted and dirty, looked entirely in keeping with the place, as was the man who got out and made his way to one of the units. He entered through the door, pushing hard to overcome the resistance of the rusted hinges, and pushed it closed behind him. Inside was cold and gloomy, as dirty as the outside. In what might once have been the office were two others. The man was big, broad-shouldered, dark skin and obviously of African descent. He entered the office and stopped. Sitting on an upturned packing crate was a blond man, head bowed, eyes closed. Standing over him was an Asian looking man, thinner build, thinning hair. They both watched as slowly the blond man came out of what might have been a trance. He blinked, yawned, and seemed only then to realise that there were others present.

'Well?' said Marshall.

Bullock looked round at him. 'Browning is such a boring man,' he said, 'I can't stand being inside his head for long.'

'Yes, but did Sanders get the message?' Marshall asked, exasperation creeping into his voice.

'They've got the memory stick but they haven't cracked the encryption.'

'The picture?' asked Singh.

'No mention. After I got Crossley I saw Sanders pull it out of his pocket, but he's not said anything about it.'

'You sure they're going to fall for this?' Marshall asked, talking to Singh.

'Soon enough. The encryption's good, they'll have to work hard to break it, but the harder they work the more they'll believe it's real.'

'We can always give them a nudge if we need to,' said Bullock.

'Right,' said Marshall, a firmer tone in his voice, 'let's plan our little welcome for them.'

He led the way out of the office and into the warehouse area. Three large wooden workbenches had been pushed into the centre of the room, a fourth bench was against the far wall, and around the place were piles of sandbags and assorted building materials. Three other men were working over the items on the table. All were dressed in worn jeans, work boots, heavy jackets. Their expressions and demeanour shouted menace. They looked around as Marshall, Bullock and Singh entered.

The three at the benches moved aside to let the others see the items on the table. Marshall, Bullock and Singh took a few moments to survey the assortment of automatic pistols, submachine guns, anti-personnel mines and a variety of electronic devices.

One of the three at the bench spoke first. 'Most of it here, basic stuff later.' The man's voice was heavily accented, Eastern European of some flavour.

Marshall looked at him. 'Get rest from lockup later,' said the Eastern European man.

'Good,' said Marshall. 'Here's what we need to do.' He looked first at the bend, then at one of the three. 'Mister Singh,' he gestured to the Asian man, 'will show you where to place the cameras and the motion sensors. I want to make sure we've got a good view of anyone approaching.'

He continued, looking at the other. 'Mister Bullock,' he gestured to the blond man, 'will show you where to place the mines. When you've done that, I'll show you where I need you to be when the time comes.'

One of the other three spoke up, his accent similar to the first. 'What about helicopter?'

'No,' Marshall said. 'They'll need to avoid announcing their arrival, they'll only bring the helicopter in later, but if we need it that's one benefit of having those,' he pointed at the shoulder-held rocket launchers on the bench.

'So how we make sure we have good exit?' asked one of the other three. 'This place,' he looked around, 'become trap.'

'We've planned the way out, I'll show you in a minute. Now, get busy.'

They each went about their assigned duties. To all intents and purposes they looked like a bunch of men who might work in a back-street car repair, shop wandering around the industrial estate talking about the state of the units, the few vehicles parked in the yard, or whatever else such men might talk about. There would be time later, when it was dark and the estate was completely abandoned, to come back and place their weapons and explosives in just the right places.

As he watched the three Eastern European men finish their tasks Marshall beckoned to Singh. The two spoke in quiet voices, to keep their conversation from the other three.

'How are preparations for our intervention?' Marshall asked.

'Most of it's done. It's nearly time we had a quiet word with the man who's going to have his finger on the button.'

ANNA SAT AT HER DESK, surrounded by pages of handwritten notes, scraps of paper with half sketched ideas, sticky notes adorning her monitors. Kingston had helped, he'd contributed ideas, some had led to a step forward, some hadn't, but overall Anna was no further ahead in decrypting the files from the memory stick. She did now have some idea what kind of encryption had been used. Michael had been right, or at least half right, it was a form of encryption used by the British military. But this application also included some new variation Anna had never seen before.

She'd logged two of the files from the memory stick with the Crackers, the team who ran the main computer used for brute force decryption. The computer, wherever it was—Anna didn't know its physical location—was a warehouse full of servers which simply tried every possible password in turn. Using thousands of computers at once the idea was that it was actually possible to try every combination of password. The servers themselves were a proprietary design and not the "off the shelf" servers you might find in any ordinary data centre. But a password was only any use if you knew the kind of encryption used. The Crackers would be running billions of passwords through millions of encryption protocols applied to the sample files.

Anna doubted it would work, but it would have been silly not to try. She imagined going into a meeting and having to confess that the encryption was the simplest possible and the password was "Fred." That would be embarrassing, more embarrassing than losing a target during a surveillance operation.

'Maybe they used a recursive bit algorithm,' Kingston suggested.

Anna sighed. 'Tried that, even tried double recursive bit, still doesn't work.'

'Did Tech Services say anything about hardware encryption in the stick?' said Wayne from the other side of the divide between their desks.

Anna looked up. 'There wasn't any. Some unpleasant physical protection of the stick, but the contents were encrypted before they copied it onto the stick,' said Anna.

'We need those files decrypting, Anna,' said Wayne.

'I know,' she said, trying not to sound annoyed. She did appreciate that this was important, and urgent.

Anna got up and walked away from her desk, trying to make it look like she was just going to the drinks machine and not storming off in a huff. She really wanted to storm off. Sometimes she liked the open plan of the office, being able to talk to people easily, being in sight of other people, able to bounce ideas of them, and contribute ideas to their problems as well. Other times she hated it, the continual interruptions made it hard to concentrate. She'd like to have put her earphones in and listen to music, but that was banned, there had been a memo not long ago.

Anna decided that the coffee from the vending machine was even less appealing than usual, so she headed off to the canteen. To call it a canteen was to do it a disservice. It was a large, bright and well-decorated area that served a huge choice of hot and cold food, and most of it was really good. The coffee in particular was Anna's favourite, a decent cup, or mug, of properly made coffee. It was a preference she and Wayne shared, which often made for harmless banter across the desk.

The Doughnut, the GCHQ building, was actually two circular office buildings one inside the other. Two circular buildings with a wide open enclosed walkway between them. The more secure areas were in the inner structure. The canteen, like Anna's office area, was in the outer section of the building, but on the other side. It meant that sometimes it was an inconveniently long walk to and from the canteen, but at times like this it meant Anna had a reasonable time away from the desk to think without interruption.

Having bought a mug of coffee, Anna sat down at a vacant table near the window and looked out at the car park. The car park surrounded the building, so every external view was of the car park. Only the offices on the upper floors could see over the car park, either to the hills or to Cheltenham town.

"What would Alan Turing do?" she sometimes wondered. She knew that this was a ridiculous question. Turing had been an absolute genius. Even people who appreciated his genius didn't know just how genius he had been, since many of his papers were still classified and held in locked rooms here in the GCHQ building. Anna had seen one of the papers. She and a group of analysts had been the latest to try to understand his reasoning behind a particular idea. As part of the project they'd been shown the paper itself, with his pencil jottings in the margin. Anna was clever, she knew that and had no problem admitting it. Straight A grades at school, reading Mathematics and Philosophy at Oxford, she could crack most of the problems that had come her way, but this one was more challenging than most.

She had to make an effort sometimes to stop thinking about Crossley. Whatever was going on was serious, and it was no exaggeration to say deadly serious. A man shot by a sniper, military strength encryption of files stored on a military-grade memory stick with a built-in explosive, Russian design, Chinese made. Something happened. A thought. She couldn't put it into words, but something had made a connection somewhere in her mind. Something about Russia. No. Something about China. Something she'd read. No. Something she'd read about. A report from some other project. No. Something she'd read about while analysing the Turing paper. Something about a Chinese paper on cyphers which referenced the Turing paper, which had been flagged for investigation because the Turing paper was supposed to have been classified. If the memory stick had been made in China then perhaps the encryption software had too, and perhaps it was the cypher based on the Turing paper.

Anna picked up her coffee and walked as quickly as she could without spilling it. She got back to her desk and started sifting through the papers. Kingston and Wayne both looked over at her.

'What's got you in a tizzy?' asked Wayne.

'China,' Anna said.

'What's China done to ruffle your feathers?' asked Kingston.

'No, China, the China connection to the Turing project. Ah, found it.' Anna picked out a sheet of paper she'd been scribbling on earlier. The China idea looked sound, but something was still missing. She typed at the keyboard, putting her ideas into the decryption algorithm. She hit the enter key and hoped. It took only moments for the same message to come back, still no successful decryption.

'What China connection?' asked Wayne in a calm voice, trying to sound soothing.

Anna paused. 'I read about a Chinese encryption algorithm based on one of our Turing papers - no we don't know how they got hold of the paper. Since the memory stick was made in

China, I thought maybe that was the encryption they used. It hasn't decrypted the files but it does decrypt the file headers.'

'Getting closer,' said Wayne. 'All you need now is the magic key.'

Anna stared at him, she could feel another thought slotting into place. She could feel it again, something was connecting with something else. She went back to the keyboard. What was it?

'Ah,' she said. She didn't mean to say it out loud at all, but she had.

'What?' Kingston asked. 'You look like you've got something.'

'Magic,' said Anna. 'Magic was the codename used by the US military in the Second World War for their decrypts of Japanese messages. Having decrypted them they had to translate them from Japanese into English. If these files were encrypted by a Chinese algorithm then maybe the seed files were in Chinese not English, and so...' her voice trailed off as she typed as fast as she could.

She waited for a few moments, and was rewarded with a window opening on her screen and pages of information went scrolling past. A grin spread across her face and she sat back, looking hugely satisfied.

'That was lucky,' she said to Wayne, 'You mentioning magic, it was just the thing.'

'Pure luck,' said Wayne. 'Now send the contents of those files over to Thames House.'

TEN

The Command and Control rooms in Thames House were one of the few features of the MI5 head office which did look like they came straight out of a James Bond film, although to be accurate the designers and engineers had modelled them more on similar rooms in bank IT data centres. The oval table had a full multi-media control station for each seat with a flat-screen computer monitor set into the desk at a discrete angle, line of sight to the big monitors lining the walls, and the place at the head of the table being the obvious seat of power.

Power, in this case, was an appropriate word. Seated at the head of the table was the Head of Operations. She didn't go in for "power dressing", she didn't need to. She was smart, not a single steel grey hair out of place, a stern expression on her face. This was a woman who was quite at ease with her personal and professional power. Having reviewed the memory stick data from GCHQ she had called a planning session. The Command and Control rooms weren't supposed to be used as meeting rooms, but this was not a problem for her. This was part of an ongoing high priority mission, and no-one was going to tell the Head of Operations where she could or could not hold a meeting.

Most of the attendees had already taken their place in the room or had dialled in. Michael was the last to enter the room. He shut the door and took his seat.

The Head of Operations asked for a roll call. Each member introduced themselves. In addition to Michael, there were three others from MI5 operational directorates, two MI5 analysts had dialled in from another location, and from GCHQ were Anna and Wayne.

The Head of Operations began. 'Miss Hendrickson, you decrypted the memory stick, perhaps you can summarise its contents for us.'

The screens relayed the information from Anna's screen and her voice came over the loudspeakers set into the table. 'The files seem to be part of a larger set, some files reference folders not found on the memory device.' Anna said "device", it sounded more professional than "stick." 'In summary, the files contain inventories of weapons, some maps and photographs.'

'Maps of where?' asked the Head.

'Central London,' replied Anna. The screens flashed up images of the maps. 'There's a collection of maps which join up, almost like a jigsaw.'

'What's the picture on the box?' asked Michael.

'Unknown,' said Anna, 'there might be other photographs not in this collection.'

In the room, the loudspeakers relayed the sound of muttering and half-concealed whispering from parties on the conference call. The Head ignored them.

'Do the maps relate to the pictures?' she asked.

'Yes,' came Wayne's voice, 'the pictures cover parts of the area inside Central London, and the maps extend wider.'

There was more muttering and whispering from the phone. For the Head, this had obviously crossed a threshold.

'Does someone have something they'd like to contribute?' she asked in a stern voice. There was quiet, waiting for an answer.

'I think we have a problem,' came another voice from the loudspeakers, one of the MI5 analysts.

'What problem?' asked the Head.

'Collectively the maps cover the route of a forthcoming transfer of gold bullion to the Bank of England from a secure storage facility.'

'How much gold?'

'About two hundred million pounds worth.'

There was a collective exhalation from those in the room and on the conference call.

'I think our Mister Crossley was into far more than throwing petrol bombs at mosques,' said Michael. 'He seems to have had eyes on large scale bank robbery.'

'Bank robbery big enough to count as a terrorist threat to the nation's financial stability,' said the Head, without a trace of humour or sarcasm. Michael had come to believe that the Head of Operations had never lost her sense of humour because she'd been born without one. 'When is the transfer?' she asked.

'Two days' time, Thursday morning.'

Michael spoke next. 'Is there any chance this is a coincidence? Could the maps and pictures cover something else?'

'It's possible,' said the analyst, 'but the maps cover the whole route and the pictures show key parts of the route inside the capital, it would be a very big coincidence.'

The other MI5 analyst spoke up. 'Our surveillance of Crossley never showed any connection to any serious weapons, but the inventory here is enough to equip a small army.'

'Agreed,' said Michael. 'Crossley may have been mixed up

with something but there's no way he was running this. Whoever it is looks like they've got access to some serious firepower.'

'Miss Hendrickson, do the files suggest if the weapons have been acquired or if this is just a wishlist?'

'We've no hard evidence to identify who owns the data so we can't verify if these weapons exist as a single arsenal.'

'I want full surveillance on Crossley's previous associates, as deep and intrusive as possible. If you need Ministerial approval for anything then don't bother with the approval, do it anyway. Mister Browning, work with our analysts and look at the route of the bullion transfer, identify potential ambush points. Miss Hendrickson, you've shown quite a skill in data analysis and tracking people, work with Sanders on analysing that data. Find out where that memory stick came from. I want an update from everyone at noon.'

The Head of Operations ended the meeting. The conference call attendees all dialled off as she got up and left the room. Michael looked at his watch, the Head would be back in an hour and a half.

Michael thought for a moment what this might mean, Crossley now being associated with a far bigger and more dangerous plan. It was clear that they knew far less than they thought about what was going on, and his mind was drawn back to the picture he'd taken from Crossley and the message it carried. Perhaps now it was time to share some information. He got up and followed the Head out of the room.

'I NEED A WORD,' Michael said to the Head of Operations as she walked up the corridor away from him. She stopped walking.

Almost without looking, she stepped sideways into a vacant office, leaving the door open. Michael followed and closed the door behind him.

'What do you need to tell me?' she asked, her voice as firm and direct as ever. Michael thought "cold" would be a good word to describe her at this moment.

'I've reason to believe a certain three individuals might be back on the scene,' Michael said.

There was silence. The Head was obviously taking a moment to consider the implications of this new information.

'What reason?' The Head was never one to use too many words.

'Something I sensed from Crossley.'

'What did you get from him?'

'Not much,' Michael said, he was trying to give away as little as possible, but lying to the Head was a dangerous game. 'He had some kind of barrier to my interrogation.'

'Is that how he resisted your control?'

'Possibly, but I've got a strong suspicion that they're mixed up in this.'

'So what do you want me to do about it?' The question was a good one. Michael had to almost bite his tongue and stop himself from saying that he wanted her to give him control of any and all MI5 assets and GCHQ support that he needed, and carte blanche to go and do whatever he needed. He didn't think such a request would go down too well.

'I need to interrogate Crossley's associates, without interference,' he said. Interference was shorthand for an individual's right to legal representation, or for interviews to be recorded. It could be quite inconvenient to have a physical record of some interviews and sometimes it could be quite awkward having a legal representative tell someone what questions they could refuse to answer. Michael also felt that having someone from outside observe his particular style of "interrogating" would lead to questions that he, and the Head, would rather not have to answer.

'No chance,' said the Head, an even sharper tone now in her voice. 'We took you back on the understanding that if these three ever appeared again you would be able to take care of them, completely off the radar. Can you? Or not?'

'I can,' said Michael, as firmly as he could, without sounding like he was trying to start an argument. 'But I need some resources to do it.'

'Off the radar, Sanders,' repeated the Head. 'No official support, nothing that gets onto anyone's mission log. No-one else can be involved.'

'If it is them and if they are planning an attack on a Bank of England gold shipment then they've moved up a league,' said Michael.

'This is your problem Sanders, a problem you said you could handle.'

It was Michael's turn to go on the offensive. 'This is our problem,' he stressed the "our". 'You're as involved in this as I am. If I can't stop them who do you think they'll come for next?'

'I'll remind you again, you're only here because you said you could take care of them again. If you can't, there are people who will insist we go back to square one.'

'Square one resulted in the kill-squad being wiped out, what makes you think you'll have any better of chance stopping them this time?' Michael could feel himself being backed into the corner. This wasn't where he wanted to be.

'Find out Michael,' she said, an uncharacteristic use of his first name. 'Find out if it really is them. But the deal remains the same, off the radar, no official support, no-one else involved. Square one remains a threat if you can't deliver.'

She left the room, leaving Michael to his thoughts. That cold night in Afghanistan seemed like a world away, it was a world away, almost a different lifetime. But now he couldn't escape the fact that his past was coming back. Not to haunt him, but to meet him on the battlefield.

ELEVEN

Michael didn't want to join the mission controller and the others in the Command and Control room. It would have been useful to listen in as they reviewed the details of the bullion transfer and possible opportunities for an ambush, but Michael needed some privacy. He went back to the office area and found an unoccupied seat. He logged on to the computer and put on the telephone headset, dialling a now-familiar number. Thoughts whirled around in his mind, possibilities, options (though they seemed few.) Here, Thames House usually felt familiar, almost safe, but the Head's lack of support made the place feel foreign. Perhaps he had expected too much.

'Mr Sanders, nice to hear from you again,' said Anna, sounding upbeat.

'Open the files from that memory stick and copy your screens to mine,' Michael said, a sharp edge in his voice.

'Sorry,' said Anna, 'here you are,' her voice now flat.

The screens in front of Michael showed what Anna was looking at, lists of the files retrieved from Crossley's memory stick.

'What do you want to look at?' asked Anna, her voice now flat and emotionless.

'We need to establish if this data is credible, or if someone's just written a shopping list of guns and downloaded a few pictures of London.'

'I've looked at some of the pictures, the advertisements on buses and the like are recent, so they're not from some stock photo website,' said Anna, her voice monotone and business-like.

'Do we know when they were taken?'

'No, the encryption removed the date and time stamps from the pictures. But there are some...' Anna's voice trailed off.

'Some, what?' asked Michael, sharply.

'I'm sorry Mister Sanders, have I done something wrong?'

Michael took in a deep breath. He should have had more self-control than this. Perhaps here, in The Office, he thought he had less need to keep up a pretence. Perhaps the Head's response should have convinced him that he was not safe, not here, not anywhere. He was never safe, not now.

'No, Anna, I'm sorry,' he said, his voice more calm. 'I was cross about something, and I shouldn't have taken it out on you, I apologise.'

'Apology accepted,' said Anna, her voice back to a more friendly tone. 'I remembered some of the pictures looked like they were from CCTV cameras, yes, here they are.'

The first picture came up on the screens, complete with a date and time in the bottom left corner. Five days ago. The screen showed a succession of CCTV images; buildings, streets, people.

'Can you scan through the images from CCTV?' asked Michael

'I can,' said Anna, 'what are we looking for.'

'It's a long shot, pardon the pun, but if someone was out and about taking photos and they've used CCTV images from the same time and place, then maybe there's an image of whoever took the photographs.'

'Right then, here we go,' said Anna, keys clicking in the background. Images flashed in various windows on the screens from a variety of CCTV cameras. Each showed a typical central London street scene with cars and buses and lots of people. After several minutes of images flickering past, it stopped on one image. Standing in the doorway of an office building was a man with a camera. He could have been one of millions of tourists taking pictures of London, but he looked more like a factory worker wearing heavy industrial boots, a dark and heavy jacket, a dark shirt of some sort. The image was grainy, obviously from a low-resolution camera.

'Can we,' Michael began, but he could hear the clattering of Anna's keyboard and assumed that she already was. The centre of the image enlarged, the man's image enlarged, but pixelation made it a blocky and fuzzy image. Regardless of the resolution, the man had a large camera in front of his face.

'No chance we can get a face from that,' said Michael.

'No, but we can see the design on his shirt,' said Anna. Michael looked. The shirt was dark but across the front was a large design, perhaps a lion's head, with lettering above it.

'Is that helpful?' asked Michael.

'Oh yes,' said Anna. 'Unless he teleported there he must have walked to and from that location, past other cameras. If I can find him on another camera, when he's not got his camera in front of his face, we might get a good look at him.' She paused, obviously working her keyboard and mouse.

The image on the screen changed. Another street scene. In the crowd of people was the unmistakeable design on the shirt, and the man was looking almost at the camera. The picture was not perfect, but it was a clear face shot of the man.

'Before you ask,' said Anna, 'I'm already running this through facial recognition. If he's ever appeared on an official database or any social media platform then we'll have an ID for him soon enough.'

'While that's running, can we tell anything about the list of weapons? Does it match anything else we know about?

'No,' said Anna. 'We did look at that, the list doesn't match any lists of stolen weapons, and it's fairly ordinary stuff.'

'Ordinary?'

'Heckler and Koch submachine guns, a few AK47s, Glock pistols, Claymore mines, there's nothing exotic on the lists, nothing that would stand out.'

'Wouldn't stand out at all,' said Michael, mocking, 'it's stuff I buy all the time in the supermarket.'

'I can believe it,' said Anna, just as mocking. 'But there were a lot of files, and some reference documents which weren't on the stick.'

'Reference in what way?' asked Michael.

'There's one that looks like it lists which weapons would be carried by each individual, no names of course, but there are two individuals assigned to something described in a document we don't have.'

'So there might be more weapons we don't know about,' suggested Michael, 'something bigger and more significant.'

'Oh,' said Anna with a note of surprise, followed by 'Ah,' as though she'd found something unpleasant on the floor.

'What?'

'Our mystery photographer, the system's found a match. He's Luka Petric, Serbian mercenary, with a very disturbing history. Mr Crossley had some very unpleasant friends.'

'I think we need to find Mister Petric. Can you cross-reference mobile phone data from that area? Get any kind of lead we might use to trace him,' said Michael. 'Don't bother trying to follow him on CCTV, I bet soon after that image he dropped out of sight. He might be on MI5 watch lists, there might be some current intel' on him. And take this all into the noon briefing with the Head. And one more thing.'

Anna paused. 'Yes?'

'If I give you a project name can you bring up recent GCHQ monitoring for the project?'

'I can,' said Anna with a hint of caution. 'Is it relevant to this case?'

'It might be relevant, it's something I need to check. The project name is PsiClone.'

'Cyclone,' repeated Anna.

'Yes, but it's not spelled like "cyclone", it's spelled P-S-I-C-L-O-N-E."

'Never heard of it,' said Anna.

'You won't have, and the files will be locked, but send them over to me.'

Anna typed and clicked and within a few moments Michael saw on his screen that the files had landed in his personal work queue.

'Anna, thank you,' said Michael. 'Keep on looking for anything that might locate Petric, and I'll speak to you at the noon briefing.' He hung up the phone and took off his headset.

The password to open the files was a long one, but one that Michael had committed to memory. He opened the first of the files Anna had sent. It detailed profiles of the subjects of an ongoing surveillance exercise, subsequent to a classified military project. He looked at the three mugshots and the summaries of the three individuals; an African man, Vince Marshall; a blond-haired man with boyish looks, Evan Bullock; and an Asian man, thin face, Julian Singh. Were they back? Why now? What were they planning? Questions Michael had chosen not to think about. He closed the file. For now, his aim was finding Petric.

TWELVE

LONDON - TUESDAY AFTERNOON

The team assembled quickly in the Command and Control room. Before the Head of Operations arrived Wayne and Anna and the MI5 analysts had already dialled into the conference call line. All the screens were up with summaries of the bullion route, pictures of Petric, details of the weapons listed in the files. The Head of Operations entered the room and closed the door. Time for business.

'Petric is our only solid lead for the moment. We can assume he's not alone, so our priority is finding him and anyone he's working with.'

Browning spoke up. 'We've got active monitoring in place over the capital, watching traffic cameras, other public CCTV, it's been running all morning but nothing yet.'

'Keep up full surveillance,' said the Head, 'what else do you have in place?

'We're monitoring the mobile phone network, but there's no guarantee he'll use the same phone that he had last time.'

'Can we identify that phone?' Michael asked.

Anna replied. 'Not uniquely, there were eight hundred and twenty-seven possible phone IDs, but if Petric has the same phone with him then very few of those others will happen to be in the same place, unless he's back in the centre of London.'

'If Petric's here then he's likely storing the weapons somewhere,' said the Head. 'Other than his little reconnaissance venture I doubt he'll stray too far from his toys.'

'When we find him, we need to intercept him and question him as soon as possible,' said Michael.

'No,' said the Head. 'When we find him, we keep him under surveillance and let him lead us to the weapons store.'

'He's slipped back under the radar once, he'll do it again,' said Michael.

'If we get the weapons then we stop their plan,' said the Head, firmly. 'They can't carry out an attack like this without their weapons, all of them.'

Michael hadn't finished. 'There's more going on than we know.' The Head shot him an angry look. 'Crossley was involved even if we don't know how. They shot him at long range and we don't know why. We have to question Petric and find what's going on.'

A bleeping came over the loudspeakers from the conference call line. In the Command Control room they heard Browning in the background asking what was happening.

Anna's voice came over the loudspeakers. 'We've spotted him, we've located Petric.'

'That was quick,' came a comment from someone on the conference call, probably more audible than they had meant.

'Don't lose him,' ordered the Head. 'I want continual surveillance on him.'

'Where is he?' asked Michael.

'Heading west on the North Circular Road, just passing North Middlesex Hospital. White Transit van.'

The image from a traffic camera came up on the screen, traffic heading towards the camera. The old Ford Transit didn't stand out in the traffic, except for the big red square outlining it on the screen. The driver was wearing a baseball cap and had pushed it up just enough for his face to be clearly visible to the camera. A moment's mistake, and it had given them a break.

'I'm cross-referencing all mobile phone signals in that area,' said Anna, 'with the IDs we collected from central London.'

'We can't assume he'd be stupid enough to be using the same phone,' said the Head.

'No match at the moment, it may be switched off,' said Anna.

'We have to intercept him,' said Michael, more to the Head than to anyone else.

'I said we'll keep him under surveillance,' said the Head.

Michael paused, but only for a moment, then stood up sharply and left the room. As he strode down the corridor he pulled out of his jacket pocket a small case, smaller than a cigarette packet. He took out of the case the small flesh coloured ear-piece and pushed it into his ear. As he reached the staircase he pressed the switch built into the case and heard the soft beep in his ear, he also heard the beep come from the loudspeakers in the Command and Control room behind him. As expected the next thing he heard was the Head's voice in his ear as he entered the stairwell.

'Michael, we need surveillance on him.'

'And if remote surveillance loses him we're at square one, we can't assume he'll make the same mistake again,' said Michael.

There was a pause, perhaps the Head was weighing up whether to pick a public fight with Michael, maybe order him back into Thames House.

The Head's voice came back in his ear. 'The car's being brought to the front of The Office, we'll direct you en-route to an intercept location. We can't get spotters or support out there fast enough, if you confront him you're on your own.'

'Suits me,' said Michael.

MICHAEL WAS SOON DRIVING up the A1 as fast as the traffic would allow. The blue lights and sirens made life easier, but there was always London traffic to fight through. It was a gamble, driving from Thames House trying to intercept a vehicle further north, through the London traffic. There were so many chances for surveillance to be lost, but Michael had rolled the dice.

MI5 and GCHQ were tracking the white Ford Transit. Wherever it was heading, Michael was heading towards it. Eric, his co-driver sat in the passenger seat working at a laptop computer, tracking the position of the Ford Transit, keeping Michael headed on the best intercept course. As they passed Holloway heading for Highgate Michael realised they were heading back towards the place where Crossley was killed. This fact was not lost on those in Command & Control. The Audi's audio system kept Michael's ear-piece connected to the MI5-GCHQ network, he could hear the Head's voice coming over the car's loudspeakers and directly in his ear, a disconcerting experience.

Eric kept track of the Transit as it passed Brent Cross, drove past the M1 junction and continued heading west.

'These boys don't travel too far,' someone said.

'Far enough,' said Eric. 'He's about twelve minutes ahead of us, almost at Wembley.' The Transit had travelled further West than anticipated. The interception would have been easier, and quicker if the Transit had stayed in the Finchley area, or turned South more towards the city centre. Instead, it had carried on West. Michael now had to join the A406, the North Circular Road and follow.

'Change of direction,' came the voice in Michael's ear, it was Anna's voice.

'Miss Hendrickson, where is our friend going now?'

'He's come off the North Circular road onto the A4088

heading south-east. There are plenty of traffic cameras in this area.'

There was a pause. 'Now he's turned round and heading north-west.'

Michael and Eric looked at each other.

Eric looked at his laptop. 'He's heading towards Kingsbury,' he said, 'there's quite a lot of open space around there.'

'He's spooked,' Michael said.

'Are you being followed?' the Head asked.

'Can't be,' said Michael, 'anyone following us at this speed would get caught by speed cameras. I think he's just checking for a tail.'

'We're ten minutes away,' said Eric.

The minutes ticked by. Michael was mindful that sooner or later they'd get close enough to the Transit that they'd have to turn off the lights and siren and blend in with traffic, but at the moment their target was heading out of the built-up area and towards the more open spaces of Kingsbury. Eric with his laptop and the surveillance power of GCHQ kept him up to date with his target's location.

'He's turned around,' came Anna's voice. 'Heading back the way he came, heading back towards town. He'll reach the junction with the North Circular at about the same time as you.'

'How long?' Michael asked Eric.

'Two minutes to the junction with the A4088,' was the reply.

Michael turned off the blue lights and the siren and slowed down. The grey Audi became just another car in the London traffic. It seemed like only seconds before they reached Neasden and the exit off the dual carriageway of the North Circular Road and swept down onto the A4088.

'Where is he now?' Michael asked.

'About half a mile ahead of us,' said Eric, 'he's turned again, he's either heading out for open space or he's heading towards

Wembley.' They both hoped Petric was heading for Wembley, where there were far more surveillance cameras.

They were close now, but not too close. Michael hoped that Petric had taken a detour off the main road and satisfied himself that he hadn't been followed. If that was the case the hope was that Petric would feel confident about driving to his destination, which hopefully was somewhere significant. It would be disappointing to find that Petric had simply gone out to pick up the dry cleaning. But as someone had once said: hope is not a strategy.

Anna's voice came back on the loudspeakers. 'Petric's reached a crossroads. If he goes left or right he goes out of sight of the traffic cameras.'

Michael kept in with the flow of the traffic, avoiding doing anything to make the car stand out. It would start to get interesting if they lost camera surveillance now.

Anna's voice again. 'He's turned left, but he's turned on his mobile phone, same ID when he was on his sightseeing trip.'

The Audi approach the crossroads, and the traffic lights turned red, which let them sit there and look down the road to the left. The side road led away from the main road into a world of light commercial units on the left and houses on the right, a typical street for the area, but the Audi would look suspicious driving down the road at low speed. The lights turned green and Michael drove forwards, over the crossroads. He pulled the car off the road and into a bus stop.

'I'm going on foot,' he said and got out of the car. He knew that Eric would keep the car close enough to maintain the communications link. He walked back towards the crossroads and turned into the road Petric had taken.

'Update,' he said. He needed to talk as little as possible, he didn't want anyone to see him walking along apparently talking to himself, any unwanted attention could be a problem.

'A quarter of a mile further on and his phone would have handed on to another cell transmitter,' said Anna. 'It hasn't so it's likely he's still in your immediate area.'

Michael walked on, noticing the industrial units out of the corner of his eye. He wasn't blind to the houses, it was possible Petric had gone to a residential address, it just seemed less likely.

'Mobile signal lost,' said Anna. Petric had obviously kept the phone switched on just long enough for a call, apparently still ignorant to the fact that GCHQ had logged the phone's ID, although it was more than possible that Petric would soon destroy that phone and change to a new and untracked one.

A couple of hundred metres down the road Michael passed what looked like a disused unit. The single window in the front was boarded up, the business name sign had been taken from the front, a heavy padlock secured the front door. A driveway led down the side of the unit, and at the end of drive, just visible from the rear of the building, was the unmistakable profile of the front of an old Ford Transit.

'Found them,' Michael said.

'Extreme caution,' came the Head's voice, 'there is no backup or support available. Are you armed?'

'No.' This little excursion had been unplanned, so the Audi was lacking the small arsenal it sometimes carried. MI5 surveillance vehicles did not routinely carry firearms, nor did their agents.

Walking down the drive seemed like a bad idea. There was nowhere to hide so Michael would have to act as though he was lost, or "looking for the previous owner" or whatever other story he could imagine. That was unlikely to work. He had noticed that the unit next door had a similar driveway and the two drives were separated by brick wall high enough to obscure him.

'All quiet,' said Michael, an instruction to everyone on the radio to keep quiet, no distractions, nothing to break his concentration.

Michael crossed the road and walked back to the unit next door. As far as he could see the road was fairly quiet, only the occasional passing vehicle and no pedestrians, so no spectators. He walked down the drive, taking care to make his footsteps as quiet as possible. He knew that to anyone watching he would look suspiciously like he was trying to walk quietly, but he couldn't avoid that now. He kept his head bowed slightly so he was out of sight of anyone on Petric's side of the wall. He could hear heavy footsteps on Petric's side, then the metallic echo of something heavy being dropped into the back of an empty Transit van.

Michael reached the end of the wall. Rubbish and broken wooden pallets littered the back yard of this unit, as derelict and abandoned as the one Petric was visiting, but he did spot a wooden box. It wasn't big, but it only needed to be big enough to see over the wall. It looked sturdy enough. With great care he picked up the box and placed in on the ground against the wall. He put one foot on it and slowly put more of his weight on it. It held. He put all his weight on it and stood up, peering very slowly into the yard of the unit next door.

He was almost directly in front of the Transit. He could see its doors were open at the back, like dirty white wings spreading out on either side of the vehicle. Petric was behind the door standing between the van and the back door of the unit. Michael could see his legs from the knee down below the door. The door was solid, no glass in it. For now, Michael was out of Petric's line of sight, but also couldn't see what Petric was putting in the van. He listened, straining to hear any clue as to what Petric was doing. He could hear the man walking into the unit and then back out to the van. It sounded like he was taking things from the unit and putting them in the van. But what things?

There was a loud crack as the wooden box gave way beneath Michael's feet. He dropped a couple of inches and narrowly escaped hitting his face on the wall. Petric shouted something, it sounded like an Eastern European language but Michael didn't recognise it. Michael looked around. The only immediate exit was back up the drive but running up the drive would keep his back to Petric, not something that struck Michael as a healthy option.

Michael's analysis of the situation was interrupted as Petric's head appeared above the wall, followed rapidly by his shoulders. He spotted Michael in an instant and was already starting to vault the wall. Michael looked around for anything he could use as a weapon. As Petric cleared the wall Michael spotted some broken timber, only short off-cuts of wood but it would make do as a club. Michael reached the wood and snatched up a baseball-bat sized piece as Petric pulled a pistol out from his jacket. Michael swung the wood and caught Petric's hand.

Petric only grunted and staggered as the club smashed the back of his hand, but he managed to keep hold of the gun. Michael closed the distance, keeping the club in his left as a guard to prevent Petric raising the gun and with his right punched hard at Petric's head. Petric grunted again and went down on one knee, but he kept moving and turning allowing a gap to open where he could raise the gun. Using the wood almost as a sword Michael swung it at Petric's head, but Petric got his arm up in a guard and the wood struck his forearm. Michael swung the club-sword down at Petric's gun hand and succeeded in knocking the gun free. It scattered across the yard, but Petric lashed out with his other arm and sent the wood flying across the yard in the opposite direction. They stood and looked at each other for a moment, both thinking the same thing, how to reach the gun before the other.

'Who killed Crossley?' Michael asked, not expecting an answer, but testing Petric nonetheless.

'Head shot, too clean,' Petric said, with an almost dismissive tone. His English was clear but heavily accented.

'Who was it, Bullock?'

'Too quick,' Petric said, 'should have sent more personal message.'

'Like what?'

'Like his head, and wife's head, in a box.'

Michael saw Petric glance down and to his left, just for a moment. The gun.

A car horn blared and the sound of an engine roared as the Audi came charging down the drive, headlights on full, like the proverbial cavalry charging over the hill.

In the moment's distraction Petric had the gun back in his hand and was clearing the wall at the end of the yard. As the Audi reached Michael he saw that Petric was already over the wall and out of sight.

'Situation clear,' said Michael, the all-clear signal to the team in the Command and Control room.

'What's happening?' demanded the Head.

'Petric got away.'

'Can you follow?'

'Negative, he's armed, I'm not and he's got choice of territory. Where's he heading?'

It was Anna's turn to speak. 'Your location backs onto waste ground bordering the railway lines into Neasden depot, then into a big industrial estate. Lots of ground, minimal CCTV coverage, multiple exits.'

It was obvious, Petric had escaped and they had little chance of picking him up again.

THIRTEEN

The Bank of England's main building in London was, in Jason Mason's opinion, one of the most impressive in the capital. The Old Lady of Threadneedle Street, named after the ghost who was supposed to haunt the building's garden, was an imposing building. It was also, in Mason's view, one of the worst offices to work in. The offices were cramped, badly laid out, and completely unsuitable to the hi-tech world of twenty-first-century banking. Which is why Mason was glad that he worked in the Bank's offices at Canary Wharf.

Many major banks had offices at Canary Wharf. The modern high-rise office blocks formed the power-house of one of the world's leading financial centres, and Mason never tired of reminding himself how important his job was in this financial monster. Mason was the IT security manager for the Bank of England. To be accurate he was one of the IT security managers, but Mason saw his role as the key one. One of the few drawbacks to his position was having to deal with GCHQ and their so-called experts. His team were the experts when it came to securing the Bank's IT systems, and he resented the interference from Cheltenham. They were never easy to deal with, almost enjoying their ability to hide behind "national security" when they didn't want to answer a question, and then using the same argument when they needed to persuade others to answer their questions.

GCHQ's recent success, down to blatant cheating in Mason's view, was a major cause of irritation. He now had no end of reports and summaries to write explaining how he would address the weaknesses that the test was supposed to have uncovered. Today's meeting was likely to bring up the same questions. Mason never liked these meetings, planning for various business activities, non-technical people wanting simple answers to questions that were really very complex and technical.

Mason took his seat in the meeting room, the blinds were half-closed, keeping out the view of the Thames stretching back into the City. The conference call line was open and he could hear people gathering in other offices and dialling in. Managers and senior managers and experts of various flavours, all gathering to make arrangements for some business exercise or other.

The most senior manager closed the door, took her seat, and the meeting began.

As Mason had expected, most of it was about the business arrangements; who needed to sign off what, whose approval was needed, what record keeping was required. He was never quite sure he understood Quantitative Easing, other than it was one of the measures the Bank used to prop up the economy in the wake of The Financial Crisis. He knew that at some point in the process the Bank actually created more money, and that this money was moved into special accounts within the Bank. It always brought to mind a dark dungeon somewhere with enormous printing presses churning out steaming sheets of fresh ready-to-be-cut bank notes. But he also knew that it was all done by computer, the money only existed as an accounting entry in the Bank's databases, and the security of those databases and computers was his responsibility.

'Mr Mason,' the most senior manager asked, turning her gaze in his direction. Here it came. 'Can you assure us that since GCHQ's breach of our defences, you have put in place sufficient measures to ensure the security of this exercise?'

Mason made a conscious effort to stifle a sigh and to keep his eyes from rolling. Stupid. All so stupid. None of them knew what they were talking about. But they had to ask the question to make it look like they were the one who truly understood the importance of things.

'The GCHQ test was of a completely separate system, which has now been remediated and secured against any similar incursion.' He got that last bit in before anyone could ask any even-more-stupid questions. He continued. 'The accounting system has no outward-facing aspects and so we remain completely secure.'

'And what if some hostile entity should decide to mount an attack while we're creating and transferring the funds?'

Always the same. What would you do if someone did something unexpected?

'As per our usual procedures, GCHQ will be helping monitor our outer defences and firewalls.'

There were nods of approval from around the table and the discussion quickly moved to the next agenda item. Sometimes Mason felt like saying that if they didn't think the Bank was secure unless GCHQ was standing guard then maybe they should just move the whole damn bank to Cheltenham. The discussion soon moved to the security around a physical shipment of gold, and Mason tuned out. No IT aspect meant no interest on his part.

THIS TIME there was no need for the Head to inform the police. They knew that a man with a gun was on the loose somewhere in the Greater London area, but that was hardly news. An MI5 tech' team were on their way, but would take at least half an hour to arrive. They would examine the area in forensic detail, literally, to discover if Petric's presence had left any tangible clues as to his intentions or current whereabouts. The half-hour wait also gave Michael a chance to look over the van and the warehouse. With Eric and the Audi stationed at the front he could be sure of an undisturbed half-hour to poke around.

What he found was disappointing. In the back of the Transit van was a pile of sandbags and a shrink-wrapped tray of bottled water, a mix of still and sparkling. Michael had obviously interrupted Petric retrieving basic supplies, but little more. They had used the warehouse, such as it was, as a temporary store, but only for basics such as the bottled water, energy snack bars and the like. One box contained pairs of gloves, boots, but again nothing of any obvious military significance.

Michael had a look in the driver's side of the Transit's cabin. There was the usual assortment of empty drinks cans, chocolate bar wrappers, yesterday's newspaper, and a baseball cap. This looked like the cap Petric had been wearing when the traffic camera had first picked him up. It was likely something that belonged to Petric, something that was personal to him.

Michael looked around and made sure that Eric was still out of sight. He held the cap lightly between his fingers, and felt his attention being drawn towards it. He got a sense of Petric. It was hard to describe even to himself what this sense was like. It was different to making a direct mind-to-mind connection. That was exciting in a strange way, taking control of someone else's mind, being able to dominate them so directly and so completely. Making a psychic connection with someone had become familiar, it was almost becoming ordinary, except in cases like Crossley. He still didn't understand how Crossley had been able to resist his direct telepathic control. Michael was powerful, even amongst people like himself. Granted, there were very few like him, but Michael was still one of the strongest. But connecting with a physical object was different, and reminded Michael that he was different.

The cap had no mind of its own, it had no personality, but it had the imprint of whoever had handled it. It had the imprint of Petric. Michael started to sense it, and he sensed anger, a cold and focused anger. Petric was someone whose mission was to do violence, as much violence as he could. Michael focused and tried to move beyond the sense of hostility. He let himself be carried by the sense, to connect with the recent history of the object he held in his fingers. He got the fleeting image of being in the Transit van, driving along a busy road. He smelled exhaust fumes, sweat, gun oil. He saw the outside of a dirty industrial unit, not here but somewhere like here. He saw a table laden with guns of varying sizes and types, other ordnance. He saw other men, he saw the three that he recognised; Marshall, Bullock and Singh.

He tossed the cap aside and focused on the world outside. Breaking the connection with Petric was like leaving a claustrophobic room full of the smell of rotting meat, and coming out into the fresh and sweet-smelling air.

'Any sighting of Petric?' he asked, not expecting any.

'No, none,' was Anna's reply.

'I found something,' he said, not quite sure how to explain this, knowing that apart from one, the people listening had no idea about his "unique" way of gaining information. 'There are six of them altogether, Petric and five others. They're amassing their weapons in a lockup somewhere, can't tell where.'

'So the list on the memory stick isn't just a wishlist?' said the Head.

'No, it's real.'

'Any clue where this lockup is?'

'None, a dirty and disused lockup somewhere, that's all I've got. Have we got anything more on Petric?'

Anna's voice. 'Yes. Mister Petric is a thoroughly nasty piece of work. He has a list of murders and assassinations credited to him, along with a long list of beatings and tortures. I think he wasn't joking when he said he'd have chosen to give you Crossley's head and his wife's.'

Something tugged at Michael's thoughts.

'Miss Hendrickson,' said the head, 'I want you to focus on cross-referencing all our surveillance data from Crossley with that of Petric. Crossley had that memory stick and they killed him for a reason.'

'Yes,' said Michael, 'they spent a lot of effort setting him up.'

'But why?' asked Anna.

'To use him to send us a message,' said Michael, 'like Petric said, he'd have sent us Crossley's head.'

There was a silence, they all shared the same thoughts - what message, and why? Michael knew part of the answer, but there was still a piece missing. And then it struck him, the thought coming fully formed into his mind.

'I need the car,' he said, knowing that Eric would hear this and be ready with the Audi in moments.

'Where now, Sanders?' asked the Head with a cautious tone.

'Crossley's widow,' said Michael, 'I need a quiet word with her.'

IT TOOK an hour and a half for Michael and Eric to reach the quiet suburban street in Redhill, south of the City. The houses were new, or no more than ten years old. The area was quiet, little traffic, most of the houses' occupants were at work. The grey Audi looked in keeping with the few cars parked on the driveways. It swept up the road and onto the drive of one particular house.

Michael made sure he left his ear-piece in the car. This was an interview to which he did not want an audience. He got out of the car and walked towards the front door. He knew that his visit had been arranged with the local police with the assistance of Commander Halbern. Crossley's widow had already been interviewed at length by the local police force and by SO15. Michael wasn't expecting to be welcomed with open arms and a fresh pot of tea. Sure enough, the door was opened before he reached it. The woman standing in the hallway was middle-aged, but the lines on her face looked older, and her eyes were etched from a day of crying.

Michael approached the door.

'Mrs Crossley, I'm Martin Edwards.' He offered his hand to shake, she kept her arms folded across her chest. She turned and walked away, leaving the door open, inviting him in. Michael closed the door behind him.

Once inside, she led the way into the living room. The room was a comfortable size and opened through into the open plan dining area. Bright sunlight streamed through the large patio windows at the far end. The woman sat in one of the easy chairs.

Michael motioned at the other chair. 'May I?' he asked, and sat anyway. Joanna Crossley was not going to make any effort to engage him in small talk.

'Mrs Crossley, I need to ask you some questions about your husband.' He didn't expect her to answer that. He continued. 'I know the police have been here several times and asked you a lot of questions already, but there are some things I need to ask you. Did your husband ever mention a man called Petric?'

She looked at him, eyes blank. She shook her head, slowly. 'No,' was all she said.

Without having made physical contact Michael had no direct mind-to-mind connection with her, and couldn't make one, but even without that he could see that the name evoked no reaction from her.

'What about Bullock? Or Marshall? Or Singh?'

Again, no reaction. It had been a long shot, he hadn't expected any of them to have used their real names when they'd dealt with Crossley. Even if they had, he would probably not have shared them with her.

She fixed him with a stare. 'They asked me if Gerald had ever talked about attacking mosques,' she said, 'whether he'd ever expressed extreme racist views. My husband worked for a printing company. I don't know what you think he did, but he didn't do it.'

The desperation in her voice was written across her face. Marshall and the others had brought devastation into this woman's life. She had no idea what was going on or how to handle it.

'Do you know what they've done?' she said, her voice sounding as broken as her soul.

'What who have done?'

'Your lot, the police. They questioned all our friends and neighbours, and now they won't talk to me.' She sounded so desperate and so alone. 'The bank has closed all our accounts and won't explain why. What am I supposed to do?' The tears were close, Michael could see.

He noticed a small framed picture on the mantelpiece, of the Crossley's together, holding hands, some holiday location. He stood up and walked over, and picked up the picture.

'Where was this taken?' he asked, trying to sound casual.

'Florida,' she said.

He considered the picture for a moment, and then handed it to her. As expected, she reached up to take it from him. In a deft movement Michael reached out with his other hand and intercepted hers before it reached the picture. As his hand took hers and before she could react he extended his mind out through the physical contact. He allowed himself to relax and felt a sense of calm come over him, he allowed the calm to spread out through the contact and into Joanna Crossley's mind.

She exhaled slowly and relaxed back into the chair, her eyes half closing. Michael went down on one knee, half kneeling in front of her chair, still holding her hand. To any casual observer it might have looked like he was about to propose to her.

'Joanna,' he said, 'Gerald was a good man, and a bad thing happened to him. I need to find who did this to him, and I need your help.'

Joanna Crossley took a deep breath, letting it out slowly.

Michael went on. 'I know you loved Gerald, and I know he loved you, and I know that in the days ahead you will find a strength within you to help you live through the grief.' He maintained the contact, letting the feeling of calm continue to flow through him and into her.

On the journey here, the Head of Operations had sent Michael a text message. She had been quite specific. He was to use any amount of psychic force necessary to get information out of Joanna Crossley. Michael had replied that he would use as much force as was safe to overcome any resistance on her part. The Head's reply had made it plain that she placed no value on Joanna Crossley's state of mind. But here, now, sensing Joanna Crossley's vulnerability, Michael wondered what would happen if he pushed deeper into her mind.

He let his thoughts form around the idea of Gerald Crossley, and felt a wave of anger and grief as Joanna Crossley tensed and inhaled sharply. It was like touching a bruise, it didn't hurt, but pressing harder would. He let his mind return to the idea of calm and peace, and she relaxed and exhaled slowly.

Michael let go of her hand and it sank gently into her lap. He knew she'd remain in this light trance for a while, so he stood up and looked around the living room. He walked around slowly, looking at the various ornaments and keepsakes, the usual collection of family photographs, trinkets from favourite holidays, nothing that was both uniquely personal to Gerald Crossley and out of place.

He walked around the rest of the ground floor of the house, again finding only the kind of family belongings found in any ordinary home. There were a few books, but most were on travel or were "chic lit", nothing even remotely approaching political. He walked up the stairs. Bathroom, two bedrooms, and a room that looked like Crossley had used it as a home office. On the desk were empty spaces where the police had already removed the computer and any papers they thought might be relevant. The remaining papers looked to be all related to the printing supplies business Crossley worked for. Had worked for.

If his three former colleagues had spent time and effort exerting their psychic control over Crossley then it was reasonable to suppose that they had left him with some kind of object, something that Crossley would touch and through that maintain the strength of the mind-to-mind connection. Even after all this time, he wasn't entirely sure of the rules of this telepathic phenomena. Mind-to-mind connection through a direct physical contact was becoming more familiar, and controllable. He knew how it felt, how to use it, how to push strongly and how to back off. But as Gerald Crossley had reminded him, Michael could still be surprised.

Connecting to physical objects was a different kind of skill, and a very different kind of experience, and a more unusual one. Only he and Julian Singh had shown this ability. All of them had the ability to connect with another person and to exert direct mental control, even at a distance. But the ability to exert control through an object, using it as some kind of relay transmitter, only the two of them had that ability.

Michael looked around the room. It was all very ordinary. This was not the lair of a man who had been planning hate crimes, this was not the home of a violent racist. They had used this man as a pawn, and had shown no hesitation in killing him simply to deliver a message: we're coming for you.

And then he saw it: a book, red cover with gold lettering, lying on the desk, half-covered by a printing magazine. "Psi: Psychic Discoveries Behind The Iron Curtain." Michael had read the book once, out of curiosity. It was an innocuous book, not out of place, no reason for the police to have taken it. But its topic spoke to Michael, it was obvious to him. He reached out his hand and touched his fingers lightly on the cover.

This time the experience was different. He had the sudden feeling that he was standing on the edge of a precipice, that a vast nothingness lay before him, that he could step off and fall into the void. He felt like he was within a hair's breadth of a vast and deafening silence. Crossley. What he was experiencing was the absence of Crossley. The object had been a telepathic link to Crossley and now Crossley was dead, so the book was a psychic link into a void. Michael made an effort and focused. The book had been a link to Crossley, but it had also been a link to Julian Singh. He focused on the other sensations he could sense.

Images flashed into his mind. At first he thought it was the industrial unit where he'd run into Petric, but he saw differences. The sounding buildings were different, it smelled different, it was more dirty. He heard voices, some of them familiar, voices he'd not heard since a dark and violent night in Afghanistan, others were foreign speaking and unfamiliar.

He got a flash of Crossley, of fear and confusion, a flash of anger at something being said but then a sense of confusion and then a sense of submission, that it wasn't worth fighting. Images ran through his mind like a disjointed pop video; a mobile phone, an area of parkland with a bench seat and rain, back to the dirty and smelly industrial unit, a broken sign from a closed taxi business.

The images stopped, he took his fingers off the book. An unused industrial unit whose neighbour had been a taxi firm. He had no doubt that Anna's databases of locations would pin down the location. They had a solid lead.

FOURTEEN

AFGHANISTAN - THREE YEARS BEFORE

Bullock dragged the dead Afghan back into the hut and covered his body with a rough blanket from the makeshift bed inside.

'So where are they?' hissed Michael, 'did you find out before you broke his neck?'

'Yeah, they're close and moving in, one from each point' said Marshall. So now they knew. Four soldiers, four of their own, were on their way to kill them, approaching one from each point of the compass. They'd be equipped with night vision goggles and silenced weapons, and orders to kill on sight.

The three looked at Michael. He thought for a moment. Their options were few; run, fight, surrender. Unless there was another way.

'We'll form a perimeter,' he said. 'Let them enter the village, then we trap them and subdue them.'

'What!' said Marshall, more loudly than he intended. 'Fuck that, we let them enter the village then we kill them.'

'No, we don't,' said Michael, still their commanding officer, 'they're four of our own, they don't know what we can do, we can do this without killing them.'

'I don't know,' said Singh, his middle eastern accent coming through more clearly, a telling sign of the stress of their situation. 'It's a nice idea, but they're not here to play nice, they aren't simply going to give up to us.'

'He's right,' said Bullock, 'they're not going to let us get close enough to subdue them.'

'Look,' said Michael, 'they're not here because of some personal grudge, we know there's just one person who's ordered them here, our fight is with him.'

Marshall spoke next. 'My fight's with anyone who wants to kill me. You stay and have a friendly chat if you want, I'm going to stop them.'

Michael faced him, looking up into his eyes, shoulders square on. Marshall was a big man and was a head taller than Michael, they both knew who was naturally more violent. They were supposed to know who was the superior officer.

'You'll follow orders, we trap them and subdue them,' said Michael.

Marshall lifted his weapon and held it across his chest. 'My following orders stopped when someone gave the order to have me killed.'

Behind him the other two lifted their weapons, a visual sign, "we're with him."

'Sorry boss,' said Bullock, 'but if they're here to kill us then that's just bad luck, we stop them, end of discussion.'

Marshall never broke his stare into Michael's eyes as he gave his own orders. 'East and west access is this track, south is up that stream bed. Best ambush is the north approach, he's going to have to come between those rocks, natural pinch point. Trap him there, suck his brain dry, kill him, pick the others off.'

Without another word Marshall pushed past Michael, and Bullock and Singh walked with him, disappearing into the darkness towards the rocky crag on the north side of the village. The night seemed to close in around Michael, and he welcomed it. He always felt like the darkness was a blanket that kept him safe. But now he shared the darkness with three who should be protecting him, but had instead deserted him, a betrayal compounded by a betrayal. They all knew who it was, back home, who would have given the order and sent a squad of soldiers here to kill them. Michael knew that his colleague was wrong, slaughtering their own people was not the answer, but he was also right, survival was going to be a fight, and success was not guaranteed.

Michael stepped into the hut and pulled out the radio receiver the old man had used. There was no point trying to connect with the corpse, no psychic connection could be made with a dead body. He found it curious that he could create a connection with an inanimate object but not with a dead body. There was still so much about this phenomenon he didn't understand.

He took off his gloves, the cold air biting at his fingers. He held the small radio device lightly in his fingers and let his mind be drawn to it. Brief images flickered into his mind, a taste of the dust that blew around in the air, villagers staring, other soldiers dressed the same as Michael. He had a flash of the soldiers tracing out a map in the dirt with a stick, but no details. He had an image of a dried river bed, of guns being loaded with bullets.

He put the device down, and focused on the silence around him. Unfortunately his abilities didn't extend to psychically sensing people around him. His attackers could be within a few feet and he'd be as unaware as any "normal" person.

He pulled his gloves back on, slipped on his night-vision goggles and looked around. He drew comfort from the stillness, from the absence of movement. He had sensed that the leader of the attacking group would be the one coming up the dried river bed a short distance to the south. Michael had a chance to intercept him, and perhaps prevent a slaughter, on either side.

London - Present Day - Tuesday late afternoon

MICHAEL WAS BACK in the Audi, Eric driving them through the afternoon traffic towards Thames House. The lead he had gained from Crossley's home was tenuous, but it was a direct lead to where his adversary was amassing its arsenal. The team were still online both in Thames House and in GCHQ, so he knew he had an audience.

'Anything?' asked the Head. Michael knew she'd be careful about what she said and how she said it. There were things the two of them needed to talk about, things that they needed to keep private.

'There was something,' said Michael. He left just a moment's pause, to listen for any question from anyone else. He continued, 'I think we're looking for an industrial unit, either disused or in a largely disused commercial area, near to a unit used by a defunct taxi business.'

'Miss Hendrickson, is that sufficient information?' asked the Head.

'Yes,' said Anna, 'don't know how many candidates we'll get, but I can do a search on those parameters.'

'How was the widow?' asked the Head. Michael was disappointed she couldn't call Mrs Crossley by her name, only refer to her as "the widow".

'Grieving,' was all Michael could find to say.

'How long will the search take?' asked the Head.

'A few hours,' said Anna, 'I'll need to pull in data from

various offline sources, particularly around taxi companies, it may not even have been a registered taxi firm.'

'Head back to The Office,' said the Head, 'we need to plan our surveillance.'

'When we find it we need to go in hard, as soon as we can,' said Michael.

'I said we'll plan our surveillance,' the Head said again, more firmly.

'With respect, any time we give them just makes them stronger, we can't wait and watch them.'

'And I'm not prepared to send men in to storm an unfamiliar target which could be a trap.'

'When we find where they're accumulating their weapons we need to attack as soon as we can, whether they're at home or not, it's the only way to stop whatever they're planning.' Michael tried to sound as firm as he could without being mutinous.

'When we find the location,' said the Head, slower, colder, 'I will line up SO15 and SO19 and have them ready to storm the place. In the meantime we will effect total surveillance and know exactly what we're sending those men into.'

Michael was about to say something else when the Head cut him off. 'And in the meantime Mr Sanders, you are ordered to support the surveillance effort, and are specifically forbidden from launching any unilateral action of your own.'

There was silence from the loudspeakers, no-one else on the call wanted to join in what was obviously a personal confrontation between the two, and some might have been embarrassed at having to witness such a public dressing down. This wasn't normally how field agents were spoken to, not in public.

Michael said nothing, he wasn't going to give the Head the satisfaction of breaking the oppressive silence.

FIFTEEN
CHELTENHAM - WEDNESDAY MORNING

Anna sat at her desk in the Doughnut, the dull grey morning a world away. She looked closely at the screens in front of her. Overnight a plethora of computer programs had worked away, pulling information from a variety of sources, making connections, identifying patterns. The results appeared in one window after another on her screens, most leading to dead ends or obvious non-starters. Occasionally she'd look up and see the top of Wayne's head. He had his head down working on something of his own.

It had seemed a simple task; find a disused, small industrial unit close to a similar unit which had probably at some time been used by a taxi company. It had not turned out to be so easy. No estate agent databases described their properties as dirty or disused. Not all taxi operators had been appropriately registered or licensed. Not all registered taxi companies who had ceased trading or moved location had registered that fact in any database or on any website.

And so Anna had set the massive computers of GCHQ the task of trawling social media sites and estate agent websites and taxi company web sites and databases of phone records to piece together clues that might point to potential sites. Despite the awesome computing power available, at the end of it all, someone would have to go and actually look at each location and decide if it was what they were looking for, or not.

Michael was on the line to Anna. This was not a full operation, there was no Command and Control room running, no team of spotters or surveillance vehicle to support Michael. There was no team of analysts on standby to support Anna, ready to run searches or investigations at a moment's notice. There was Anna at her desk and Michael in the Audi, somewhere in the London morning traffic.

'It's going to be in the last place we look, you know that, don't you?' said Michael in a jovial tone.

'It's going to be in the last place we look by definition,' said Anna. She knew full well what he meant, but the banter helped pass the time.

'No, not because when we find it we stop looking,' said Michael, 'but because out of your three potential sites it will be the third site.'

'So do we ignore logic and go straight to the third site?' she asked, this time only half-joking.

'No, logic wins in this instance.'

Anna heard someone's car horn blare, and didn't envy Michael the task of driving through rush hour traffic. No doubt he would feel the temptation to use the car's lights and siren, but that would have defeated the purpose of covert surveillance.

Anna had identified three potential sites and mapped out the most efficient route from the first one to the third. She looked at the screen showing Michael's location.

'You're almost there,' she said.

'Yes, I know, I can see the road signs,' said Michael.

'Sorry, just trying to help.'

Anna was sure she heard a suppressed snigger from Wayne's

side of the desk. She watched the scrolling map display on her screen, and saw Michael's car arrive at the end of the road where the first potential site lay.

'This doesn't look like it,' came Michael's voice over Anna's headset.

'Why not?'

'Too many people, there's a mobile burger van doing a greasy breakfast, a newsagent's on the corner opposite and a bus stop on each side of the road. There are far too many people.'

'Worth a look anyway?' suggested Anna.

'No,' said Michael, 'no-one's going to be moving guns and explosives in and out of vehicles with this many people walking past.'

One down, two to go.

'On to the next one,' said Michael.

Anna tapped a few keys. 'I've sent you the details of the next site and a route. Or you could make up your own route.'

Michael chuckled. 'No, this route looks fine.'

She heard the sound of the car's engine as Michael set off again into the traffic.

After a suitable pause, Anna decided it was time to ask.

'Michael, what did you mean when you had a "quiet word" with Crossley?'

There was a pause, Michael wasn't going to launch into a full and frank explanation.

'That's not something I can really talk about,' he said.

'I've never heard the term used like that before, and the Head said it a few times.' Anna decided it was worth pushing a little, not that pushing and being assertive was really her thing.

'It's a questioning technique,' he said, and added, 'just verbal, there's no rough stuff, but I can't tell you any detail, and no I can't explain why not either.'

Anna left a suitable moment's silence before very clumsily changing the topic.

'Who's behind this? You suspect someone, don't you?'

'I suspect that Petric and his colleagues aren't the driving force, yes.'

'You know who is?' It was as much a statement as a question. Anna still wasn't sure how far she should probe.

'I have a suspicion about who might be behind it, but no evidence.'

'How do we get evidence?'

'We,' Michael stressed the "we", 'focus on finding this location, evidence will either be available or it won't.'

'And if there is evidence?'

'Then I,' and now Michael stressed the "I", 'will decide how to tackle them.'

'We're a team you know,' Anna tried to sound as casual and light-hearted as she could, but couldn't help meaning it. There was something exciting about working with a real-life secret agent, but something disturbing about knowing what had been done to an innocent man and what else might be being planned.

'We are a team, Anna,' Michael said, without joking.

It took another half hour for Michael to reach the next destination. Google Earth, Maps and Streetview had been a Godsend to Anna and her colleagues for doing basic research. From the comfort of her desk she could look at aerial photographs of a location and get an idea of its appearance. The next candidate site looked hopeful, and while Michael had been driving Anna had checked again for bus stops and newsagents. This location looked quieter.

Anna heard the car stop and Michael switch over to his in-ear transceiver, the signal boosted by the comm's system in the car. Provided he stayed within range of the car she'd maintain communications with him. The map showed the car stopped at the end of a short road, the industrial site at the other end.

After a short while, Michael came on the radio. 'I think we can rule this one out, too.'

'How come?' asked Anna, 'it satisfies all the criteria, I can't see any bus stops and there's a distinct lack of newsagents. Don't tell me there's another burger van?'

'No,' said Michael, 'but I think we can rule it out on account of the only vacant unit has burned down.'

Anna swore, quietly.

'I heard that,' said Michael. 'Send me the details of number three, let's hope it really is in the last place we're going to look.'

'If not, we're snookered,' said Anna, sending the next set of details and directions to the car's navigation system.

Wayne looked up and grinned. 'Stuffed, more like,' he said, 'if it's not the next one then you're stuffed.' He got up and walked off in the direction of the coffee machine.

Anna and Michael said little during the twenty minutes it took Michael to drive to the next location. Anna could hear the engine rev's dropping as Michael slowed.

'How does it look?' she asked.

'Not good,' was the reply.

'Oh now what? Don't tell me, there's a police station opposite it.' Anna couldn't keep the frustration out of her voice.

'I'd have thought you'd have noticed something like that,' said Michael. 'No, but there are tower blocks near-by, residential and office. This place looks possible but it's just overlooked by too many people.'

'So now what do we do?' Anna sighed and slumped back in her chair. Obviously unable to resist the temptation Wayne popped his head over the divide, grinning.

'Told you,' he said, 'stuffed.' He disappeared again.

'Back to square one,' Michael said, 'can you widen the search parameters?'

Anna thought for a moment. 'No, let's go back to the original parameters. You said a disused light commercial unit.'

'Probably disused, or at least several of the surrounding units are disused.'

'Next to a unit which is used or was previously used by a taxi company.'

'Yes, or at least a business which had a sign saying taxi. I saw...' Michael's voice trailed off. Anna waited for him to continue.

'What were you looking at? Don't tell me, you can't tell me.'

'I can't tell you everything, but the information is incomplete,' Michael said, stressing the word "incomplete" as though it might have some other meaning.

'So it may or may not have been a taxi company,' Anna said.

'Possibly, any other type of company uses the word taxi?' Michael asked.

'Not that I can think of,' Anna said, 'unless it was part of another word like "taxonomy" or "taxation".'

'Tax is more likely to be an accountancy practice, probably an office location, this needs to be more commercial,' said Michael.

'So maybe it's "taxidermy",' said Anna.

There was a silence between them. It couldn't really be that obvious, could it? Before Michael could say anything Anna was typing away, adjusting the search parameters in the various programs she'd been using.

'Bingo,' she said quietly. 'There is only one company in the Greater London area with the word "taxidermy" in its title which went out of business in the last twelve months. It's in a small industrial estate on Willbury Lane, near Edmonton, about fifteen minutes from your location, details are on their way.'

Anna pressed the final key with a flourish and the navigation details were on their way to the Audi.

Anna felt like there was an extra tension in the air, and kept thinking that this would prove Michael right, that the location would be in the last place they looked. She scribbled down some notes, ideas about what else to search for if this didn't turn out to be successful.

Soon enough she heard the tone of the car's engine drop.

'Looks promising,' said Michael, 'the units are at the end of a small road, narrow access. What's on the other side?'

Anna looked at the maps on her screen. 'The far side is a wall, then railway tracks.'

'Even better. Quiet area, not overlooked, access to open ground. I need to go and have a closer look.'

'Be careful,' Anna said before she could stop herself.

'Don't worry, I'll be careful,' Michael said in a teasing tone of voice.

There was the sound of the car door opening and closing. She was tempted to ask for a running commentary, but bit her tongue. She tried to imagine Michael walking nonchalantly along, sneaking a crafty glance down the road, or however field agents did it. She couldn't hear much over the comm's system, it screened out a lot of background noise, and it took what felt like an age before she heard the car door open and close again.

'Bingo,' said Michael triumphantly, 'now we know where they live.'

MICHAEL COULD SEE in the car's rearview mirror the entrance of the road into the industrial estate, such as it was. He could see the pile of car tyres on one side. They looked innocent enough, a pile of car tyres at the entrance to an industrial estate, they looked in keeping with the location. Yet he had touched them, and sensed something. He had sensed the purpose with which someone had put them there. It would be easy to look at them and miss their effect, the pile of tyres narrowed the entrance to the estate, it made the beginning of the road just a little narrower, just enough to make a bottle-neck. Any incursion into the estate would be slower.

He started the engine and drove further down the street, turning into a side road and parking at the side of the road. He pressed keys on the car's control panel and the telephone ringing tone came over the loudspeakers.

'Yes?' said the Head of Operations.

'Sanders,' Michael said, knowing that the Head almost certainly knew who was calling. 'We've found their location.'

'Stand clear,' said the Head, 'we'll continue covert surveillance.'

Michael was very tempted to state clearly just how little he thought covert surveillance would achieve. 'I'm going to stay and observe, I want to see how much activity there is.'

'Agreed. I'll line up SO15 and SO19, we'll ready for a planned assault. Until then, observation only.' The Head sounded even more firm than she had before.

The line went dead.

'So,' Anna said, 'no going in for another look around?'

'No, but if anyone comes out, I might have a word with them.'

'I can get the video feed from the car's camera,' Anna said, 'and do real-time face recognition. If anyone comes out of that road, we'll know who they are.'

Michael had the thought that he wasn't sure he knew everything this car was capable of doing. He did wonder if it really was equipped with machine guns or rockets, or maybe even an ejector seat. He was, however, sure it wasn't fitted with an invisibility device.

'Unfortunately Petric has seen the car,' Michael said, 'I really don't want him getting sight of it, we lose all our advantage if they know we're sitting here keeping tabs on them.'

'Ah, so what do we do now?'

'We,' said Michael, again stressing the "we", 'go for a walk and do it the old-fashioned way.'

'You could use the body cam kit that's in the boot,' Anna suggested.

Michael wasn't sure how Anna knew about the kit in the car's boot, but decided the quickest thing was to have a look. He got out of the car and sure enough, one of the things in the boot was a miniature camera attached by a thin wire to a transmitter pack. He slipped the pack into his pocket, ran the wire up the inside of his jacket and used the adhesive backing on the camera to attach it to his lapel. It looked a little odd, he thought, but only if someone were looking for it, or at close quarters, and he didn't intend to let anyone get too close. He zipped up his jacket and felt the solid presence under his left armpit, the pistol in a concealed holster. He and the Head had agreed that there was too great a chance of coming face-to-face with someone unpleasant to risk being "unprepared". He and the car were now fully equipped. He put on a baseball cap and pulled it down. As disguises go, it wasn't brilliant, but it might avoid being recognised from a distance by someone who had only seen him in a photo.

He walked to the end of the road. Not far down the adjoining road was the entrance to the industrial estate, but he could hardly just stand there waiting to see who came or went. He would also have to assume that Bullock and associates had provided Petric and friends with a photo' of him, and that they would likely recognise him if he got too close. Fortunately, beyond the entrance to the industrial units, was a parade of shops and what looked like a cafe, with seats outside for smokers. Michael started walking down the road towards the entrance to the industrial estate and the cafe beyond it.

Michael was within a dozen metres of the industrial units when a man walked out of the road and turned to walk in the same direction as Michael but ahead of him with his back to Michael. Michael adjusted his walking to keep pace with the man.

'I didn't get a look at his face,' Anna said.

They walked past the cafe, the man showed no sign of stopping. Wherever he was going it wasn't for a coffee break. Michael could see ahead that there was a passageway at the end of the row of shops. He'd like to have asked Anna where the passageway went, whether it was secluded or opened immediately into a populated area, but he dared not speak openly, he was too close to the man to avoid being heard.

The man had almost reached the end of the row of shops and was almost level with the passageway. It was decision time.

Michael took three big strides forward to close the distance on the man. As he closed in the man turned to face Michael, but Michael had already reached into jacket and half pulled out the gun, not enough to be obvious to anyone in the shops but obvious enough to the man.

'Turn around,' Michael said, keeping his voice as low as he could. He could see the man thinking through his options as fast as he could; maybe run (but Michael had the gun), maybe fight (again, the gun), go for the gun (very risky). 'Turnaround,' Michael hissed, making sure he kept just out of arm's reach of the man.

The man turned around slowly. Michael spoke again, just a little louder to make sure he was heard. 'Keep walking, put your hands behind you.' The man walked, slow steps, and put one hand behind his back. Was the other hand going for a gun? Michael didn't wait to find out. He stepped forward and reached out, taking hold of the man's hand. He connected to the man through the hand-to-hand connection, overwhelming the man's mind as suddenly as he could, projecting a rush of mental energy. The man's shoulders sagged.

'Positive ID,' Anna said, 'he's Ilija Dulic, a known associate of Petric's.'

Michael looked at the alleyway, letting the thought permeate through the connection. Without a word the man turned and walked to the alleyway, and he and Michael walked off the road and into the relative cover of the alley. It wasn't ideal, the alley led to the car park of a gloomy office building, but it would have to do. Michael had the man stop and turn to face him. Michael put his palm across the man's forehead. He let his thoughts extend into the man's mind. It was like pushing at a brick wall. Michael's former colleagues had obviously done some work here, preparing the man to resist a psychic interrogation. Michael pushed harder. Any mental resistance could be overcome, it was just a case of how hard you pushed.

Michael got flashes of images; guns, the industrial unit, faces of his former colleagues (at least that confirmed who was giving the orders to Petric and friends), a flash of Crossley's face. Michael pushed harder, a strange sense of concentrating and of deliberately feeling strong and holding the desire to win a staring competition. The wall in the man's mind was strong. The man shuddered again. More images, flashes of other places, streets filled with soldiers, civilians lined up against the wall, terror written across their faces just as bullet holes defined the wall behind them. The man's mind was as much a sewer as Petric's had been. Michael had the sense like someone had told a joke but he didn't get it, that feeling of everyone else knowing a secret but you don't. How hard to push? Enough to demolish the wall? Then what? Michael pushed, and had the sense that he was pushing against glass. He could push hard enough to break through, but it would shatter, be destroyed, irrevocably changed.

Michael looked into the man's eyes. 'Carry on with your day,' Michael said, 'you will remember meeting me like you remember a dream, forgotten quicker than you realise.'

Michael dropped his hand. The man blinked, looked around slowly as though waking from a brief sleep. He turned and walked away, back to the road, and in moments was gone.

Michael waited a few moments, and then strode purposefully back towards the car. He remembered with a jolt that the camera and ear-piece were still active.

ANNA SAT at her desk with her headset on waiting for the meeting to begin. Only minutes after Michael had called in and reported some of what he'd found the MI5 Head of Operations had called a planning meeting to plan the assault on the industrial unit. Anna heard the team from Thames House dial in, Wayne had dialled in, other analysts from MI5 and GCHQ had dialled in, as had Michael. Anna imagined Michael sitting in the car, parked at the side of the road somewhere. She wondered what passers-by would make of the man sitting in a car having a conversation on the hands-free carphone. She imagined they'd think him a sales rep' or something similar, and it amused her to think that none would imagine him being an MI5 field agent taking part in a call to plan an armed assault on a gang of mercenaries hiding in a disused industrial unit near the heart of London.

Two more joined the call, Commander Halbern of SO15, the Metropolitan Police's Counter Terrorism Command, and Commander Straker of SO19, the Met's specialist firearms unit.

The call began. The Head invited one of the MI5 analysts to review their current intelligence.

'We now have reason to believe that the murder yesterday of Gerald Crossley was committed by one or more of a group of three former special forces soldiers.' The pictures of the three came up on Anna's screen, they would be appearing on everyone else's screens. She imagined Michael was viewing the video feed on his mobile phone, via the car's communications system.

The man continued. 'Vince Marshall, Evan Bullock Julian Singh. We believe Crossley was being used as a reluctant courier, probably unaware of who he was working for. These three have employed three Serbian mercenaries.' Three different pictures came up. 'Luka Petric, Ilija Dulic, and an individual we know only as "Vlad". They're wanted by the Hague for war crimes, it seems they've committed virtually every barbaric act any country has a law against.'

The Head cut in. 'Intelligence shows they intend to ambush a delivery of gold bullion, being transferred to the Bank of England from a secure storage facility. They have enough weaponry to bring World War Three onto the streets of London. That will not happen.' The Head paused. In any other conversation it would be for dramatic effect, here it served to let the seriousness of the situation sink in.

The analyst continued. 'The six have been confirmed as using this location to store their arms.' The maps and pictures of the industrial unit came up on the screen.

The Head cut in again. 'As soon as we know all six are at the location we need to be able to launch an assault with maximum force. Commander Halbern, Commander Straker, how long to prepare?'

Straker spoke first. His voice was softer than Anna expected. 'We can mobilise at a moment's notice once we're on-site, I'll have our unit in situ and ready to move within the hour.'

Halbern spoke next. 'My command team will be on-site within the hour, strike team will be ready. SO15 will lead the assault.'

There was a moment's pause. Anna wondered if there was going to be a pissing competition to see who was in charge.

'Commander Halbern will have operational control,' said the Head. So, no pissing. 'MI5 and GCHQ will have assets on-site to provide surveillance. Mr Browning?'

Anna heard Wayne both in her headset and directly from across the desk. 'Surveillance vehicle will be on-site to provide full access to the intelligence network. Comm's will be up for all police personnel and for MI5 spotters.'

'Spotters?' someone asked, Anna wasn't sure who.

Wayne explained. 'Covert MI5 personnel who can track any individual who escapes the scene. They'll coordinate additional forces intercepting any such individual.'

'I want your men to be very clear,' said the Head, addressing no-one in particular but probably talking to everyone, 'these individuals are highly trained soldiers, skilled with guns and knives. If your men find themselves going hand-to-hand with these people, they will lose.'

'Our primary aim will be to apprehend and arrest these individuals,' said Halbern, 'but if they present a threat to any police officer then we will have no hesitation in using deadly force.'

For some reason it was that phrase that made Anna realise how serious this situation was. This was the most serious operation she had ever been involved in. She had a quick glance around the office, and took comfort from being inside a secure building, miles from anyone with a gun. She was an office worker, a very clever one who worked with top-secret material, but her battlegrounds were intellectual. She was glad other people were tasked with taking the battle out into the field.

'Mr Browning, I want you leading the GCHQ support,' said the Head. Anna looked up. Wayne didn't look phased by this.

Wayne replied, 'Certainly, and I'll have Miss Hendrickson online with me to provide operational intelligence support.'

Anna stared at him, wide-eyed, and felt that she'd suddenly taken a definite and unwelcome step closer to those people with guns.

SIXTEEN

WEDNESDAY AFTERNOON

To the north of the small industrial estate was a sports ground, which Michael thought looked worryingly like the place where he'd watched Crossley be killed. It was, however, the best venue for the command centre. The large function room in the sports club building was an ideal staging post for the police assault force to use for their preparations. The function room had comfortable seating, tables and chairs, a small stage, and a bar, which was closed. On one side of the room were several tables laden with hi-tech equipment. A bank of monitors showed the images from CCTV cameras to which GCHQ had "granted" access, and images from covert surveillance cameras placed close to the entrance to the estate.

From here it was a short dash across the playing fields to the north wall of the estate, easily scaled to reach the rear of the industrial unit. Another force would make its way along the embankment of the railway line and over the east wall, while another force entered down the road into the industrial estate approaching from the west. A forth force would prevent any escape to the south into the residential area. The force entering down the road would assault the front of the building, blowing the door of its hinges and throwing in stun grenades and tear gas grenades. All very SAS. Michael noticed that there was no plan for anyone to shout "this is the police, you are surrounded, come out with your hands up". Perhaps, wisely he thought, they considered it very unlikely that any of the six would be so obliging.

There was something that worried Michael. Something annoyed him, like he'd forgotten to do something very obvious and very important. He looked at the policemen (all men he noted) on the other side of the room preparing their weapons, black coveralls, gas masks, radio equipment and the like.

Michael pulled out his phone and picked a number from the contact list.

'What?' answered the Head, not exactly giving the impression she was up for a friendly chat.

'This isn't right,' Michael said.

'If you're going to suggest that you lead the assault then forget it, this is a police operation, and you're there to provide intelligence and support. So be intelligent and follow orders.'

'We both know what those three can do,' said Michael, meaning the three ex-soldiers, his ex-colleagues, 'they know we'll storm their position, they know what's coming.'

'They don't know that we've found them,' said the Head, 'they've no reason to believe they're any less secure today than they were yesterday. If they come back to the unit the police will go in, and you won't.'

The line went dead.

He went over to the desk covered with maps and diagrams. He looked at the plans for the industrial estate. Sure enough, the front door to the unit was the only usable access. There was a fire exit at the rear, but it led straight into the narrow alley that ran along the rear of all the units; it looked like a trap made by the units and the wall between them and the sports fields. There had to be an escape route, and that wasn't it. But neither was the wall to the east. True the other side was scrubland bounded by a railway line, but in the event of an assault on the unit the wall was a barrier, not an exit. The pile of car tyres had narrowed the entrance to the estate, but it had also narrowed the exit. The only clear exit was to the south, through the estate and over a low wall and into a residential area. But it was a long run past all the industrial units, nowhere to hide, no cover. It didn't look right. It looked like a trap, like Marshall and Bullock and Singh had created a trap for themselves.

Whatever was going on, or going to happen, Michael wasn't going to sit and watch it from the command centre. He went to the flight cases containing the assault clothing. He pulled out one of the black suits and all the associated equipment. He took off his shoulder holster, planning to wear it over the top of his suit. He noticed some of the police were wearing body cameras, larger versions of the unit he'd used earlier. Smile, it's all on camera. Why did he still feel like being amongst turkeys celebrating the arrival of Christmas?

'Contact,' called someone seated at the table of monitors. An instant silence fell over the room.

Halbern marched over to the table and studied the monitors. He spoke into his microphone, all the assault teams wearing earpieces, Michael included, heard his words.

'Targets are entering the industrial estate.'

SEVENTEEN

There was immediate activity, all very calm, all very quiet. The assault teams picked up their weapons and filed out of the room. Michael knew they'd make their way to the corridor at the back of the building, not risking being seen outside until they knew their targets were inside the industrial unit and out of sight.

The camera covering the road leading to the industrial estate showed a dark coloured van, possibly a Mercedes, pulling up outside the unit. It stopped right outside the door. That could be a problem, the van was providing a barrier right in front of the door to the unit. They watched as two men got out of the front of the van. The back doors opened and two more got out of the back. They all watched as the four made their way into the unit, and the van was driven over to the side. A fifth man got out of the driver's side of the van and went into the unit. They saw the door close.

'Five targets are now in the unit,' said Halbern.

'Is it Marshall and the others?' Michael heard the Head ask, her voice coming over his ear-piece. There was a pause. He could see others had heard the question over their comm's link, they all stood almost motionless waiting for the confirmation.

Anna's voice came over the channel. 'Positive confirmation of Singh, eighty per cent certainty of Marshall, Dulic and Vlad, less certainty about Petric. No confirmation of Bullock.'

'Bullock's no threat on his own,' said the Head.

Halbern made his decision. 'All teams to assault positions,' he said.

Michael moved quickly out of the room and down the stairs. The police assault team were already out of the door and running quickly across the playing field, carrying black coloured step ladders with them. Despite the speed of their approach, it all seemed very calm. The black uniforms stood out against the green of the sports field in broad daylight, but that hardly mattered now. Michael ran with them, keeping low, listening to the updates over the police radio.

'Unit three in position,' Michael heard through his ear-piece. The unit on the south side, covering the egress to the residential area, was in position. They would stay out of sight until the assault began.

The men ahead of Michael were almost at the bushes between them and the wall.

'Unit two in position.' The men on the railway embankment were in position, ready to scale the wall and enter the industrial estate from the east.

Almost immediately he heard, 'unit one in position.' The small group of police would be crouching down just out of sight at the end of the road to the industrial estate. They would be in full view of any passing public, or any residents in the houses opposite. There had been no time, or opportunity to evacuate them, so now they were committed.

Michael got a flash of an image. It just flickered in his mind, like something he'd forgotten. It had a particular sense about it, almost a familiar smell, an unpleasant one. It was the sense of Dulic, it was an image Michael must have picked up from this connection. It was a brief glimpse, of a Claymore anti-personnel mine, and the briefest image of the front door to the industrial unit. And in that moment Michael realised what Dulic had kept from him: this was a trap, it was always planned to be a trap.

The men ahead reached the wall.

'Unit four in position,' one of them said.

There was no hesitation, Halbern's voice came over the radio. 'Go. Go. Go.'

THE SPACE WAS CRAMPED and dark, the five men and their equipment barely fitted. All were dressed in dark battle dress, similar to the police, heavy helmets protected their heads. The dark features of Vince Marshall's face were picked out in the ghostly white light from the small video monitor he held in his left hand. The others watched him as he watched the screen.

'The team by the wall are in place,' he said, 'now the team by the road.'

Petric, Dulic and Vlad watched him intently, sub-machine guns cradled in their laps. Julian Singh sat with his eyes closed as though in deep meditation, which he was.

Singh spoke next. A slow and deliberate voice, his eyes remained closed. 'They've decided the south entrance is the least likely escape route. Browning has no CCTV coverage of this area.'

'Team at the rear are in place,' said Marshall. 'Stand by.' At this they each lowered ear defenders into place and pulled their face masks down, polycarbonate visors covering their eyes. Marshall cradled in his right hand a small device with a flip-top.

With his thumb he flipped the top off, revealing the button beneath. His thumb hovered over the button.

He stared closely at the images on the monitor. He saw the feed from two concealed video cameras, one showing the police group on the other side of the rear wall and the other showing the group at the front of the building. The group at the front had their weapons held ready, two of them were readying shotguns to blow the front door off its hinges.

He saw them move as one. The group to the rear launched their ladders at the wall and climbed over, dropping into the space behind the building. The group at the front raised their shotguns to the door. They never completed their move. Marshall pressed his thumb down on the button.

Even inside their protected space, even with their noise-cancelling ear defenders and eye protectors, even dressed in battle-kit, the noise and force of the explosions was almost unbelievable. They could actually make out the two separate sets of explosions, one from the rear and one from the front. The percussive bangs ceased in an instant, but the ringing in their ears continued, despite this they moved with frightening speed.

Singh was "awake", he pushed open the door/hatch to the bomb shelter they had built inside the industrial unit. Sheets of blast-resistant armour surrounded by sandbags and protected overhead from any roof collapse by steel girders welded into a frame. As they climbed out of the shelter, they were met with a scene of complete devastation. The entire front of the building had been blown away. Smoke and flame swirled around them. Pieces of debris continued to fall to earth. Beyond what used to be the wall was carnage. The Mercedes van had gone, in its place a small mass of twisted and burning metal sitting in a shallow crater. All the other buildings and units were either smoking or on fire.

The five men walked through the carnage without hesitation, stepping over bits of bodies, some recognisable, some not. They walked quickly towards the length of the industrial estate and the residential area at the end.

To their left was a movement, a policeman lying twisted, bleeding and smouldering, moving an arm. One of the five raised his gun and shot the man with a short burst of automatic fire. They marched on, an occasional burst of shooting here and there as they shot any man they thought might still be alive.

Ahead of them was movement, members of unit three, outside the immediate blast radius from the bomb in the van. The five men marched on seemingly unconcerned by the two soldiers peering from behind the edge of a building, visible just enough to aim their weapons.

A single shot rang out and one of the men dropped to the floor, the other man flinched and looked around, desperately trying to see who had fired. A second shot and he collapsed, neither moved again.

There was sound from the left of feet treading in the dirt, more police trying to find a better position, not clear whether they should seek a clear shot or seek cover, but cover from where? Another shot, another policeman fell. The two with him scrambled for cover now fearful of the sniper they couldn't see but who they knew could see them.

The five soldiers walked past them all and strolled out of the residential area. With no more drama than if they were out for an afternoon saunter, they walked through the gate at the side of one of the small apartment blocks and into the small garden at the rear. Another soldier appeared from out of the building, carrying a rifle equipped with a telescopic sight.

The six walked to the end of the garden and through the gate onto the road, then to the two black Land Rovers parked by the side of the road, the blacked-out windows making the vehicles look sinister. They could hear shouts coming from inside the apartments. Every single window had been shattered by the blast waves from the explosions and the residents were still cowering inside, not daring to raise their heads.

Without even a backwards glance Marshall said to the others, 'that will keep them busy for a while.'

MICHAEL SAW the policemen ahead scale the ladders and drop over the wall, barely a moment later came the explosions, enormous percussive bangs that knocked him to the ground. Even though he had been shielded by the wall his ears still rang and his head swam for a moment. He knew he had to get to his feet, but even as he struggled to stand he heard the short bursts of automatic weapons fire.

He ran towards the ladders and scrambled up the nearest one. He heard an individual shot. As he dropped over the wall he heard another shot, and another. Soldiers with automatic weapons and at least one sniper. The trap had been sprung.

He couldn't see for the smoke swirling around him. He put his hand out and felt for the back wall of the industrial unit. He could feel it was blown full of holes. Through his goggles he could begin to see the wall, and he found the door. The explosions had destroyed the lock and the hinges. He was able to pull the door open. Something at the bottom of the door stopped it opening. He looked down at a black bin bag, smoking and crumpled on the floor. As the smoke cleared a little more he saw that the black thing had a blue badge; he couldn't tell which part of the man's body it had been.

He wrenched open the door and staggered in. Smoke and flame picked out holes in the wall. The internal walls separating the warehouse space from the office spaces had been destroyed, but still completely intact was the imposing shape of the bomb shelter. Michael pulled out his gun and advanced. He emerged from the smoking ruins of the industrial unit into the smoking ruins of the industrial estate. He saw bodies, blood, body parts.

It was only then that the ringing in his ears subsided enough that he could hear Halbern screaming over the radio, demanding to know what was happening.

Michael lowered his gun. Nothing was happening. It had all finished.

EIGHTEEN

It seemed like an eternity before more police arrived at the scene, followed minutes later by the first of a fleet of ambulances. Michael muttered something into his police radio when he heard his name. No doubt the Head would be going apoplectic wanting to know what was happening. Because it was a police operation they would have heard everything but been able to do nothing. He'd muted his ear-piece. For the moment he didn't need a tirade of questions and orders in his ear.

Michael looked around him. It reminded him of a battlefield. He'd seen this before, several times. After an airstrike, after heavy artillery had pounded a target. This wasn't how a street in London was supposed to look.

Someone passed in front of him, someone in green, a paramedic, asking him if he was hurt. Michael waved the man away. People were starting to work on saving those who could be saved, there weren't many. Michael holstered his gun.

He turned and walked back into the remains of the industrial unit. Most of the smoke had cleared but the smell of burning and the acrid fumes hung in the air. He could see more clearly now. The imposing black shape of the bomb shelter made it frighteningly clear that this had been a well-orchestrated ambush. They had been lured here, with the single objective of killing as many police as possible, and Michael. The conclusion was inescapable. Everything from Crossley onward had been a trail of breadcrumbs to lure them, him, here. The memory stick, the picture of the cyclone imprinted with a psychic message, the book in Crossley's house, finding Dulic on the road outside.

Other than the bomb shelter there was little left in, or of the inside of the industrial unit. What had been workbenches, chairs, light fittings: all destroyed.

Michael stuck his head into the shelter. It was dark, and small. He pulled out the small flashlight from his jacket pocket. Inside the shelter were five rudimentary seats. One of them must have been hiding somewhere else. He remembered the single shots he'd heard. A sniper position, to pick off any individual police who survived the explosions. On one of the seats was the miniature video monitor device, its screen now dark. Michael didn't think it was worth trying to make a connection with the device. There were too many distractions here for him to focus on creating a psychic connection, and the device just seemed too impersonal to have been imprinted.

He picked up the device and turned it over. There were no distinguishing marks, no manufacturer's logo, nothing except for something written on the back in dark ink. It was hard to see, so Michael carried the device outside into the light. He glanced over at the entrance to the area and saw Halbern talking to some paramedics. Michael looked at the device. What was written looked like the address of a website. The writing was small and dark, but he could make out the address:

. . .

WWW.PSICLONE.NET.RS

He pulled out his mobile phone. The screen was flashing, the Head was trying to call him. He thumbed the cancel button and selected the phone's camera function. The built-in flash flared and the screen showed him the captured image of the back of the monitor device and the writing. He had no doubt that he'd remember the address, but he also knew that shock could play tricks with memory. Even with his experience of battle and combat he knew there was a risk of waking up tomorrow and not remembering the address, a photograph seemed prudent.

He used his thumb to work the phone and pulled up the number of the most recently missed call and dialled it. With his other hand he rubbed the writing off the back of the device, leaving just a dark smudge. PsiClone was not something he wanted the police forensics team poking their noses into. Nor would the Head.

The Head answered. 'Did they escape?' An interesting first question, it showed her true priorities.

'I'm fine, thank you,' he said, not bothering to mask the sarcasm. 'Yes of course they escaped, this is what they planned all along.'

'You mean they always had an escape route planned?'

'No, I mean this whole place was a trap, everything was done just to lead us here.'

The Head sounded like she was on the verge of shouting. 'So not only are they still at large, they are still working on ambushing the bullion delivery and we now have no idea where they are.'

'That's about the size of it.'

'So we are now back at square one,' the Head said.

'No, we now know it's them, we know what they're planning and there's only one time and date when they can do it.'

'But apart from knowing they're going to try and steal millions of pounds of gold we have no idea where they are or how to stop them.' Michael had to admit, the Head did have a point. She went on, 'and you've shown you can't stop them. So what use are you to me?'

'This happened because you wouldn't give me the resources to stop them,' Michael hissed, 'I can't stop the three of them on my own and you know it.'

'What I know,' said the Head in a slow and deliberate manner, 'is that there is only one option left and no reason not to use it.'

'Go on, send a kill squad after them, that worked out so well last time. Where do you propose to send the squad? How are you going to find them without me?'

He heard the Head take in a breath ready to respond, Michael didn't let her. 'We do things my way now. As far as anyone else is concerned this is still a regular anti-terrorist operation, but if I need resources then I get them.'

There was a pause, which went on, and on. Finally, the Head spoke. 'The deal remains the same, you find them and you stop them. I'll provide you with resources if I can without revealing what you're doing.'

Michael didn't give the Head the satisfaction of a reply. He let her speak next. 'We need to review recent events, I want you back in The Office now.'

'On my way.'

'Did they leave anything at the scene that might help?'

'No, nothing,' said Michael, 'they don't make mistakes like that.' He ended the call.

ANNA AND WAYNE sat in silence. They were due to dial back into the conference line of the MI5 Command and Control room, the review meeting would start soon. Even with the headset off they could both still hear the bangs, the shouts, the screams.

Anna looked over at Wayne. He was sitting with his eyes closed. Anna didn't want to close her eyes, when she did she started to imagine the scene at the industrial estate. She had several windows open on her screens with scrolling updates from the police and from the various Internet news services. Reports were mixed, especially in the number of dead. Eye witness accounts from members of the public painted the scene of a miniature world war having taken place.

The latest official figures were eleven dead, seventeen seriously or critically injured, dozens of walking wounded. She had closed all the images of the men they knew were responsible, she couldn't bear to look at the faces of men who had just committed multiple murders.

Wayne stood up and walked off. There would be counselling, that would be standard, and Anna was almost surprised that she was looking forward to being able to talk to someone about this. She now wanted today to end. The phrase "I never signed up for this" had flitted through her mind, but she dismissed it. She knew that stopping events like this was exactly why she had signed up, having to come so close to it was probably inevitable.

Her reverie was interrupted as Wayne returned, and put a large cup of coffee on her desk. She smiled at him, not a very big smile, but it was the biggest she could manage. He smiled back. Neither said anything, they didn't need to.

They both put on their headsets and dialled into the conference call.

As usual, the Head was chairing the meeting.

The various participants announced themselves, and when

Michael (who was obviously in the room in Thames House) introduced himself, Anna had to suppress a gasp of relief. Overall the noise and confusion she had listened to she hadn't been able to hear Michael's voice. The live audio feed had been cut once it became clear that the assault had failed and that there were many casualties. Anna kept wondering if Michael had survived.

The Head began the call.

'Bullock, Marshall and Singh escaped the confrontation, along with the three Serbian mercenaries they have working for them. It seems likely Gerald Crossley never was involved with any far-right group.'

'So what was Crossley's role?' someone asked, Anna didn't recognise the voice.

'They set him up to get our interest, to get us to follow their lead to the warehouse. Their aim all along was to kill as many as they could.'

'And the bullion raid is also a ghost?' the unrecognised voice asked.

Michael answered. 'No, that's genuine. They've made sure they've seriously damaged our ability to interfere with the raid.'

'Why drop hints about the raid?' asked the unrecognised voice, 'we'd possibly never have known about it otherwise.'

'We only committed such a large force to the assault at Edmonton because we suspected what they were planning,' Michael said.

'Basically,' said the Head, 'they had to dangle a big enough carrot in front of us to lure us into a trap, and it bloody well worked.'

'So now what?' asked the voice, 'is the bullion delivery cancelled?'

'Not yet,' said the Head, 'we're considering our options. First order of business is to analyse whatever was left at the scene of the assault.'

A new window opened on Anna's computer, a video conference link to somewhere she'd not seen before. It showed an office, a man was just coming into view of the camera and sitting down at the desk. He looked tall with fair hair.

The Head's voice introduced the man. 'This is Doctor Wilders, he and his team have been analysing materials retrieved from the scene.'

'Good afternoon,' the man said. Anna could hear a trace of Dutch in his accent. The man didn't waste any time with small talk, he launched straight into his report. 'We have not yet completed autopsies on all bodies, but the bullets retrieved so far are all regular issue ammunition. The weapons used were likely Heckler and Koch submachine guns. We can confirm the sniper used the same weapon that was used to kill Gerald Crossley.'

There was a moment's pause. This itself was no great surprise, but it was confirmation that bits of the jigsaw fitted together.

Wilders continued. 'The mines used at the rear of the building were Claymore mines, one either side. The explosives in the vehicle at the front of the building were shaped C4 charges, designed to disintegrate the van and cause maximum shrapnel dispersal.'

Anna tried to focus on the words, or his accent, or the office behind him; anything but imagine what happened to the men caught in the blast of the explosives he was describing so dispassionately.

'Did they leave any evidence that might be of use?' asked the Head.

'No,' was Wilders short but simple answer. 'They left their surveillance equipment, so we know they had three cameras covering the police assault. But they took everything else with them.'

The conversation was interrupted by the sound of an alarm at Wilder's location. They watched Wilder look around. The phone on Wilder's desk rang and he answered it.

'Ja?' Wilders said, dropping into his native language without realising it. He listened for a moment, then put the phone down and spoke to the camera. 'The building has gone into automatic lock-down, I will be back.' And with that he left the office.

There was a long pause, no-one seemed to know whether to wait or speak, or no-one was brave enough to break the silence.

'Whilst he's gone,' said the Head, 'I want the route of the bullion delivery circulated to this team. Analyse it. Tell me where they'll strike. Tell me how we trap them.'

'The delivery's going ahead?' someone else asked.

The alarm at Wilder's location ceased. Everyone waited for a moment. Nothing happened.

The Head replied, 'that's not a decision we make here. But if it's decided to proceed we need to be ready.'

Wilders came back into the office and sat down, facing into the camera. He took a moment to compose himself.

'The laboratory was analysing dust and residue samples from the scene,' he said, 'we detected something quite unexpected, it set off the sensors and locked down the building.'

'What was detected?' asked the Head.

'Uranium.'

'Uranium?' the Head asked. Anna thought she'd never heard the Head sound so surprised before.

'Yes, uranium 235. Metallic dust, from someone working with uranium metal.'

'There are only two things they're likely to want uranium for,' Michael said, 'either a nuclear bomb or a dirty bomb.'

'They can't be making a nuclear bomb, they don't have the

skills or the tools,' someone else said. Anna recognised the voice as one of the MI5 analysts who'd been on previous calls.

'I agree,' Michael said, 'but they do have the capability to make a dirty bomb.'

'Why? Possible strategies?' asked the Head.

Michael speculated. 'Possible options: blow up the bullion delivery with a dirty bomb, contaminate it and the surrounding area with radioactive material, the economic damage would be catastrophic. Threaten to do that but demand a ransom. Distract us with the bomb while they steal the gold?'

'Distract us with an attack on the bullion while they plant the bomb somewhere else,' someone else suggested.

'The inventory on the memory stick,' Anna said, 'it referred to one of the weapons requiring two people to carry it.'

'So there's a strong chance they've built a dirty bomb and intend to use it somewhere in London within the next twenty-four hours,' said Michael.

'There were only traces of uranium found,' said Wilder, 'nothing conclusive.'

'Okay,' said the Head, with a degree of finality. 'We'll pause there. Do your analyses. I need to refer this matter to others. We'll reconvene in an hour.'

The conference call line went dead, meeting over.

Anna took off her headset and looked across at Wayne, who was taking his off.

'As the old Chinese curse went: may you live in interesting times,' said Wayne.

Anna sighed and reached for the coffee cup Wayne had delivered. The coffee had started to go cold. She drank it anyway.

NINETEEN

Michael was back at the desk in the office area and logged on to the computer. It seemed the usual occupant of the desk was on holiday. He took out his phone and brought up the picture of the web address he'd taken. He picked up the phone and dialled.

'Hello Anna,' he said when she answered.

'You're alive,' she said, and then hesitated, maybe embarrassed by what she'd said.

'Yes, I am alive, thank you,' he said, and smiled.

'I haven't finished looking at the bullion route,' Anna said, changing the subject,

'Not a problem, there's something else I'd like you to take a look at.'

'Of course, what?'

Michael cradled his phone between his shoulder and ear as he typed an email. 'I'm sending you a web address. Without actually opening up the website, can you tell me what's there?'

'Of course,' Anna said.

Michael pressed the Send button. There was a few moments' wait.

'Okay,' Anna said in a curious tone, 'let's have a little prod at this.'

'Prod?' asked Michael, and then wished he hadn't. He really should learn, never ask a techie to explain what they're doing, because they will explain, in a painful degree of detail.

'Yes, just prod the address and see what's there and where it is,' said Anna, with a helpful lack of tech-speak, 'just in case it's got any unpleasant surprises.'

He could hear her tapping away again at the keyboard.

'Well,' she said, 'despite having a dot RS address the site isn't in fact in Russia, it's hosted on a web server in Armenia.'

Michael thought that was curious, but probably not important. Anna continued, 'it's a web host we've come across before, these sites disappear very quickly, usually used to host a single message.'

'A message?'

'Yes, usually used by unsavoury people who want to send a single message. The site typically disappears if the message isn't read quickly and it disappears once the message is read. Do you want me to try to download the video?'

'No, thank you, I'll speak to you at the next briefing.' Michael hung up the phone.

A one-shot message, for him. He used the phone to select the computer as the audio source for the headset. Whatever the message was it wouldn't be for public consumption.

He opened the browser window on the desk computer and entered the web address. As expected the MI5 firewall blocked him, warned him about unauthorised access to suspicious web sites and asked for his security clearance to continue. Michael entered his personal ID number and password and clicked the Submit button. It took a few moments for the web page to open. A plain black page with a single word and next to it a text box.

The word was "Evan". The page obviously wanted the user

to enter Evan's second name. Obvious. Bullock. Too obvious. This was a message for Michael. It could only be a message for him for in case he survived the assault. If he didn't, the message would disappear within hours.

Evan Bullock, nickname Evan Bollock. Only Michael would have thought to enter that. He typed in the word and pressed Enter. After a few moments, a video window opened, and the video started to play.

It was a picture of three men sitting on a sofa, looking into the camera, looking at Michael. The big, dark presence of Vince Marshall, the blond-haired Evan Bullock, and the thin frame of Julian Singh.

Bullock spoke first. 'Hi Michael,' he waved, the others gave a small wave. Michael had to almost hold down his hand to stop himself from waving back. 'So you walked away from our surprise party? We did tell you we'd come back for you, we are coming for you Michael.'

Singh spoke next. 'We've had to go to a lot of trouble Michael, all because of you. But don't worry, it will all be over soon.'

Bullock spoke. 'Sorry about Crossley, but hey, have to break an egg to make an omelette and all that.'

Marshall again. 'You must know by now Michael that you can't stop us. We've got some friends working with us. With the three of us, the three of them, and just you on your side, odds aren't in your favour.'

Bullock, 'We'll be seeing you buddy, up close and personal.'

Singh, 'You should have stayed with us Michael, we've had so much fun, can't imagine your life has been as much fun. Still looking over your shoulder? You know you can never trust her?'

Marshall, 'You had your chance Michael, you chose your path. They made us what we are then they wanted rid of us, and you chose to side with them. We've got bigger ambitions, much bigger ambitions.'

The three of them waved at the camera and the image faded.

Michael sat there. It had been three years since he'd last seen the three of them, since that freezing cold night in Afghanistan where choices had been made. But Michael had to focus on the present, on the here and now. Something, a thought of something irritated Michael. Something one of them had said. There would be no point trying to access the video again, the website would have deleted itself by now. "Much bigger ambitions." It was the emphasis Marshall had put on "much", teasing Michael.

He pulled out his phone and composed a text. He had to speak to the Head before they went into the next briefing.

MICHAEL WAS ALREADY SITTING in the windowless meeting room when the Head arrived. The room was one of the many small meeting rooms in Thames House. Being in the centre of the building it had no windows, no natural light, just the harsh glare of strip lights set into designer light fittings. The room was bare and functional, just a meeting table and chairs and the obligatory video conference equipment. He sat facing the door.

The Head closed the door behind her and looked Michael in the eyes. Michael stayed seated.

Straight to the point, he said 'the bullion delivery's not the target.'

She continued to stare at him for a moment. 'How can you be sure?'

'I'm sure. They'll still stage some kind of attack, but it's not their primary target, they're after something else, something bigger.'

'What?'

'Don't know.'

'Come to me when you do know.'

'The delivery is a trap, but it's not a bluff or a feint.'

Again the Head eyed him, as though looking into his soul for answers. 'What's going on Michael?'

'You told me my role was to stop them, that's what I'm working to do.'

'So what do you propose?' asked the Head.

'Find them, but the only leverage we have now is to stop the delivery, thwart whatever they're planning.'

'We only have one lead, and that's the delivery.'

'And if we let them make their play, more people will get killed.'

'Not if we're ready for them.' The Head was standing firm, she seemed solid in her confidence.

Michael took in a deep breath, and exhaled slowly.

'When you came onto the PsiClone project the four of us had already been working together for years,' said Michael.

'Yes, I did read the files,' there was more than a hint of sarcasm in the Head's voice. She remained standing.

'We'd been a special forces unit together for four years. We'd been in battle together. We'd saved each other's lives.'

The Head remained impassive. Michael watched her face, but she never gave anything away, nothing that Michael could ever read.

'By the time you joined the project we'd already realised what powers that drug gave us.'

'That drug,' the Head said, 'was never meant to give you any power, it was only meant to boost your stamina.'

'But it didn't, and instead you ended up with four powerfully psychic soldiers.'

'Three of whom have now run amok using those powers for God knows what purpose.'

'Yes,' said Michael, emphasising his point, 'because someone decided that they were too powerful to have around and sent a kill squad after them, after me.'

'An unfortunate outcome,' the Head said, leaving the ambiguity hanging in the air.

'Yes, unfortunate,' said Michael.

'So now the three are in London threatening a Bank of England bullion delivery.'

'Which brings us back to the point that the only thing we can do to interrupt their plans is to stop the delivery, force them to do something unplanned.'

'Something that we can't predict or control,' said the Head, 'the only time and place we know they will be is when they go after that delivery.'

'They know you'll be waiting, your ambush for them is what they're expecting, you're doing exactly what they want you to do.'

'I'm sorry, Michael.' Michael didn't think he'd ever heard the Head use the word "sorry" before. 'But we all report to someone higher up the food chain, and the orders are that the bullion delivery will happen as scheduled.'

Michael up looked at her, physically if not metaphorically.

'They still believe it was you who sent the kill squad,' he said.

She said nothing. He said nothing to indicate his opinion on the matter.

'Stop the delivery, force them to change their plans, when they do they'll have to do something which makes them visible,' said Michael.

'And if they don't? What if they just melt away, we'll never find them, you'll never find them.' The Head made the last point as an accusation.

'I'll find them,' said Michael, 'they've invested too much to just walk away, this is as much about revenge as it is profit.'

'The delivery goes ahead, that's already been decided.'

'What about the threat of a dirty bomb?'

'The Bank needs that delivery of gold, so the delivery goes ahead. Our orders are clear, stop the attack and make sure the delivery gets through.'

'It doesn't make sense,' Michael said, more passion in his voice, 'they're powerful but they're still just soldiers, what would they do with a thousand bars of gold? Start making ear-rings?'

The humour, of course, was lost on the Head.

'Enough,' said the Head, an added edge of finality in her voice. 'It has already been decided, the delivery goes ahead. We need to be ready when they make their move, and I need to know that I can rely on you.'

Michael stood up, and looked her squarely in the eye. 'You and I both have the same aim, and that's to stop them. If someone's made the decision to keep the convoy on schedule, then that's what we'll have to work with.'

She considered him for a moment, and then walked past him and out of the meeting room, back towards the bigger room where the planning meeting was about to resume.

Michael looked at his reflection in the window between the room and the corridor. He paused, and looked into his eyes reflected in the glass. He wondered if he had what it would take to stop them, but he knew he did. He wondered if he really would do whatever it would take. Perhaps now was the time he would find out.

TWENTY

The black Land Rover Discovery swept down the road, large anonymous warehouses on either side sat behind fences and security gates. The vehicle swung into the entrance of one such unit, dark and without any sign to identify its owner. The vehicle stopped at the solid barrier blocking the entrance. The driver's side window slid down and an arm reached out, holding an identity card up to the scanner. The enormous gate slid to one side and the barriers sunk into the road, clearing the way for the vehicle to enter the site. It drove swiftly down the road along the side of the warehouse and turned sharply right into the loading bay towards the rear of the building. As the barrier rose again to block the entrance and the gate slid shut, the shutters of the loading bay descended and the vehicle disappeared from view.

Inside the warehouse, the inner shutters of the loading bay rolled up and the vehicle drove forward into the rear part of the building. Inside was a tennis-court sized room, bright lights, polished floor, clean, almost antiseptic, everything the previous industrial unit was not. The vehicle stopped alongside the other Land Rover and a similarly black BMW X5. All three had darkened windows. To one side were stainless steel workbenches, covered with the group's arsenal. Knives, small arms, submachine guns and other more powerful weapons were lined up in neat rows, clips of ammunition next to them, a plethora of hi-tech communications devices completing the collection. On the other side of the room were the sources of all the noise. Petric and Dulic were facing a large flat-screen TV playing a video game, the object of which seemed to be to kill as many innocent bystanders as possible, while Vlad was amusing himself punching a floor-mounted bag.

Marshall left the vehicle and strode across the room, not glancing at the weapons or his mercenary employees. Whilst he, Bullock and Singh had exerted a degree of psychic control over the three Serbians he wasn't sure how far he trusted their ability to control them. The Serbians were violent, but more than that they enjoyed violence, they were driven to inflict pain and suffering. The sooner they could complete this mission and get rid of the three (permanently) the better.

He didn't like this mission, and the thing he disliked most was having to employ the Serbians. They were unstable. The profits however, the potential profits, were enormous, but it was too messy for his liking. He preferred operations like their Hong Kong venture. That had been most satisfying. Using their "additional" skills they'd created tension between rival drugs gangs, killed a few to prompt some violence between the gangs, taken control of key figures in the two gangs, had them organise huge drugs deals which they then "interrupted" and took the money, and left the gangs to kill each other in a blood bath. It had been simple, quick, relatively low risk.

This current operation was taking longer, required more risk. It needed them to gain psychic control of more people over longer distances for more time in more complex and unpredictable situations. He still wasn't sure the profit was worth the effort. But every time he thought this he reminded himself how much profit was involved, and was satisfied, for a while.

He left the loading area through a security locked door on the far side and walked through into the office area. He walked a short way down the corridor, subdued lighting and soft carpet made such a change from the shit-hole they had endured at Edmonton. At another locked door he held the ID card up to the scanner and heard the lock click as it unlocked. He entered the room. It was a large office space, similar carpet and lighting, no windows. Like the rest of the building, it was secure and safe from any prying eyes.

Bullock lay on a reclining chair, eyes closed, as though asleep. Against the long wall was a wide desk and above the desk a bank of computer monitors, two high and six wide. The light from the images lit the room. The monitors showed images from the security cameras outside the building, various maps, images from traffic cameras, while others showed tables of figures and information. Julian Singh sat at the desk, fingers on a computer keyboard, typing in response to the changing details on one of the monitors.

'Well?' said Marshall, 'what's new in the world?'

Singh turned around. 'Finance set up is done, that's all ready. Now we just need some money to pay into it.'

'And the message?'

'Sanders accessed the website twenty minutes ago.'

'Shit,' said Bullock, 'why won't he just be good mannered and die?'

Bullock spoke without opening his eyes. 'Browning's in another meeting. The bullion delivery's going ahead, route unchanged. Sanders is in the meeting.'

'Where's everyone else?' Marshall asked.

'Where they're supposed to be, at the moment,' Bullock said. 'Browning and his team are all at the Doughnut.'

'What about the schedule for the delivery?' asked Marshall. He sat down in one of the executive chairs. He preferred the rooms with wooden floors, he could roll around the floor using the castors on the chairs. He couldn't roll around on the carpeted floor, but they needed the security around this room to keep the Serbians out.

'Schedule unchanged,' Singh said.

'Are the kids ready?' Marshall meant the Serbians.

Singh looked up at the monitor, at the three mercenaries playing their video game and punching the bag. 'Oh yes,' he said, 'they're ready. We just need to keep them occupied until tomorrow.'

'Fine,' said Marshall, 'they need to stay in tonight, I don't want them causing any trouble.'

'Are we set for our next recruitment?' asked Sigh.

Bullock, eyes still closed, answered. 'We're ready. Our candidate will be home by about six-thirty tonight. It's not too far from here.'

'Good,' said Marshall. 'Now, what are we going to do about Sanders?'

Singh spoke. 'It's not what we're going to do, it's just how and when.'

'Much as I'd like to take our time and kill him really, really slowly,' said Bullock, 'the sooner we get him out of our way the better.'

'Agreed,' said Marshall. 'When we hit the convoy do we know where he'll be?'

'No,' said Bullock, 'they're discussing plans, but no decisions yet on who's going to be where. But as soon as they know we'll know.'

'And Browning has no idea we're listening in to his head?' asked Marshall.

'If anyone does realise then we'll just get rid of him,' said Bullock.

Marshall just nodded in agreement. Tidying up after this was feeling more like knocking over a row of standing dominoes, it was fine so long as all the dominoes were in just the right place. He'd rather they had a plan that involved fewer but more positive actions.

'How will we know if our candidate does what we expect?' asked Marshall. He looked up at the monitors. One of them showed the expanse of the pedestrian area outside the tower blocks at Canary Wharf.

'We're keeping an eye on him,' said Singh, motioning to the monitor. 'We've got facial recognition running on the public CCTV system. We'll pick him up as soon as he leaves work.'

'Impressive,' said Marshall. 'How did you manage that?'

'He didn't,' said Bullock, 'I had our Mister Browning set the surveillance running and pipe the output to us.'

'Traceable?' asked Marshall. The last thing he wanted was doing something clever but leaving a digital trail which led straight to them.

'Eventually it will be, but not in time to be a worry to Mister Browning,' said Bullock. He opened his eyes and sat up, blinking as his eyes adjusted to the light. 'They've just taken a break.' He swung his legs over the side of the reclining chair, elbows on his knees, rubbing his temples. Maintaining a psychic connection and listening in to someone for a prolonged period always gave him a headache. It wasn't the reading that was the problem, it was maintaining the block that prevented the target from becoming aware. Without the block the target would get the feeling that someone was watching them. Left unchecked they could become mildly paranoid.

'Okay,' said Marshall. 'We've got a couple of hours before we need to leave. Let's review our options for getting rid of Sanders.'

Anna and Wayne were both back at their desks and dialled into the conference call line by the time the Head started the meeting. The usual suspects were involved; the GCHQ analysts (although Anna thought they never seemed to contribute much), the MI5 analysts (who didn't seem to contribute much more), Michael, and the Head. Anna hadn't "figured out" the Head. The woman was certainly headstrong, focused, and it was obvious that only Michael was prepared to challenge her. Anna wondered what history there was between Michael and the Head. What was the Head's background? She was Head of that section of MI5, although Anna wasn't entirely sure which specific section that was.

Anna's speculation was interrupted by the Head.

'It's been decided,' said the Head, 'the bullion delivery will go ahead as planned.'

There were gasps of disbelief from the people on the phone and those in the room in Thames House. One of the MI5 analysts asked the question everyone wanted to ask: why?

'The Governor of the Bank of England made it clear to the Director General that the Bank requires the bullion to be delivered on time. So it will be.'

'Surely they can delay it, even just a day,' protested one of the other MI5 analysts.

'What about the threat of a dirty bomb?' asked another, unrecognised voice.

'It's been decided,' said the Head, in a tone that left no room for further challenge. 'The threat of a dirty bomb is credible, but not likely, more likely is the threat to ambush the delivery. Our responsibility is to anticipate any ambush of the delivery and thwart it.'

Anna had opened several windows on her computer, ready for what she expected to come next.

'What options are there for ambushing the convoy?' asked the Head.

Anna spoke up, before anyone else could.

'I've analysed the route,' she said. 'Assuming that they're not going to do something like ambush it in the middle of the motorway...' she was interrupted, by one of the other GCHQ analysts dialling in from another location.

'How can we assume that?' the analyst asked.

It was Michael who answered. 'Reasonable assumption, given the weaponry we believe they have and their limited numbers they can't do something like close the motorway and control that big an area.'

Anna continued, glad that the people in the room couldn't see her smile. 'Given the size of their force, six people and mainly hand-held weapons, it will have to be a small and focused attack. Depending on traffic conditions at the time there are only three locations where the traffic is caught in a bottleneck and slowed down but there's still enough access for them to assault the vehicle and make a getaway.'

Anna clicked with her mouse and the maps and diagrams from her screen appeared on the screens in the room in Thames House and on the screens of those dialling in.

Anna began her analysis. 'The convoy will take the M4 from Heathrow towards the City. It will then join the A4 and go through Chiswick, Hammersmith, Knightsbridge, Covent Garden, along the Embankment and into the City of London.'

'That's passed all the most significant sites in London,' said one of the analysts, 'Downing Street, Buckingham Palace, Westminster. An attack there would be catastrophic.'

Anna was ready to respond. 'And for that reason we don't believe the attack can happen at any point closer than Earl's Court, security around significant buildings is too intense, far too much CCTV coverage, concentrations of police and security services. They have to strike some time after the motorway and before Earl's court.'

She paused, waiting to see if there was any challenge. None came, so she continued. Our analysis suggests the three most likely points are the M4 to A4 junction, the junction with the A316 at Chiswick, and at Hammersmith.'

'So how do we stop the assault?' asked one of the MI5 analysts, 'assuming we want to stop them before they blow up the delivery truck.'

'Yes, we do,' said the Head, sharply.

Anna went on. 'All three locations form a bottleneck where the traffic slows, but it also means there's only a limited number of ways the attackers can approach. All three locations, however, give easy access to the river as an escape route.' She clicked her mouse and more detail appeared on the screens showing arrows and labels.

Anna said, 'we can assume they'll have their sniper providing cover, the only reasonable locations for a sniper will be here.' A click and red circles appeared on the maps picking out where the sniper might cover each location.

'Plan for a counteroffensive?' the Head said.

Michael spoke. Since Anna hadn't shared any of her thinking with Michael he must have been making it up as he went along, but he sounded like it was all planned out. 'Armed teams in vehicles surround the delivery truck, out of sight but keeping the truck inside a protective box. Surveillance vehicle ahead of the truck maintaining the communications network.'

'And the potential ambush locations?' the Head asked.

'SO15 and SO19 teams to cover the expected approaches to each of the locations, teams in situ to intercept the sniper as he arrives, so in place two hours ahead of time.'

There was a silence as everyone digested the plans and suggestions. Anna looked up at Wayne, who was looking over his shoulder. He turned and met Anna's stare, smiled and looked back down at his screen.

Wayne spoke. 'This is all based on what we know at the moment, things could change very quickly, even traffic conditions could change things.'

'Agreed,' said Michael, 'but what they're planning is high risk, and only works if they're able to get away, so their ability to change is limited.'

'We still need to be able to respond to surprises,' said the Head, 'we'll need complete electronic surveillance and all analysts running real-time scenarios to predict changes.'

'I think Miss Hendrickson should be in the Command Room in Thames House,' said Michael.

Anna's heart almost stopped. She knew she had to say something now, like "no", but the words wouldn't come out. She could feel her throat tightening and now her heart was pounding. She looked up at Wayne, who looked up and met her stare.

'I think Anna should be in the surveillance vehicle,' said Wayne.

Anna shook her head vigorously. She waved her hands, drew a finger across her throat. She looked around her desk for anything she could throw at him.

'Good idea,' said Michael, 'the closer to the action the better.'

'No,' Anna finally managed to say.

'I agree,' said the Head, cutting Anna off before she could say anything else. 'Mister Browning, I assume you can arrange for Miss Hendrickson to access all her IT resources from the surveillance vehicle?'

Anna sat down, nearly collapsing into her seat. Wayne was

looking over his shoulder again, then back down at his keyboard, no longer making eye contact with Anna.

'Yes, the surveillance vehicle is fully equipped to access the computer services,' said Wayne, still not looking up.

The conversation moved on, and Anna sat staring at her screen. She had been excited, nervous but excited, about being involved in such a high-profile operation. But she had never wanted to leave the Doughnut. This was where she was meant to be. This was the world she knew.

'Miss Hendrickson?' she heard someone saying over her headset, realising she'd missed a good part of the conversation.

'Sorry,' she said.

It was the Head. 'Has any useful intelligence been gained from the site of the Edmonton assault?'

It took Anna a moment to refocus, to bring her imagination back under control and focus again at the screens in front of her.

'Er, at the scene, no mobile phones,' she struggled to bring up the right screen of information, everything suddenly seemed more difficult. 'They didn't use mobile phones.'

'Was there any CCTV in the area?' asked the Head.

'Not directly,' Anna answered. 'But we analysed car number plates from CCTV cameras on the surrounding roads, reviewed the owners, we've identified twelve possible vehicles.'

'Can we narrow it down?' asked one of the other analysts on the call.

'Not yet,' said Anna, 'but on the morning of the operation we can set up alerts for any of the twelve that enter the area of the operation. And we have an ongoing alert set up for the mobile phone that Petric used on his recce.'

'Very good,' said the Head, drawing the meeting to a close. 'I assume you'll be ready to join the surveillance vehicle tomorrow morning Miss Hendrickson?'

'It'll leave its base at four-thirty tomorrow morning,' said one of the other GCHQ analysts.

'Yes,' Anna managed to say. She couldn't find the words to say anything else.

The call ended, and Anna took off her headset, feeling like she'd just been given the worst news ever. Being told she'd been fired wouldn't have compared. She struggled to believe that she'd actually heard what had been said on the call.

She looked up at Wayne Browning. He was sitting with his elbows on his knees, rubbing his temples. She said nothing. Finally, he looked up.

'Sorry,' he said, 'I have a headache.' He got up and wandered away.

TWENTY ONE

WEDNESDAY - EARLY EVENING

The houses in this part of Clapham were grey, three-storey terraces. All the windows were clean, the doorknobs polished, a selection of expensive German cars parked on both sides of the road. The black Land Rover cruised into the road and parked at the end. Two men got out; a big dark-skinned man and a not-quite-so-big blond-haired man. Dressed in dark business suits, they looked in keeping with the rest of the street. They walked to one of the houses, up the steps, and the man in front pressed the call button for one of the apartments. There was a pause before the door opened. A man looked out from the foyer of the house. Casual but smart dress, grey hair combed over, professional but retired.

The big man at the door smiled. 'Mr Green? We spoke on the phone, I'm Detective Sergeant Baker from Thames Valley Police.' He held out his hand, and the man in the house accepted the handshake without hesitation. In that moment he took in a deep breath and his eyes half-closed. He exhaled slowly and swayed slightly where he stood.

The big man said, 'shall we go inside, Mr Green?' Without letting go of the handshake Mr Green led the way into the house, the telepathic dominance making his steps slow like he was wading through water. The blond man followed and shut the door behind him.

In the foyer their voices echoed off the tiled floor and bare but very smart plaster walls. One of the dark wooden apartment doors was open, and Mr Green lead them towards it. Mr Green stopped and turned to look at the big man. The big man looked down at Mr Green, allowing his mind to envelop Mr Green's consciousness. Mr Green did not offer much in the way of resistance, his mind was like wet clay in the hands of a master potter.

'Go back inside, Mr Green,' said the big man, 'and sit down comfortably. In a few moments you'll remember what you were doing and you'll never again think anything of me.' He let go of Mr Green's hand.

Mr Green blinked a couple of times and turned very slowly to go back into his apartment. He closed the door behind him.

Marshall turned to Bullock, 'are you sure I can't kill him?' He grinned.

'Sorry, no,' said Bullock. 'Mason's flat is on the first floor.'

A wide staircase led from the foyer to the landing on the first floor. Three doors, one in front and one either side. They walked to the door facing them. Bullock pulled out a small pouch and from it pulled a set of skeleton keys. He selected the three most likely keys and tried each in the lock. Nothing. He selected the next key and tried again. The lock was stiff, but as he turned the key it clicked loudly and unlocked.

At that moment a door behind them opened, and an older lady stepped out. Before she realised they were there Marshall had drawn his pistol, the long cylinder of the silencer pointing at her forehead. Her mouth fell open. He watched as she inhaled, no doubt to scream. In just as deft a motion, Bullock stepped forward and put his hand across the woman's mouth, the surge of mental energy subduing her in a moment. She sagged and Bullock held her arm to keep her from collapsing. Marshall was still thinking through whether killing her was the easiest option, but of course it wasn't planned, and unnecessary deviations from the plan could only cause problems.

He looked at Marshall. 'No, you can't kill her either.'

There was a buzzing from Marshall's jacket, his mobile phone. Slowly, Marshall lowered his gun, then put it back in the holster inside his jacket. The phone buzzed again.

Bullock looked into the woman's eyes. She looked at him, staring without seeing.

'Go back inside,' he said, 'you came out and no-one was here. You might remember something from the television last night, a faded memory, a man with a gun. The memory will disappear, you will enjoy your day.'

Slowly he let go of her arm. She stayed standing. He took his hand away from her mouth. Without speaking she turned and went back inside her apartment and closed the door.

Marshall's phone buzzed again. He pulled it out and tapped the screen. 'Yes,' he said. He listened for a moment then tapped the screen again and put the phone back in his pocket. 'Mason's on his way.'

The two of them turned back to the door they'd opened. They went into the apartment and closed the door behind them, just as they heard the buzz of the electronic lock of the front door opening.

The house was old but the apartment was modern. Polished wooden floor, flat-screen TV with soundbar and surround sound speakers. A smoked glass coffee table and a dark leather three-piece furniture set. It was all a little too modern for Bullock's taste. The owner was a yuppie and belonged in the 1980s. They stood either side of the door, backs against the wall, waiting. It was only moments before there was a key in the lock and the door opened.

Jason Mason strode into the apartment, shiny suit and shiny shoes, smart attaché case in one hand and keys in the other. He never saw either of the men before Bullock had his hand on the back of Mason's neck as Marshall closed the door. The psychic control was almost instant. Mason let go of the attaché case and it fell to the floor, Bullock reached with his other hand and took the keys before they fell. He led Mason into the living room and they both sat on the sofa. Mason's eyes closed as he relaxed deeper.

Marshall took out his phone and selected a number, his call was answered almost immediately. 'We've got Mason, come up,' was all he said.

Bullock was already talking to Mason, speaking softly and slowly, giving instructions, Mason nodding gently as the commands sunk so deeply into his psyche. Marshall opened the door and Singh joined them, dressed similarly, dark business suit.

'Is this going to take long?' asked Marshall.

Singh huffed. 'Why? You got somewhere you need to be?'

Bullock stood up. 'He's all yours,' he said to Singh. Singh sat next to Mason, Bullock stood next to Marshall to watch.

'For all his bravado,' said Bullock, 'he's actually a really weak minded little shit.'

'That's alright,' said Marshall, 'all he needs to be is a useful little shit and then we can get rid of him.'

They watched as Singh took from his inside jacket pocket a small, faux leather diary. It looked smart, but was cheap. He took Mason's hands and placed them over the diary, then he placed his hands on top of Mason's.

'Jason,' he said, his voice soft, well-spoken. 'This diary is important. You can feel it, can't you.'

Mason nodded slowly. 'It's a connection between us, it connects our minds.'

Marshall had always wondered about Singh's ability to connect with physical objects. He'd finally got his head around the idea of controlling someone's mind, a psychic connection with another individual, especially when he realised how useful it could be. But the idea of connecting with an inanimate object was just weird. But, it seemed to work, at least for Singh, and Sanders.

'Keep this with you,' said Singh, 'know that I am with you, you can hear my thoughts, you can share your thoughts with me, I can protect and guide you.'

Mason seemed to smile slightly. Singh kept hold of Mason's hands for a little while longer, then stood up. 'He's done, our very own cash machine is ready for business.'

'We just leave him like that?' said Bullock.

'He'll be fine,' said Singh. 'Twenty minutes he'll wake up and remember none of this, not consciously.'

'Right,' said Marshall, 'one more member of our merry band and we're in business. Let's go.'

They left the apartment, Mason still sitting on the sofa holding the diary.

TWENTY THREE

LONDON - PRESENT DAY - THURSDAY MORNING

Paddington Green Police Station was a regular police station, an ugly 1960s concrete monstrosity. It was also a high-security police station and was just the other side of Hyde Park from the nearest potential ambush location at Hammersmith. With the large surrounding fence and solid security gates enclosing its forecourt it made the idea staging post. Police milled around the courtyard, many in riot gear carrying a variety of shields and automatic weapons. Few spoke, the absence of talking was noticeable. Michael stood and watched. Many of the men here would have known colleagues who had been killed at Edmonton. He had no doubt they could all remain professional, but if any of them decided on a little personal revenge it could complicate matters.

The aim of the operation was simple, ambush the ambushers, attack and destroy Marshall and the others before they could launch their ambush of the bullion convoy. It would have been simple, if they knew exactly where and when the ambush was due to take place. But they didn't, they would all have to rely on GCHQ and their cyber-surveillance, and their ability to recognise the initial moments of the ambush. Marshall had obviously matured in his planning and preparation since their last encounter.

Michael heard the Head's voice in his ear-piece. 'Are you ready, Sanders?' She never did manage small courtesies like saying "good morning".

'I'm here, just waiting for the surveillance vehicle,' said Michael.

'Just a few minutes,' came a familiar voice. Anna was in the surveillance vehicle. Her voice sounded like someone trying to sound cheerful when they really weren't.

'Where are the spotters?' asked Michael.

The Head replied. 'They're heading for the convoy's departure location.' Good, thought Michael, they'd have full surveillance of the convoy from the moment it left. He looked at his watch, two hours before the convoy was due to leave.

Michael looked across the courtyard as Commander Halbern came striding towards him.

'Mister Smith?' the Commander asked, stressing a slightly disbelieving tone on "Smith".

'Commander Halbern,' said Michael, reading the name from the badge on the man's jacket, and aware that the Head could be listening.

'Are your lot confident we can get these men?' Halbern asked, 'before they do any more damage?'

'We'll find them, you arrest them,' said Michael.

'You find them,' Halbern said, 'we'll deal with them. I'm not expecting many arrests.'

Halbern looked at him for a moment, then walked off. Michael wasn't sure if Halbern blamed him or MI5 for the death of his men. It had been Michael's investigation that led them to the industrial unit, that led them into the trap.

Michael's pondering was interrupted by the sound of the main gate opening, the armoured steel gate rattling as it slid open. In drove a truck, an ordinary-looking, dark brown lorry. Other than the slightly tinted windows in the cab the Battle Bus looked like any other lorry. It parked in a parking bay at the side of courtyard and the gate rattled its way shut.

A set of stairs unfolded itself from the rear of the truck, revealing a door, the only obvious means of access to the body of the vehicle. The door opened and a man about Michael's age exited the vehicle and walked across to meet Michael.

The man held out his hand. 'Mister Sanders,' the man said in an appropriately low voice, 'my name's Kyle Blake, GCHQ.'

Michael shook the man's hand, making no attempt to initiate any psychic connection. 'Nice to meet you Kyle. Are your team ready?'

'They are. We'll leave soon and be ready to meet the convoy as it leaves.'

Someone else appeared in the doorway of the lorry. Michael looked at the dark haired, olive skinned young woman who stood there. She looked like she had dressed as casually as she knew how, and had just arrived in a completely foreign land. She looked around, taking in the scene of police milling around, the guns, the armour.

Michael walked forwards. 'Anna, I presume,' he said, smiling.

'Oh, yes, hello,' she said, smiling as best she could.

'I'm Michael,' he said, guessing that she was so overwhelmed she hadn't recognised his voice.

'Oh Michael, hello,' she said with more enthusiasm. They shook hands.

Michael had a sudden temptation to let a connection happen, but he resisted the urge. He had no need to exert any undue influence over her, and as a rule he tried to avoid using his ability to gain an advantage over colleagues, unless absolutely necessary. But there was something more, it somehow just felt wrong. He shook her hand and released it. There began an awkward silence.

'Shall we get set up?' Michael said, gesturing to the lorry.

'Oh, yes, let's,' said Anna. She let him lead the way, even though the vehicle was the domain of GCHQ, not MI5.

Michael walked up the steps and into the vehicle. Inside was cramped, minimal lighting, enough room for four small workstations, two on each side. Each station had a chair bolted to the floor, facing a small desk with keyboard and mouse and bank of six large monitors. To the left side of each station was a communications panel, single button access to the various communications networks and channels. There was a man already seated at the front right station. Michael didn't recognise him, assuming him to be another GCHQ analyst. The man had a headset on and was in the middle of a conversation, but he smiled and waved as Michael took up his position at the front left station.

Anna took up her position at the rear left station, next to Michael. Anna put on her headset (Michael still had his ear-piece fitted and had found he couldn't stand hearing a double conversation from the ear-piece and a headset) and logged in to their workstations. After a moment Kyle Blake joined them, pressing the button next to the door. The external steps started to fold up and he pushed the door shut and locked, and took up the final station.

The Head's voice came over the private GCHQ channel, not shared with the police. 'All stations make ready,' she said, 'police personnel are on their way to cover the approaches to the target locations.'

They looked up at their monitors and saw the video feeds from the vehicle's external cameras. They saw the courtyard gate sliding open and two police vans ready to depart.

'Comm's vehicle ready to depart,' said the Head.

Blake spoke, he was the senior GCHQ analyst in the vehicle,

the leader of this particular team. 'Comm's vehicle ready, we'll be in position to pick up the convoy as it leaves.'

They heard the vehicle's engine start and felt it begin to move. Michael watched the others pick up and secure their safety belts, he followed their lead.

The unknown analyst stabbed a button, giving him priority broadcast over the private channel, even over the Head. 'Alert, alert,' he said, 'the convoy has already left the depot.'

'What?' shouted the Head, 'who authorised that?'

'No authority from us,' said Blake, 'they must have taken a local decision.'

'All stations alert,' said the Head, 'make all speed to intercept the convoy.'

Michael looked up at his monitors and saw a rear view from the vehicle, as it left the courtyard he could see armed police running to their vehicles, the news had reached them as well.

TWENTY TWO

AFGHANISTAN - THREE YEARS BEFORE

Michael crouched in the darkness. He knew that the cover of the bushes at the side of the dried-up river bed wouldn't hide him from anyone else with night vision goggles, not if they were looking for him. His only real cover was the hope the approaching soldier believed he retained the element of surprise and that Michael and friends would be in the village. The world around him was swathed in blackness, but he stared into a sparkling green world. He kept as still as he could, knowing that any movement might give him away.

After what seemed like an age he saw a movement, a man crouching as low as he could, crawling inch by inch up the river bed. Each movement of arm and leg as slow and deliberate and as quiet as possible. He could see the man had night vision goggles on, but was looking at the ground immediately in front of him. His submachine gun was slung across his back, his pistol secured in the holster strapped to his leg. The man was approaching almost silently, not yet ready to engage in fighting, not yet ready, not expecting to have to be ready. Michael waited. A face to face confrontation could go very wrong. There was no guarantee the man would have any inclination to engage in dialogue.

Michael waited as the man drew level, and slow inch after slow inch moved ahead, still only a metre away from him, up the slight incline and towards the rise beyond which was the village. Slowly, so slowly, Michael raised his own submachine gun. He pointed at the back of the man's head and pulled with gentle pressure on the trigger. The targeting laser came on and through the image intensifier goggles the point of laser light looked like a flare on the rock in front of the man's face. The soldier on the ground shuddered, caught between the urge to freeze and the urge to find a weapon and start shooting. Slowly the man opened his hands, extending his fingers, as much a signal of surrender as he could manage, the gun on his back and the gun strapped to his leg was too far out of reach.

Michael spoke as quietly as he could. 'I'm behind you, I can fire, you can't. Listen to me.'

The soldier on the ground stayed silent.

Michael continued. 'My colleagues and I obviously know you're here, we are ready for you. I'm afraid my colleagues have set an ambush for yours. Your friends will shortly be dead. I can't stop that.'

Still the soldier on the ground said nothing.

'I don't want to kill you. Whatever they told you about us was false, just a story to justify you killing us.'

The silence of the night was shattered by a round of automatic gunfire. Marshall or one of the others had killed one of their would-be assassins and made sure everyone for fifty miles heard about it. The soldier on the ground flinched, his arms almost defying the soldier's will and reaching by themselves for his weapons. Michael took a stride out of the bushes and pushed the barrel of his gun into the small of the man's back.

'Keep still. If I wanted to kill you, I would have done. I want you and I to both get out of here alive.'

'Sorry, no can do,' said the man on the ground.

'Put your hands behind your back,' Michael ordered.

Slowly the man moved his hands behind him, no doubt trying to calculate where he might have a chance to reach a weapon. As soon as his hands were in clear view Michael reached out with one hand and grasped the man's left hand. Michael sent a surge of psychic energy through the connection, subduing him in a moment. The man relaxed and became still.

Michael was acutely aware that the clock was against them. He had no doubt that the other three would soon dispatch their would-be assassins, and then they would turn their attentions back to Michael.

'Get up,' he ordered, and the man on the ground stood up, as though it was the most natural thing in the world. His face was relaxed and his breathing calm, completely at odds with their situation. 'Where's the evac' point?'

'Ten clicks from here, due west,' said the man, divulging secrets he would normally have died to protect.

Throughout the night they'd heard no motorised vehicles, so this man's team must have walked in. Ten kilometres was a long way to walk, especially if they had to maintain a lead on Marshall and the others.

'Walk,' Michael ordered. The man started to walk back down the river bed, he and Michael both walking slowly, their footing uncertain over the rough ground, the night vision goggles robbing them of their depth perception. Michael had to let go of the man's hand. He knew he could maintain a psychic connection for the moment, but having had no time to consolidate it he wasn't sure how the connection would hold if the man was surprised, say by someone shooting at them.

Another burst of automatic gunfire punctured the night.

'Do you have an alternative extraction point?' Michael asked, trying to keep his voice as quiet as possible. Even as the man formed the words Michael had an image flicker in his mind; a map, co-ordinates, closer, south-west, a radio transponder.

'Call them,' Michael ordered, 'signal you're going to the alternative extract point.' The man pulled open one of the pockets in his jacket and pulled out a small radio device. Almost by feel he fingered the controls and pressed a button. There was no light, no sound, the device gave no confirmation, but Michael felt the sense of certainty from the man that the signal had been sent. The man turned left and Michael followed.

As they left the river bed the ground was just as rugged, littered with dry and bare shrubs, the branches scratching at their legs. The night vision goggles lit the way, but each stumbled every so often over a rock or hollow. Progress was slow, Michael estimated it would take them five hours to reach the alternative extract point, just in time for sunrise.

There was a loud clicking from the man's radio. His eyes flicked open, and before he could say anything Michael reached out and laid his hand on the back of the man's neck, re-establishing the psychic connection, making the man relax and forget the significance of the radio.

It was Marshall's voice that crackled over the radio. 'Sanders, where are you going?' Michael thought it was none of his business. 'Michael, we need to talk about this.' Michael had no doubt, Marshall was not the talking type.

Marshall continued, 'we've got another of them here. He wants to talk to his friend.' There was a pause. Another man's voice came on the radio, it sounded slow, as though the man speaking was half asleep.

'Dave,' said the unfamiliar voice, 'Dave, you need to come back.' Michael made his companion relax even more, he subdued the man's response to his colleague's voice.

Michael and his companion kept walking. The voices on the radio hadn't sounded like they were walking, so Michael was gaining a lead on them. Michael made no attempt to reach the man's radio, he had no intention of responding. Silence and darkness were their only hope.

A single pistol shot made Michael jump. His companion's colleague was dead. There was a single click from the radio and it went quiet.

In the strange loud-but-silent form of telepathic voice, Michael heard Marshall's voice in his mind. 'Michael, we're a team, don't do this. They won't have you back. They sent them to kill us, all of us, you too. You think they're going to welcome you back? Forgive and forget? Won't happen man.'

Michael knew that Marshall was a good soldier, and aggressive, and determined, but not the brightest man in the world. Michael had no doubt that there had been no chance of saving any of the other three soldiers from his former colleagues, all he could hope was that Marshall had killed them before thinking there might be an alternative extract point. If that was the case Michael and his new companion had an advantage, Marshall and the others would have no idea where to look for them. If not, events would turn very ugly very quickly.

He heard Marshall's voice again. 'We're supposed to be a team, Michael. Don't do this.' There was a silence. And then, 'if you turn against us Michael, we'll come for you, I promise man, we'll come for you.'

Michael used his thoughts to create a mental wall around him, imagining the world to be quiet inside the wall, no voices penetrating from outside. It was a crude way of keeping out telepathic communication, but for the moment it was the best he could do. He needed to make sure Marshall and the others got no telepathic clues about Michael's location or destination.

As they stumbled their way forwards, Michael tried not to

think of the enormity of his gamble. If Marshall, Singh and Bullock had gone rogue, then he (Michael) was the only man in the British Army who stood any chance of finding them. That, potentially, gave him some bargaining leverage. If, on the other hand, the Army simply wanted them all dead either one-at-a-time or all-at-once then he was walking to his own execution. Between his former colleagues and the organisation which had sent a kill squad after him, Michael had only one thing to figure out: which was the rock and which was the hard-place?

TWENTY FOUR

Michael wasn't sure if it was a surveillance vehicle or a communication's vehicle, everyone seemed to have their own name for it. Whichever it was the Battle Bus was making its way through the London traffic as fast as it could, with a police patrol car ahead clearing the way with its lights and sirens. Taking separate routes, illustrated on various animated maps on their displays, they could see the other police units, all rushing out of London to meet up with the convoy. Without windows he couldn't see the landmarks rushing past, but on the animated map he could see they were passing White City, Wormwood Scrubs, heading west towards North Acton. From there they'd turn south on Horn Lane and head to the first potential ambush location.

Michael watched the graphic of the convoy move across the map. The "convoy" was in fact just two vehicles, the lorry carrying the gold, and another vehicle following close behind. Both would be plain, unmarked vehicles, nothing to mark them out as any different from any other delivery lorry on the road. None of the other drivers and passengers on the road would have known that almost two hundred million pounds of gold and twenty armed police had just driven past.

Anna kept up a running commentary on the progress of the convoy. Michael suspected this was to keep herself busy, everyone could see the progress on the monitors. The convoy was closer to the first ambush point than they were, partly due to lighter than expected traffic on the first part of the M4 for the convoy and heavier than expected traffic for the police. Michael could imagine some difficult conversations being had later in the day over the decision to have the convoy depart early. Maybe someone thought an element of surprise was a good idea. Ultimately, the wrong people had been surprised.

The first ambush point was where the M4 motorway became the A4 main road which carried on into the City. Michael knew the junction and could see it illustrated on his screens. At this point the motorway went over an elevated section above a large roundabout, three main roads joined the roundabout which also had slip-roads to and from the motorway. The traffic on the roundabout was controlled by multiple sets of traffic lights. There were several vacant office buildings, obvious locations for a sniper to cover the area. It would be easy to jam the traffic, jam the motorway, attack the convoy, use any of the exits from the roundabout to escape. It was large, messy, uncontrollable, it made Michael think of Vince Marshall.

If that's where it happened it would be a very public hit, and so far Marshall and friends hadn't been shy of doing their dirty work in public. Michael started to imagine the political shitstorm that would follow if two hundred million pounds of gold was stolen amid a deadly firefight with civilian casualties in such a public place. There was now a very real chance that this was all about to go very horribly wrong.

'The convoy is thirty seconds from the interchange,' said Anna. Michael looked at the monitors, three of them were showing feeds from the traffic cameras at the intersection. The traffic was heavy, typical for a Friday morning on the way into London.

'Miss Hendrickson,' came the Head's voice, 'where are the vehicles you hot listed from the Edmonton attack?'

'Four have been positively IDd on the other side of town, three IDs are out of town, currently no hot listed vehicles or suspects have been spotted on available cameras and no suspect mobile phone IDs have been detected.'

They watched as the convoy made its way along the motorway, the last section of the M4 approaching London. The traffic was heavy, bumper to bumper, frequent stops and starts. They all watched and waited when the convoy came to a stop and all breathed a little easier when it started moving again. Michael looked at the vehicles on his screens, none looked suspicious, but then he didn't think Marshall and friends would turn up in a truck with "hey look, here comes the ambush" painted on the side.

Michael saw Anna lean closer to one of the monitors, then type something on the keyboard and check the response.

'Possible sighting of one of the hotlist vehicles,' Anna said. 'Approaching the intersection from the north.'

'Why didn't we see this sooner?' said the Head sharply. It reminded Michael that in Head-world everything was possible and done in an instant. Head-world didn't seem to obey the laws of physics here in the real world.

Anna struggled for a moment to find an answer. 'The traffic's too dense,' she said, 'the cameras don't always see number plates.'

Everyone watched as a red circle picked out the vehicle on the monitor. A red people-carrier, part of the flow of traffic approaching the intersection from the north. The vehicle was caught in the stationary traffic waiting at the red light to join the roundabout. The convoy crawled along in the motorway traffic, passing over the bridge over the roundabout.

'Is the police unit near the sniper position?' the Head asked, her question directed to another comm's channel. There was a pause. The reply didn't come through on Michael's ear-piece. He looked at Anna. She looked at him and shook her head.

The lights changed and the traffic set off. The convoy crawled along over the intersection, the suspect vehicle crawled through the traffic round the roundabout, heading for the slip road up onto the motorway. For a moment the two vehicles were in sight of each other. There was silence in the Battle Bus as they watched the animated maps plot the progress of the vehicles. The convoy carried on past the entry road from the roundabout, and the people-carrier passed the motorway entry and continued round towards the exit for Kew Bridge. From there the suspect vehicle continued in the opposite direction and disappeared from view as the surveillance continued to focus on the convoy. The convoy was now into a stretch of road where the traffic was contained, access was limited, an attack would be possible but easy escape would not be, until they reached the next potential ambush point. Michael found himself breathing again.

The Head's voice came over the comm's channel again. 'I want all units covering the convoy by the time it reaches the next target location, all sniper points covered and all entry routes covered.'

'Surveillance team five minutes to the convoy,' said Kyle Blake from behind Michael. Michael watched the animated map on the screen. He felt the vehicle turn and watched the display, showing them turning right and approaching a turn onto the Chiswick High Road which, for a while, would keep them more-or-less parallel with the convoy. He saw two of the spotters had fallen in ahead of the convoy on nearby streets, probably on motorbikes. Two more were moving to fall in behind and from there the convoy would always be within the contained box of surveillance.

Michael watched as the convoy snaked its way through the London traffic, heading ultimately for the heart of the City. The next significant point was the second likely ambush point where the A4 met Burlington Lane which joined from the south. From there the A4 turned north, heading for the City, but it was a point where the Chiswick High Road would take the Battle Bus further from the A4. Like last time, the approaching traffic was at ground level, controlled by traffic lights, the A4 on a section of flyover. Here it was a narrower section of road, access less easy, but with as much potential for a small force to paralyse the traffic and contain the convoy.

'At this speed, seven minutes to target location,' said Kyle.

Another voice came over the comm's channel, Michael assumed it was one of the other analysts, probably in the Command and Control room in Thames House. 'All police units are in place, no unusual activity.'

Michael looked from one screen to another, assimilating the information about location of police units, the location of the convoy, video feeds from a plethora of CCTV cameras. There wasn't the slightest hint of anyone putting assets into place ready for a major hit. The gold weighed several tonnes, there was a small army of heavily armed police following every move of the convoy and every aspect of online and mobile communication was being monitored by GCHQ and MI5. Inside the surveillance box a rat couldn't fart without it being detected. A nagging feeling of doubt was growing in Michael's mind. This had all the hallmarks of another set-up, but what were they being set up for?

'Two minutes to target location,' said Kyle. Michael felt the vehicle slow and stop. He looked over at Anna and made a writing gesture with his hand. She realised what he was asking and handed him a notebook. She frowned at him as she realised she didn't have a pen. Anna picked up her handbag and rummaged around inside. She pulled out a smart ballpoint pen and handed it to Michael, who made an exaggerated expression of being impressed. She didn't look impressed with his humour. He scribbled a note and showed it to her. "This doesn't feel right" he had written.

She frowned again, took the pen from him and wrote a single question mark. He took the pen back and wrote "set up?". She looked at the words, then back to Michael. Their "offline" conversation was interrupted by Kyle. 'Convoy now approaching second target location.'

Another voice came over the channel, Wayne Browning. 'Mobile phone ID just pinged, it's Petric's phone.'

They looked up and saw on the map that the convoy was crawling through traffic into the section of flyover. Streets below were filled with vehicles, inching their way along. The area was surrounded by office and retail buildings, a sniper's paradise. The density of the traffic meant that bringing the convoy to a standstill wouldn't be a problem, London traffic had almost achieved that. Michael looked at the map. The surveillance vehicle was still on the Chiswick High Road, now over eight hundred metres from the junction and the convoy.

Anna almost shook as she saw something on one of the monitors and she stabbed at the button giving her priority transmission. 'Possible sighting of Bullock,' she said, 'street-level CCTV, on foot, at the junction of Chiswick High Road and Devonshire Road, carrying a guitar case.'

Everyone had the same thought, a guitar case could easily be used for carrying a sniper rifle. The location put Bullock only a few hundred yards ahead of their current location.

'This is Sanders, I'm going on foot.' Before anyone could say anything Michael was out of his seat and had opened the back door. He hit the emergency release and the mechanised steps were unlocked and swung outwards. He left the vehicle and ran off into the London traffic.

As he ran he was conscious of the Head's voice in his ear, but he couldn't make out the words over the noise of the traffic, and he wasn't sure he wanted to hear what she was saying at this precise moment. He had only run a short distance when he stopped and looked around. The traffic was moving only very slowly, pedestrians were shoulder to shoulder on both sides of the street. Chiswick High Road was wide, well-presented shops on each side, trees adorned both sides of the road. He looked ahead towards the junction of Devonshire Road where it departed the main road and led away to the right, a smaller but just as pretty road, and quieter, fewer cars and pedestrians. He walked quickly between the cars and across the road. The number of people on the main would make it hard to pick out Bullock or any of the others, but equally would work to conceal him from them. The side road would leave them both more exposed.

'Do we still have a location for Bullock?' Michael asked. He had to push his finger into his ear to block out the traffic noise to hear the ear-piece.

'Negative,' came Anna's voice, 'there's no CCTV coverage on Devonshire Road, not until it reaches the junction with the A4, but there was one more siting of him heading down Devonshire, it leads down to the next ambush point.'

'Sanders,' he Head said in a very firm voice, even for her, but not shouting, not when there was an audience. 'Get back to the surveillance vehicle,' she commanded.

'Not yet,' he said, loudly enough to be heard and loudly enough to attract some quizzical looks from the nearest passers-by.

'Where now?' he asked. There was a pause.

'No further sightings,' came Anna's voice. Michael looked around. Petric and Bullock were here, there could be no doubt that the other four were also close by, and they would be armed and working to a plan. Michael walked briskly down Devonshire Road. Despite the long and unobstructed view down the road there was no sight of Bullock. He crossed the road, passing between parked cars. With the busy traffic on the main road behind him and the quieter road stretching out in front of him, there was no sign of any of his targets. Michael stopped and looked in a shop window, a restaurant, El Toro Blanco, the white bull, the words curved around a graphic of a white bull with a ring through its nose. Michael stared at the graphic.

He pressed his finger in his ear, he needed to hear what people said. He spoke loudly, not caring what any passerby might think. 'This is a set-up, the convoy is not the target, whatever they're after it's not the convoy.'

'If not the convoy then what?' asked the Head, as he expected.

Michael looked around him. 'Where are the spotters?' he asked.

There was a pause and Browning answered. 'All four points of the box, the nearest to you is on a motorbike, five hundred metres ahead at the end of Devonshire Road.' Michael began to run, trying to ignore the growing feeling that they had seriously misread their role in this game of cat-and-mouse. The road curved to the left, fewer shops now, most of the buildings were houses, smart terraced houses, a dense residential area. There were blocks of flats on the right, sheltered accommodation. A gunfight, or worse, here would result in significant civilian casualties. 'Identify the bike,' he said as he ran.

'Red Ducati,' said Browning. Michael was breathing heavily as he ran faster. He could see the flyover beyond the end of

Devonshire Road. He could see an office building at the end of the road where it met the main road and the roundabout. As he got closer he became aware of a growing crowd ahead of him, people coming out of the corner shop and the office building, pedestrians from the main road, all milling around something on the ground. As he reached it the crowd was growing bigger, a surprising number of people had appeared. People pushed their way out of the crowd as others pushed their way in wanting to see what had caught everyone else's attention. Michael reached the edge of the crowd and started pulling people out of his way, ignoring protests and complaints, until he reached the centre.

On the ground, legs still either side of a red motorbike, was a young man, dark leather jacket, jeans, boots, and a large and growing pool of blood flowing from what remained of his neck.

'Call an ambulance,' Michael shouted at the crowd and at his unseen audience, 'call a fucking ambulance, get all our assets out of here, we're the target.' He pushed his way out of the crowd, pushing harder and harder. As he broke free he looked back up Devonshire Road and caught a glimpse of a face looking back at him from a hundred metres away, the face of a lightly built, athletic man with thinning black hair man walking away from Michael. Julian Singh. In the instant before the man turned his face away Michael registered the expression of surprise on his face, Singh had not expected to see Michael.

'I've sighted Singh,' he said, 'he's killed the spotter, we're the target, get everyone out of here.'

'Get back to the surveillance vehicle,' the Head commanded.

'No, get it out of here, get everyone out of here.' He pushed his way out of the gathering crowd of onlookers, trying to follow Singh, but he'd lost sight of the man. No doubt Singh had now pulled on a cap or a hat and with his head down he'd now be invisible to Michael and any CCTV cameras.

Michael was half aware of the Head giving orders for the

convoy, relaying orders over the police comm's channel, he heard Browning giving orders to the remaining spotters and the surveillance vehicle.

'Do we have any siting of any of the targets?' Michael called.

'Negative,' was all Anna said.

'Sanders,' said the Head, in a slightly more measured voice, 're-join the surveillance vehicle.'

'Where is it?' asked Michael.

'It's close, Bennett Street, back the way you came then first left,' said Browning. Michael turned and ran back up Devonshire Road, past the large block of flats with its neat and manicured lawn and left into Bennett Street. As he rounded the corner he saw the surveillance lorry parked on the left at the far end of the road.

Almost in slow motion Michael glanced to his right across to the tree and grass outside another block of flats halfway down Bennett Street towards where the Battle Bus was parked, and there he saw Bullock crouching on the ground, his guitar case open in front of him, out of which he was lifting a shoulder-held rocket launcher.

TWENTY FIVE

As Michael watched Bullock lift the launcher onto his shoulder, he started to pull his gun out of its holster. At that moment he saw Singh stand up from the other side of Bullock, looking straight ahead at the Battle Bus. Michael was sure he heard himself shout, bringing his gun up to aim at Bullock, but Singh saw him and was quicker, maybe he already had his gun drawn, he turned and fired at Michael.

Michael instinctively dropped behind the nearest car as he heard the sharp crack of the pistol shot and the metallic ring as the bullet hit the car. If Bullock fired the rocket launcher at him the car would provide no cover at all and Michael would be killed, he had no doubt of that. He stuck his gun out from behind the car ready to fire, but couldn't. Singh and Bullock were in front of the windows of ground floor apartments, pedestrians could be near, he couldn't fire blindly. Firing without having a clear sight of the target broke every rule there was on using firearms in a public space.

His hesitation was rewarded by five shots in rapid succession from Singh hitting the car.

'Singh and Bullock,' Michael said, recovering his sense of time and space, 'small arms and rocket launchers, under fire.'

'Withdraw,' ordered the Head, directed at Michael. A second order, directed at others, 'get the surveillance vehicle out of there.' His ear-piece went quiet, no doubt the Head was handing control over to Halbern in the full expectation his armed officers would assault Singh and company with full and lethal force.

Michael heard the engine of the surveillance vehicle revving and the vehicle start to pull away.

Michael looked around for a spot where he could get a better view without becoming a target, but before he could move came the ominous double-stage hiss of the rocket launcher firing. The first high-pitched hiss came as the rocket left the launcher, and barely a moment later was the dark and angry hiss of the rocket's second stage propelling it to its target. At such close range it was only a moment before there was an enormous percussive bang. Even behind the car Michael could see the blinding flash of the explosion and felt the heat from it.

He stayed crouched behind the car, head down, hands over his ears, waiting for whatever would come next. It seemed like an age but was probably only moments, he had to move. Ears still ringing from the force of the explosion he gripped his pistol and ducked into the space between the parked cars, pointing his gun forwards ready to fire.

The smoke was already billowing around him and it stung his eyes and nostrils as he stared forwards. It took him several moments to understand what he was looking at. The road was littered with burning debris, cars were on fire, every window in every building had been blown out, smoke swirled around with an almost other-worldly appearance. But the true horror was at the other end of the road. Where the surveillance vehicle had been there was now just a mess of twisted, burning wreckage. Wicked little flames licked at the debris, none of it recognisable.

Michael sank backwards onto the pavement, almost losing his grip on his gun. He heard nothing, not the shouting in his ear-piece, not the shouting and screaming of civilians who were escaping now burning buildings, not the clatter of debris still falling to earth. He sat there, stunned, physically and emotionally.

He was only vaguely aware of the police who seemed to swarm into the area from every direction. He held up his ID card in one hand, visible to anyone who cared to read it, he didn't care who did. The police paid him scant attention, perhaps they'd already been briefed on his description and who he was.

The police began to "secure the area", though that had little meaning any more. The area was not secure, they were not secure, they never had been. El Toro Blanco; like a bull with a ring through its nose they'd been led here, exactly where Marshall and the others wanted them, to finish the job they'd started at Edmonton.

MICHAEL WALKED towards the burning remains of the Battle Bus. Its battles were over, and it had lost. The intensity of the heat from the explosion had instantly burned out the cars closest to the vehicle. Others further away were on fire. Some of the police had hand-held fire extinguishers, but this was going to tax London's fire service. Fires were already burning in some of the nearby buildings and the police were leading civilians out of the buildings and towards holding areas they'd set up. Everyone would be identified, accounted for, tagged for further investigation. Who knew if any of them had acted as a lookout?

For the second time in less than twenty-four hours Michael found himself looking at a scene of devastation. Marshall, Bullock and Singh had brought terror to the streets of London, terror and carnage. He clenched his fists, he wanted to hit someone, something. He could feel the anger burning inside, the rage building. He would make them pay for this, he had to.

He felt almost invisible as he walked around, no-one talked to him, few even looked at him, not in the eye. Eventually, he became aware of a voice in his ear.

'Sanders, report,' the Head was saying. He realised that he'd not made contact since the explosions.

'I'm here,' he said.

'Report, what's happening?' she demanded. Still no interest in his personal welfare. If he was speaking and could add value that was all she cared about. Michael had a sudden, curious thought. He wondered why she did the job she did. Why did she spend so much energy and effort protecting the public when she cared so little for individuals? He decided it didn't matter.

'The surveillance vehicle was the target,' he said. 'They hit it with a rocket launcher, looked like a Javelin, probably a high-intensity incendiary warhead.'

'Casualties?' she asked.

'Surveillance vehicle completely destroyed.' He paused before adding the next part, knowing that Browning and others would be listening. 'No survivors.'

There might have been other questions, other voices, Michael didn't listen to them. It was like the world before him was being played out on a big movie screen and he was just standing watching it. He watched fire engines arrive, fire-fighters leap out and un-reel their hoses and put out the fires. As they sprayed the remains of the surveillance vehicle it seemed wrong, it shouldn't happen like that. He kept focused on what he saw in front of him. He couldn't think of anything else, he wouldn't think of anything else.

'Michael,' the Head's voice came in his ear so sharply it jerked him back into the world around him.

'Here,' he said.

'I said I want all personnel back in The Office, now.'

Michael stood still for a few moments. 'Negative,' he said finally, 'I'm going to find them.'

'You are not,' she ordered, 'you will do as you are told and come back to The Office, immediately.'

'Why? To plan how we're going to walk into the next trap?' said Michael, and immediately thinking that maybe his sarcasm wasn't the best choice. There was a chilling pause.

'Because there's nothing constructive you can do in the field,' she said, in a more calm and measured tone than he'd heard her use in a while. 'We have no leads on them, no current sightings. We need to decide collectively how we're going to track them down.'

Michael had the sudden thought that the task would take all their best analysts, and finally the thought of Anna sneaked into his consciousness and robbed him of his voice. He stood there in silence as tears streamed down his cheeks. He managed to avoid any sound.

'Sanders,' the Head said eventually, 'you were right, we were the target. They're still out there and so are you. I'd appreciate it if you would come back to The Office.' It was as close as he'd ever heard her come to asking for something.

'Soon,' he said. He wasn't finished here, didn't feel he could leave yet. He didn't know why, but something still held him in this place.

It was another few moments before he became aware of someone standing close to his left side. He looked up at Commander Halbern. They looked at each other for a moment. Neither spoke, neither needed to. Michael had been here before, in battle, having lost friends and colleagues, standing with the survivors and dealing with the painful mix of grief and guilt and anger and relief. He knew Halbern was still hurting after the loss of his men at Edmonton.

Michael couldn't think of a single thing to say. "We'll find them" he had said to Halbern, find them before they could do any more damage. They'd failed on both counts, and now more people were dead. He thought back to the Serbian he'd had his hands on, whose mind he'd probed. If he'd probed deeper, pushed harder, he would have discovered all of this, he could have prevented it.

'There isn't a right time to say this,' someone said. Michael took a moment to realise it was Halbern talking to him.

'Sorry, say what?' Michael asked.

'A statement, we'll need a statement from you.'

It seemed almost ridiculous that with all the surveillance they had deployed he was now going to have to sit with a police officer and describe what had happened.

'Fine,' Michael said, 'I'll talk to one of your officers.'

'It will need to be a written statement, you'll have to sign it.' Halbern said nothing more and walked away.

The idea of a written statement seemed absurd, and yet the words teased him, they reminded him of something. He looked around. Most of the smoke had cleared, most of the fires had been extinguished. He only now realised how much noise there was around him; police shouting orders, the roar of the fire engines pumping water, the sound of the water jets and the water splashing, and behind the sound of the crowds of onlookers which were pushing at the makeshift cordon the police had erected.

Only now did Michael feel strong enough to look at the wreckage of where the surveillance vehicle had been, and think of Anna. He thought of Kyle Blake, and he thought of the other analyst whose name he didn't know, but he thought mainly of Anna. He realised that he had been getting used to hearing her voice, hearing her analysis and conclusions and suggestions. For a moment he thought of reaching out psychically to her, but then realised that the only time he had made physical contact with her he had not initiated a psychic link, and then realised that of course she was dead and psychic link or no there was no way to form a link with someone who was dead. He had lost all connection with her.

The idea came into his mind quietly and without fuss, just appearing as a thought, a realisation. The pen. Anna had given him her pen and when he jumped out of the surveillance vehicle he'd put it in his pocket. Slowly, almost as though handling a delicate antique, he pulled the pen out of his jacket pocket. It was an insane thought, trying to connect to the pen, because the owner was dead, but he felt compelled to try. But not here, too noisy, too busy.

He started to walk to the edge of the cordon, towards one of the police vans. A young police officer pulled the barrier aside to let him out, she didn't make eye contact. He pushed his way through the crowd, ignoring looks from the people clamouring to see if they could catch sight of a dead body. He found a quiet corner at the side of the apartment block, close to the spot from where Bullock had launched the rocket. It wasn't exactly private but it was far enough from the crowds.

He held the pen lightly, letting his mind extend through his fingers and into the pen. He had the comical thought that it was the psychic equivalent of scratch'n'sniff. His mind connected with the pen, and he got a sudden mental image of an older woman, elegantly dressed, in a sunny garden. Perhaps a relative who'd given the pen to Anna. The images came more quickly; an office scene, probably the Doughnut (he'd never been inside); an old church hall, people sitting at rows of desks, it was a university hall, exam time; signing of a document headed Official Secrets Act, signing so carefully and clearly. Smells came with the images; perfume, nylon carpets and computers, polished wood, a heady mix of nervousness and excitement. The last one wasn't a smell, but a feeling, and felt so real, so present.

Michael was ready for the hollow, empty feeling he'd experienced with Crossley's book, the feeling of calling to someone who wasn't there. The feeling didn't come, just the idea of signing the Official Secrets Act, it must have been when she had started working for GCHQ. There was only one thing that made this make sense: Anna was still alive.

TWENTY SIX

The Head of Operations marched down the corridor flanked by three aides each taking notes as she barked orders at them. The initial shock at the scale of the attack and the destruction it had brought had swiftly given way to a wave of activity. Everyone in the Command and Control room had feared the Head of Operations would start firing accusations and recriminations, but instead she had switched into a mode only one of them had ever seen before. Her focus and understanding of the situation and what needed to be done was almost frightening. Having given the first round of orders she had left the room, no doubt to consult with senior staff in MI5 and possibly even Government Ministers, and now she was on her way back.

'Have tactical review any images we can find of the rocket launcher, I want to know what type it was. Sanders thinks it might have been a Javelin, start there,' she commanded. The analyst stopped to scribble a few notes and as soon as they were back in the Command and Control room was onto the keyboard typing furiously, orders being cascaded by instant messenger.

'I want access to the police forensics reports before they get them, I want to know what kind of warhead those rocket launchers used,' she said. More activity resulted, each analyst knew their area of responsibility, everyone knew which order was for them.

'Do we have any indication of radioactive contamination?' she asked, sending her request into the atmosphere of the room.

One of the analysts looked up, 'no ma'am, on-site forensics teams have done a sweep, the scene is cold.' Only Michael Sanders addressed her as anything other than ma'am.

'Bring me the analysis of the satellite imagery as soon as it's ready,' she ordered.

She heard a muted bleeping coming from her pocket. She took out her mobile phone and looked at the caller ID, it was Sanders. 'Yes,' she said answering the call, curious as to why he was calling and not using the comm's channel.

'I need a private conversation,' Michael said. His words came only through the phone and not also through the loudspeakers in the room, indicating he'd muted his ear-piece transceiver. The Head walked into the corridor and started to walk slowly away from the open door of the Command and Control room.

'I told you I need you back here,' she said.

'She's alive,' said Michael.

'Who's alive?'

'Anna Hendrickson.'

'Can't be, no-one survived that blast.' The Head had seen the images from one of the other spotters who'd been first to the scene, beating even the police. The police, of course, didn't recognise her, just another tourist, but her concealed camera captured all the imagery the Command and Control room needed for a first assessment.

'Of course she didn't survive the blast,' said Michael, 'which means she wasn't in the vehicle when it was hit.'

'There's no surveillance showing her out of the vehicle,' said the Head.

'I bet there's no surveillance covering the attack.' Michael was right, events had been manipulated so that the surveillance vehicle had ended up in an area not covered by CCTV.

'She was in the vehicle, Sanders,' said the Head, almost sounding like an attempt at being soothing. 'There was nothing on comm's about her leaving the vehicle, her last report was moments before it was hit.'

'I know she's alive,' Michael repeated.

'How?' As soon as she'd asked the question, the Head had a sense that she knew what the answer was going to be.

'Trust me, I can sense it, she is alive,' said Michael, offering no further detail. The Head considered it for a moment. She was well aware of Michael's unique (almost unique) skills and capabilities, and of those of the other three. If Anna Hendrickson was indeed still alive, this posed a whole new set of very perplexing questions, and right at the top of the list would be "why?"

'I need evidence,' she said, and before Michael could interject she said, 'I'll have GCHQ review all comm's records and surveillance, if she did leave the vehicle there would have to be some record. Now get back to The Office.' She ended the call.

She turned to walk back to the Command and Control room, and had barely taken another step when the phone rang again. There was no caller ID, which on her phone was almost impossible, calls into the intelligence communications network (which meant virtually all calls from any phone in the world) could be identified and traced, except this one, and she knew what that meant.

She pressed the key on the phone, 'yes,' she said. It was a man's voice. He made no attempt to identify himself, but the Head knew exactly who it was.

'I'm hearing lots of disturbing things about bombings and rocket attacks,' the man said, 'and I believe our man is involved.'

'We have a problem,' she said.

'I wouldn't call if it wasn't a problem,' said the man.

'A cyclone just hit central London.' There was silence on the phone, the man was obviously considering the implications of what she had just said.

'How big a cyclone?' he asked.

'Full strength.'

'Is our man still on side?'

'He is.'

'Is he effective?'

The Head paused. There was no simple answer to the question.

'If he's not effective then we may have to take more drastic action to solve this problem,' said the man.

'That solution didn't work last time. Kill them if you want but Sanders is still an asset with some value.'

'It's an all or nothing action,' said the man, 'anyone in range will be taken care of.' He hadn't needed to say that, the Head knew full well the implications of what he had said; kill squads weren't typically choosy about their targets, anyone and everyone in the vicinity of their targets were also targets, and anyone associated with them.

'This problem needs to be made to go away, whatever the cost,' said the man.

'And it will be.' The line went dead.

The Head marched back into the Command and Control room, her face giving no clue as to the seriousness of the calls she had just been a party to.

'Listen up,' she said. All talking in the room stopped and everyone looked at her. She liked the way she never had to ask twice for people to listen, she'd often thought that many school teachers would appreciate the kind of authority she wielded, but then parents probably wouldn't appreciate the kind of punishments she could mete out.

'Evidence has come to light that suggests the surveillance vehicle had warning of the attack, Miss Hendrickson being the likely recipient of that warning.' No-one asked her to explain what that evidence might be. 'I want a full analysis of all comm's to and from that vehicle in the five minutes before the attack, if they were warned I want to know who warned them.'

She looked up at one of the video conference screens, and looked at the face of Wayne Browning, sitting at his desk in the Doughnut. His eyes were red and sunken, the day's events had taken a toll on him. He was not a seasoned field operative, he was, let's face it, a desk jockey; death and destruction, particularly of colleagues, was not a part of his usual working day.

'Mister Browning,' the Head said, trying to sound less authoritative.

'Yes ma'am,' Browning said with a start, not expecting the Head to address him directly.

'You and your team have a particular expertise and cracking secure communications systems, wherever that warning came from, I need you to find it.'

'We will,' he said.

WAYNE BROWNING SAT in his seat, staring at the screen. He had three screens on his desk, arranged in an arc in front of him. Each screen had multiple windows, displays from various information feeds, video streams, documents, email, web browser. One window remained dark, a simple "no signal" message in the middle. It had been the video feed from the surveillance vehicle. He stared at the window and wondered what he felt. He knew it was an odd thing to think, to wonder what his own feelings might be, but somehow he felt disconnected from them. There were things he had to be doing, he knew that. He had important things to do, and he must do them quickly. He looked across his desk at the mug, sitting unobtrusively on the coaster on top of a few sheets of paper. He reached out and put his fingers on the rim of the mug. Somehow it felt soothing, it reminded him of feeling a cooling breeze on a hot day. Things became clearer in his mind.

He looked over the divide, past Anna's desk to where Kingston was sitting. He too was sitting staring at his screen. Wayne got up and walked round to Kingston, he stood next to him.

'Kingston, I need your help,' said Wayne. He had no idea how to handle the situation, but for the moment they had orders, and they had work they needed to do.

Kingston looked up at him. He didn't blink, didn't speak, he just stared.

'We think Anna may have received a warning about the attack.'

Kingston's eyes widened, daring to think before he could stop himself, allowing the possibility of her survival into his mind before the facts could crush the idea.

'I need you to scan the surveillance vehicle's comm's, scan everything, find anything that might show they had a warning.'

'Then what?' was all Kingston could ask.

'Then we find where it came from.'

Wayne walked back to his desk and sat down. He reached out and touched the mug again. He thought about Kingston's task and finding the source of the warning. It suddenly became quite clear to him that Kingston must try his hardest to find the warning, but it was vital that Kingston fail in his task, it must be shown clearly that there was no warning. That could be tricky,

Kingston was very skilled, he'd managed to breach the Bank of England's security systems. But then Wayne remembered that Kingston had only achieved it with Anna's help, and Anna wasn't going to help him in this task.

MARSHALL AND SINGH stood in their control room watching Bullock, who was sitting in one of the chairs, apparently staring into empty space.

'And?' said Marshall, with more than a hint of impatience.

'They seem to think the surveillance vehicle may have received a warning, they're trying to trace it,' Bullock said, his gaze not changing.

'Can they?' Marshall asked looking over at Singh.

Singh shrugged his shoulders. 'Browning was clever getting the message to the girl, but if they think there's something to find they'll dig until they find it.'

'Can we stop them?' asked Marshall.

'Nope,' said Singh, 'Browning's going to have to do that on his own.'

Marshall turned back to Bullock. 'Right, Browning's going to have to cover his tracks as well as set up the cascade.'

Bullock didn't say anything but he closed his eyes. The telepathic link with Wayne Browning was strong, made stronger by the physical link of the mug, but it was still difficult commanding someone to do something that they would normally refuse to do. The psychic link was the strongest form of influence, but Browning was not yet a mindless puppet, it would still be possible for someone to interrupt him and break the link, especially if he was getting Browning to follow two different orders at the same time. The control might have been stronger if Singh had created the link, because he had the direct connection to the mug, to the physical object. Bullock couldn't create a link to physical objects, but Singh could share his link. Sometimes he found it easier just to get on with things and not try to explain them.

After a few moments he opened his eyes and blinked. 'Okay, we'll see what happens,' he said.

'He better cover his tracks,' said Marshall.

'And he better get that cascade set up, or all this is for nothing,' said Singh.

Marshall turned around and scratched his head. He hated any part of a plan that relied on someone else. This psychic control thing was incredible, it was allowing them to do things they would never have been able to do otherwise, but it wasn't infallible.

'We need a contingency plan,' Marshall said. 'We need a plan for if Browning's discovered.'

'When he's discovered,' said Singh, stressing the "when", 'they will find the message he sent to the girl.'

'Can he delay them?' Marshall asked.

'He will,' said Bullock, 'he'll get the cascade set up, then he'll do what he can to cover his tracks, then he'll leave.'

'And then we go and take care of him,' said Marshall. He felt happier when plans included tying up loose ends.

'I'll go and take care of him,' said Singh. Bullock and Marshall looked at him. Singh was a capable soldier who'd done his fair share of killing, but in this plan his role had been IT more than a "hands-on" role.

'When he's done with the cascade I'll send him to you,' said Bullock.

Singh smiled and left the room. Bullock and Marshall looked at each other. Sometimes words and psychic connections weren't needed to share a thought.

A Mind To Kill

As Wayne sat and stared at his screen, fingers resting lightly on the rim of the mug, he suddenly found that it all became so clear. He set about what he needed to do. He'd have to look into Kingston's activities, but that could wait. He began by accessing one of the multitude of servers on the GCHQ network. This was a special server, because Wayne had gone to some length to hide it from the rest of the network. It didn't appear on any virus scan, it was invisible to the network's asset management system, it wasn't registered in any of the messaging systems, it was a ghost. Wayne had the logon credentials, the username and password, to access the server and to configure it. The server would only need to do one job. It would of course be discovered within minutes of starting this job, but then it would delete everything on its hard drives; all activity logs, all programs, all data. By the time anyone located the machine and took it apart there would be nothing left but a completely blank machine, as clean and clear as the day it arrived from the manufacturer.

Wayne set about configuring the one job. The job itself was easy to set up, it was a simple program, the challenge was knowing when to start the program running. Indeed, no-one knew exactly when the program would need to start running, and so it needed a trigger. This was the tricky bit; opening a communication channel to the outside world that could remain undetected until the one time it was needed. At that one time, someone from outside the intelligence community network would be able to send a single command through all the firewalls and demilitarised zones between routers and gateways, between external networks and the internal reverse proxy servers, right through the network to this one server. But Wayne could do it, and it was a work of art.

His admiration of his own handiwork was interrupted by an

alert on one of his screens, Kingston was dialling back in to the conference call line for the Thames House Command and Control room. Wayne put on his own headset. He looked up at Kingston and held out a thumbs-up gesture with raised eyebrows. Kingston gave a thumbs-up in return, and a knowing nod.

'Mister Smith,' came the Head's voice over the headset, 'do you have something for us?'

'In the few minutes before the attack,' Kingston began, but had to pause. Wayne heard him take a deep breath, and continue. 'Anna was cycling through five separate CCTV feeds.'

'Trying to re-establish a lead on Singh or Bullock,' said the Head.

'Yes, but thirty seconds before the attack she stopped, her station remained on the same feed for the last thirty seconds.'

'I'm not clear what your point is,' came another voice, one of the other analysts in the Command and Control room.

'There was no activity at all from Anna's station for the last thirty seconds, I don't think she was in the vehicle.'

Wayne said nothing. He knew full well Anna hadn't been in the vehicle for the last thirty seconds. He tried to look like he was listening to the call while he worked furiously at his keyboard. He entered the connection details for a database, used the object directory to find the name of the table containing records of comm's messages, built a query to find one very particular record. He needed to remove that record and any trace of his doing so as quickly as he could.

'Then there must have been a communication to Miss Hendrickson between thirty and thirty-five seconds before the attack,' said the other analyst.

'Focus everything and everyone on that time window,' said the Head, 'I want to know about every single byte of data going in or out of that vehicle, I want to know about every communication even if it was sent by smoke signal.' There was a pause while everyone double checked that they had just heard her make use of humour and wasn't actually being serious.

'I'm looking into all the comm's logs now,' said Kingston, 'I'll find that message.' His voice had the tone of someone who was on a personal mission, a crusade, this was not someone who would give up. Wayne realised how hard he would have to work to throw the man of his trail.

TWENTY SEVEN

THURSDAY AFTERNOON

Wayne had asked Kingston for regular updates on what he was doing and the progress he was making, it was the only way that Wayne could keep one step ahead of Kingston, and Kingston was working quickly. Kingston had started with the logs of all the voice communications, which was fine, Wayne's final message to Anna hadn't been by voice. This gave him time to access the relevant communications database, find the correct record, delete it, and remove any trace of what he'd done. The irony wasn't lost on him, that he could have done with Anna's expertise in this.

'There's nothing out of place in the comm's logs,' said Kingston. Before Wayne could suggest anything Kingston said, 'I've checked all the checksums, all the packet sizes, message lengths, everything, there was no voice message and nothing hidden in any of the voice channels.' Kingston had been very thorough, and quick.

'So what's next?' Wayne asked, trying to keep a casual note in his voice.

'CCTV feeds, it's a quick one to check,' was Kingston's reply.

Wayne thought that it would be quick, there was nothing to find there.

Wayne finished up covering his tracks in the comm's database, but couldn't shake the nagging feeling that he'd missed something.

'Have you checked the GPS channel?' Wayne asked. The surveillance vehicle sent tracking data back to the network and received navigation data. Wayne had considered using that channel to hide his message to Anna, but decided there was too great a risk that someone else in the vehicle would have accessed the GPS channel and seen the message. His message had been for Anna and for her alone.

'Not yet, I'll do that next,' said Kingston.

Wayne felt a buzzing on his desk and realised it was his mobile phone. He recognised the number, but this was very definitely a bad time for a call. The buzzing stopped, but he knew it wouldn't stay stopped for long. He thought for a moment about creating a false trail for Kingston to follow, but realised that he'd left it far too late, that would have taken a significant amount of work, more in fact than he had had time for. It would have been the best idea, but unfortunately not one he could use now. The phone buzzed again. In his peripheral vision he noticed Kingston look across at him. Without returning the man's look he picked up his phone and walked away from the desk as he answered it.

He found a corner by the coat rails, it was away from most of the desks.

'What?' he said sharply, in no mood for any idle conversation.

'I'm almost ready at my end.' Wayne recognised Jason Mason's voice, not one he had wanted to hear.

'Good,' said Wayne, 'piss off, I'm busy.'

'I need the port number,' said Jason before Wayne could hang up.

'Ninety,' said Wayne.

'No,' said Mason, 'I need port eighty-five.'

'Don't care,' said Wayne sharply, 'the cascade is set for port ninety.'

'I haven't disconnected the scanners from port ninety,' said Mason, sounding a little anxious.

'Then do it, the cascade will hit port ninety so port ninety had better be open.' Wayne hung up, he'd had enough of that conversation.

He walked briskly back to his desk. Kingston was staring wide-eyed at his screen and his fingers were pounding on his keyboard. Wayne had the desperate feeling that the man was onto something and that his time was running out. He thought of all the things he could say to explain his next action, but decided not to interrupt Kingston. Wayne picked up his mug and put it and his phone into his bag, pushed his chair under the desk and walked to the exit. He picked his jacket off the coat rail and left without a backwards glance, only half aware that he was probably leaving this part of his life behind forever.

There were always people coming and going at the Doughnut, at all times of the day and night. Wayne was just one of many as he walked through the security doors of the outer ring towards the main entrance area. The final physical barrier, inside the building, was the row of full-height turnstiles, revolving doors opened only by the relevant security pass. Wayne held his pass to the scanner and noted the flicker of green light. He walked into the cylinder of the turnstile and pushed, the door revolved gently and he passed through into the entrance area.

Like most modern buildings the single biggest space was the wasted cavernous space of the entrance area, as though visitors would be awe struck at a building with such a big open space. Wayne ignored at, as he ignored it every time he entered or exited the Doughnut, and walked quickly to the main doors and out into the sunlight. He'd forgotten what a nice day it had turned out to be, and paused very slightly as he noticed the clouds and the sun. But then he focused on the line of bus stops and headed for them.

For one bizarre moment he thought of the scene from the movie The Great Escape, the scene where MacDonald (played by Richard Attenborough) having escaped the German PoW camp through the tunnel, boards the bus in his bid for freedom. When it came to the tasks dictated by his telepathic puppet-masters, Wayne's thinking was remarkably clear. When it came to his own immediate future, his thinking was blurred and incomplete, and thus he completely missed two important points; he had no idea what he was going to do once he got home and was inevitably identified as the source of the warning to the surveillance vehicle, and he forgot that in the Great Escape, MacDonald is captured as he boards the bus and is ultimately executed.

THE HEAD SAT at the head of the table, appropriately, in the Thames House Command and Control room. She looked at the screens, her eyes flicking between them, assimilating facts and information. She could see some of the patterns, how Marshall and the others had set them up and led them ultimately to the destruction of the surveillance vehicle. She contemplated how much effort must have gone into programming Crossley and setting him up, all to use him as bait. The piece that was still missing from the pattern was the most important piece: the reason why they wanted to destroy the surveillance vehicle. The

Head considered two possibilities; that inflicting further damage on MI5 and GCHQ gave them some tactical advantage, or Sanders was right and the analyst, Hendrickson, had been abducted. For the moment the first possibility was the more plausible, although what advantage they had gained still seemed unclear.

Her thinking was interrupted.

'Ma'am,' came the smooth voice of Kingston on one of the video conference screens from GCHQ. She had the strange and fleeting thought that the man would make a wonderful continuity announcer for the BBC.

'Yes,' she said, 'progress?'

'Possibly, I've found something strange.'

'Explain.'

'I've been looking at the logs for every communication channel the surveillance vehicle had, and there isn't a single communication to the vehicle that could have been a warning.'

'But?'

'There's a discrepancy in the master sequence log.'

The Head had no time for technical talk. She had always found that if it was significant it was simple. 'Explain, briefly.'

'The log is a master list of all items of data sent to the vehicle, there's one record missing.'

'I take it that's unusual,' said the Head, hoping that the man would get to the point, quickly.

'There's never a record missing in the log, it could only be because someone deleted a record and didn't renumber the subsequent entries.'

Now she was interested. 'Is that tangible evidence that someone has been covering their tracks?'

'That's my opinion ma'am, yes,' said Kingston. The Head liked it when people were clear in their view.

'Your only focus now is to find who deleted that record. Browning!' she said to get Wayne's attention.

'He's not here at the moment ma'am,' said Kingston.

'I'll clear it with him,' said the Head, 'find who deleted that record.'

Kingston hung up his headset and turned away to focus on another screen, tapping away at his keyboard. The Head had a sense of confidence that this man was more than capable of finding who had warned the surveillance vehicle. She wasn't sure if the others in the room had picked up on the significance of what the GCHQ man had said. If someone had compromised the GCHQ communications database then the first place to look for a suspect was inside GCHQ, or MI5. She didn't like either option. This was a complication she had not considered. It would explain how Bullock, Petric and the others managed to get into central London, armed with a shoulder-mounted rocket launcher, kill a spotter, blow up the surveillance vehicle and then escape unseen.

For the moment, she would have to wait for the GCHQ man to do his work. She also needed to speak to Sanders, and then she would have some major damage limitation to do. The firing of the rocket launcher in a central London street had not gone unnoticed, especially following the explosions at Edmonton. The press had been filled with eye witness accounts and expert opinion (or "uninformed speculation" as the Head called it.) Various Government ministers were asking some awkward questions, as was the Director General of MI5. She knew that very soon she was going to have to explain how she was going to close down this problem; quickly and completely. The assault at Edmonton had been contained and explained, but no doubt the Prime Minister would soon be talking about convening a meeting of COBRA, the Cabinet Office Briefing held at times of a security crisis.

'Ma'am?' Kingston's voice brought her back to the here-and-now. 'I found something.'

The Head didn't say anything, she expected him to go straight into his explanation. Kingston took a moment to realise this. 'There's a hole been left in our firewall, I think someone deleted a record from the proxy registration...'

The Head cut him off. 'I don't need details, significance?'

'It could be where someone got in to delete records, or it could be how they got a message out to the surveillance vehicle.'

'Was it opened from the inside?'

'Almost certainly.' Kingston pre-empted her next question. 'I'll track whoever opened it.' This time he left his headset on as he worked away on his keyboard. One of the screens in the Command and Control room mirrored a window on Kingston's computer. The green text on a black screen scrolled as he typed in commands and evaluated the responses. The Head ignored the detail, simply noticing how quickly he was working. The man didn't seem to slow, being in an almost continual dialogue with the computer systems.

The Head was considering whether to call the Direct General of MI5 and explain what was happening, or go straight to the Prime Minister's office. She focused back on the screen when she noticed the scrolling had stopped.

'Ma'am? This doesn't make sense,' said Kingston. On the video phone link she saw him frown as he considered what his computer screen was telling him.

'Explain,' she said, wishing people would just get straight to the point. She was sure ninety per cent of all human communication could be avoided if people stopped trying to be polite and just said what needed saying.

'I've tracked the address of the commands which opened the firewall, and they came from Wayne Browning's station.'

Kingston was silent, the Head considered what this might mean.

'Where is Browning?' she asked.

Kingston looked past his screen, past the camera, then looked around him. He stood up and looked around the office. He sat back down and looked into the camera. 'I can't see him, he's not here.'

'Find him,' ordered the Head. 'Review all security coverage of the building, see if he left, if you need authorisation have them come directly to me.'

The Head tapped a key on the panel set into the conference table, it muted the channel with the Doughnut. She picked up her phone and walked out of the conference room, shutting the door behind her. She checked there was no-one in the corridor within earshot, and dialled Michael Sanders' number.

TWENTY EIGHT

Michael had made his way back to the Chiswick High Road. He didn't want to be anywhere near the incident site when the press turned up. He stood just inside an alleyway at the side of a baker's shop, London life walking past him, oblivious to who or what he was. He watched the crowds of ordinary people walk past, going to or from work, or shopping, or wherever. He pondered the fact that many would have heard the explosions and the sirens, and yet most now seemed to have returned to their normal routine. It was almost bizarre to think that none of these people could have any idea (or if they had would not have believed) that the slightly scruffy individual they walked past was a former special forces soldier, now an MI5 operative, with incredible telepathic powers, hunting a team of similarly psychic and powerful mercenaries who were loose on the streets of London, armed with rocket launchers and who knew what else, hell-bent on a plan that only they knew. Sometimes, he thought, ignorance must be bliss.

He'd called for the car over ten minutes ago. He checked his watch, even with the extra congestion it should have arrived by now. He heard his phone ring, no doubt Eric calling to say where he'd got held up. He looked at the caller ID; not Eric. The Head was about the last person he wanted to talk to right now.

'Yes,' he said, he didn't have the energy or the inclination to try to be polite, or engage in a pointless attempt at small talk.

She was of course, straight to the point. 'It seems your friends might have recruited Wayne Browning to their cause.'

'Browning?' said Michael, 'the GCHQ analyst?'

'It's likely he warned Miss Hendrickson about the attack, and now he's left the Doughnut.'

'Why would they warn anyone when they were about to destroy it?' Michael said, more thinking out loud than posing a question to be answered.

'I want you back in The Office, now,' said the Head, 'I need you to find out what that warning was for, what advantage it gave them.'

'No,' said Michael, 'we're missing something.'

'We're missing almost everything and I want everyone here working on this problem.'

Michael didn't like the idea of being cooped up in Thames House. There were plenty of skilled analysts there and at GCHQ who could carry out remote surveillance and review intelligence data. He had the sudden idea he knew how a cat felt when its owner was trying to coax it into a cat box, and he didn't like the feeling.

'We need to get ahead in this game,' said Michael, 'we need to find Marshall and co.'

'So follow orders and get back to The Office.' The Head's tone was unwavering, no anger or malice, just chilling.

'No, Mister Browning is our only tangible lead, if you've found what he's been doing and he really is under their control then they'll know, and they'll be on their way to take care of things.'

'I would have thought if they wanted to silence him they'd just command him to walk out in front of a bus.'

'That would take a very powerful psychic link,' said Michael, he avoided sighing and sounding like he was explaining something simple. 'My guess is their control over Browning is strong but not that strong, but they will want to silence him, so they'll have to do that the old-fashioned way.'

'They're in London, he's in Cheltenham, it will take time for them to reach him,' said the Head.

'I'm in London too, it will take them longer to reach him than it will take me. I need to find him before they do.'

'I'll have the local police find Browning and arrest him, he'll be safe in custody.'

Something about that idea didn't feel right to Michael. 'That could complicate things, I need to be able to talk to him alone, by the time I get there the police would be all over it and there'll be solicitors and other complications. No, I need to find Browning.'

Almost on cue Michael saw the grey sleek shape of the Audi threading its way through the traffic. No doubt the car had been fully equipped in preparation for the day's operation. Michael made a mental note to find out just what kit the Audi carried. Eric pulled up in front of Michael. Still holding the phone to his ear he opened the door and got in.

'I'll be in touch,' said Michael, and ended the call.

He turned to Eric and smiled. 'Cheltenham, and step on it.'

ANNA SAT in a small interview room. She assumed it was an interview room, it looked like the interview rooms in the Doughnut. A small round table, three chairs, modern office decor. No windows, so it was an internal room. She wondered which room this was, she didn't recognise it, and then remembered that she probably wasn't in the Doughnut. She'd smiled, remembering that she always thought it was an odd nickname for the building. True, the building was circular with an open space in the middle, so from the air it would look like a Doughnut. But it was the headquarters of one of the world's most sophisticated surveillance and intelligence agencies. Surely they could have thought of a more appropriate title?

But if she wasn't in the Doughnut, where was she? She tried to think back to the events of the day. Surely she had gone to work, as usual? But she had a vague memory of today being different. She hadn't gone to work today, she had gone somewhere else. She had travelled. London. She had some memory of being in London, in the back of a lorry. What a strange way to spend a day.

And then it came back to her, that she had been in the Battle Bus. How could she have forgotten that? But why had she been there? It was all a bit hazy.

Michael. She had met Michael Sanders. She had met a real live secret agent. She smiled, again. She was a secret agent, of sorts. But he was a secret agent who carried a gun, and got into danger, and got shot at. And then she remembered that she'd been shot at, and she stopped smiling. She'd always said that she enjoyed working in the office, in the Doughnut, and that she never wanted to go out into "the field". And now she had been in the field, and people had shot at her. She remembered how Wayne had saved her. She remembered the message that came up on her screen, saying that Michael was outside the lorry and needed her, that she should leave immediately and not say anything. But what happened next was hazy.

She got up and tried the door handle. The door had been locked. She wasn't sure how she'd got from the surveillance vehicle to inside a locked interview room. Why would anyone want to lock her in an interview room? Who would do that? Friends don't lock each other in rooms. Friends. She'd seen a friend. She remembered getting out of the lorry. Michael wasn't there, but someone was. She couldn't remember who it was, but she had a vague recollection of knowing the person. They'd run, she remembered running, running towards a door. They went into a building, and then there were some strange noises and then an explosion. The friend must have saved her, and must have brought her here.

The door unlocked and opened, and there was her friend. She wasn't sure of his name, but she knew he was a friend. He was a big man, tall and board shouldered, black, dark eyes, deep rich voice.

'Anna,' he said, 'I hope you're feeling okay.'

'I am, thank you,' she said. He gestured to the chair and she sat down. He sat in the chair opposite her, the door still slightly ajar. He obviously felt no need to lock the door, it wasn't like she was going to want to leave.

'Anna, we need your help,' the friend said. 'We have a big problem with our computers, and we might lose a lot of money, we need you to help us, you're the only one who can help us.' He held out his hand across the table.

Anna reached out and took his hand. She instantly felt wonderful, like she'd won the lottery, or how she imagined winning the lottery might feel. A better description would be she felt like she'd just cracked a really complicated analysis problem and helped stop something really terrible happening.

Thoughts and feelings collided in her mind. Her friend had saved her, yet she remembered her job was stopping bad people from doing bad things. She had felt deeply calm and peaceful, in a way she'd never felt before. But she also remembered being part of a team, keeping people safe, doing something really important, something she really had to get back to, that she shouldn't be here she had other, more important places to be.

Her head swam and she had the feeling that there was something she ought to remember but couldn't quite. She was here with friends and that was all that mattered, that and helping them, helping her friends was very important.

Anna had no idea how much time had passed, she just came to the realisation that she was alone again in the room. Her friend had gone, she didn't know for how long, or what they'd talked about. But it must have been a nice conversation, because she knew she had to help her friends, she was the only one who could help them, help them find their money.

TWENTY NINE

The lights and sirens of the Audi had cut the journey time from London to Cheltenham from two and a half hours to barely two, but all the way Michael knew that Marshall and friends might have had a head start. He also knew that they would be directing Browning to some pre-decided meeting point, whereas Michael had no idea where Browning might be. He had finally persuaded the Head, who had seemed somewhat reluctant, to agree to engage GCHQ to locate Wayne Browning. They were, of course, only too willing to help find one of their own who might be in mortal peril. The possibility of Browning's potential treason had been kept quiet.

Unfortunately Wayne's mobile phone had been found soon after they started searching for him, left on the bus he'd taken from outside the Doughnut. There was so much open countryside around Cheltenham that if Marshall and the others had arranged for Wayne to go to a meeting place outside the town it could be almost anywhere. There were farmland and open countryside, none covered by CCTV or any kind of electronic surveillance. They could have Wayne take a taxi to the middle of nowhere, go and stand in a field, and have Bullock kill him with a shot from his sniper rifle. There would be no way to find Browning in time, and probably no way to find him any time soon after the event. Michael's only hope was that all that would take too much planning and preparation, and that the only safe and easy thing they could rely on would be to order Browning to go home and for one of the three to intercept Wayne at his home.

There was only one small problem. Michael was certain that the Head would have tipped off Halbern who would have arranged for the nearest firearms unit to be staking out Browning's home waiting for them. Or maybe she had arranged for some more covert military personnel to be in the area, to effect a more permanent solution. The Head had seemed a little too keen for Michael to go back to Thames House, a little too keen to pass up an opportunity to intercept Marshall or one of the others.

GCHQ was, of course, attempting to locate Marshall or any of others on all possible routes between London and Cheltenham, so far without success. Michael had never been quite sure why they built the Doughnut in Cheltenham, it wasn't in easy reach of London. He knew the building was a modern replacement for the previous site, GCHQ having outgrown its previous location. But surely if they were going to build a new site they could have built it somewhere a little more convenient. Having come off the M4 at Swindon they'd blasted down the A419, past Cirencester and were now hurtling along the A417 towards Cheltenham. Michael had always liked the Cotswolds, a particularly scenic part of England, but he hardly noticed it this time. Strangely the Head had made no attempt to contact him since they'd left London, other than to confirm that GCHQ were trying to trace Browning.

As they scythed their way through the traffic in the suburbs of Cheltenham, Michael had Eric turn off the sirens and lights, and slow down, blending in with the local traffic. He had no doubt that Browning would be home by now, and most likely sitting in the middle of a cohort of concealed and highly armed police or military personnel. The more he thought about it, the less Michael liked the idea of walking naked into the lions' den.

It was certainly tempting just to let events take their course. Let Marshall and gang turn up, let the police or military take care of them. Whichever of the gang turned up would be killed. Unfortunately it was possible that whoever turned up would kill Browning, or in the firefight the police might kill him. If the military were there, they would almost certainly kill Browning. Michael could then go in, examine what was left of the representative of Mister Marshall and Friends, connect psychically with an appropriate item of clothing or equipment and determine the location of the rest of them. Michael just couldn't be sure enough though that he would be viewed as friend rather than foe. There would be too many people there with guns and with orders to kill, and too few with any intention to engage in reasoned dialogue.

'Pull over,' he said to Eric. Eric found a bus lay-by and pulled in. He frowned, but Michael just sat there, thinking. 'I'll be back in a minute,' he said, and with that he got out of the car.

Michael walked a short way from the car, and pulled out of his jacket pocket the plastic sleeve still holding the picture of the cyclone. Of course he'd recognised the visual pun as soon as he'd seen the picture. The military project which had resulted in four of its subjects developing extraordinary mental skills had been renamed as the PsiClone project, the idea being to mass produce, or clone, psychic soldiers. The picture of the cyclone would be meaningless to anyone but Michael, but Julian Singh had infused the paper with a charge of psychic energy, intended to deliver a message. Michael looked at the picture. They were coming for him, that had been made clear.

Whatever they were planning, they intended revenge on him as well.

Michael had spent a lot of time and energy making sure that there was no possibility of any psychic link between himself and any of his three former colleagues. He had no doubt that they would have done the same. The original idea of the project was that psychic soldiers would have enjoyed a completely private and reliable method of communication, impossible for any enemy to intercept. After their parting, it had been obvious that severing any psychic link was essential. It would have been useful to be able to psychically locate Marshall and friends, but that would mean they would have been able to locate Michael. Their parting company had to be complete, physically and mentally. But now they had delivered an object infused with a psychic connection to Julian Singh, and Michael Sanders was the only other in the project who had developed the ability to connect with physical objects.

He prepared himself, letting his thoughts extend out through his hands to his fingers, almost imagining gloves of light shimmering around his fingers. He slipped the paper out of the plastic sleeve. He pushed a single thought out, imagining the thought flowing through his fingers and into the paper. This time there would be no being overwhelmed by the psychic energy in the paper, he'd use the connection to his own advantage.

It was like reaching out into a dark room, expecting to feel something, never sure if the something is actually there. What came back was a surge of surprise. Whatever Julian Singh was doing at that moment he certainly hadn't expected a psychic connection from Michael. There was a pause, as though each was waiting for the other to speak first. The telepathic connection between two strong psychics had always been a strange experience for Michael, and now he was having to push past his own mental defences as well as Singh's. It made the connection awkward, Michael wasn't sure if he could think clearly enough to transmit a phone number, or if it would be better to simply think of a place, the idea and image of a location.

He held in mind the idea of armed police, of soldiers, of Wayne Browning. The meaning was clear in his mind, and hopefully would be clear in Singh's mind. He relaxed and cleared his mind and waited for a moment, and felt from somewhere else a sense of understanding; he knew that Julian Singh had got the message.

The next part wasn't going to be so easy. There was no chance that Singh would simply give up and go back to London, Michael was going to have to come up with an alternative course of action. He didn't know Cheltenham well, but he did remember a nice little coffee shop in the centre of town. Any meeting would be risky, but sometimes you just had to roll the dice. He held in his mind an image of the coffee shop, imagining its location in the centre of the town.

What he experienced next was slightly surprising; an image formed in his mind of a pub, a large white building, old, set back off the main road. The sign hanging outside the pub had the image of a king, an old hand-painted sign. The image faded, but the meaning was clear. Michael hurried back to the car and got in. He picked the laptop off the back seat and opened it.

'Looking for something?' asked Eric. Eric had never spoken much, but at times he had proved to be a mine of useless, and occasionally useful, information.

'Yes,' said Michael, 'a pub, near here, picture of a king outside.'

'The Kings Arms,' said Eric, 'about five miles up the road.' Eric pulled the car out of the lay-by.

The pub was indeed four and a half miles further along the road. Michael had Eric pull up at the side of the road, they could see the pub, but he estimated the car was out of working range of any CCTV cameras around the building. He knew that GCHQ would be tracking the car, but if the meeting turned ugly he didn't really want the local constabulary having his face too easily available from CCTV images. They were too far out of London for Halbern, the Head or anyone else to quickly smooth things over with any local police and he really didn't have time to waste.

'If anyone's waiting for you, there's no cover,' said Eric. He was right, of course. Between the car and the pub was a hundred metre walk, open space, a perfect environment for a sniper.

'Fortune favours the bold,' said Michael.

As he got out of the car he thought he heard Eric say something like 'or the foolish,' and if he did say it he was probably right. Michael walked towards the pub, baseball cap pulled down to cover his face from all but direct head-and-shoulders facing cameras. Using his peripheral vision as much as he could Michael saw that the pub was an old building, so small windows, little chance of a sniper hitting anyone inside. There was one camera covering the front door, but it was mounted so far up the wall Michael doubted it captured any more than lots of tops of heads. The car park was to the side of the building, no windows facing the car park. Michael tried to walk quickly but not look like he was hurrying. Being so exposed felt uncomfortable, but he was soon at the car park and then to the front door. He looked around. There was little traffic, and no pedestrians. To wait? Or to go in?

The question was answered. The front door, a solid wood affair, opened, and Julian Singh stood there. Casually dressed, but smart; shoes not trainers for Julian.

'Michael, how lovely to see you,' he said, with all the warmth of a rattlesnake. 'Come in, have a drink, let's talk.'

MICHAEL FOLLOWED Singh into the pub. They walked past the bar to a small table towards the back. Sitting at the table Michael recognised Wayne Browning. A pint of beer sat on the table in front of him, a glass of orange juice at the place beside him, and a glass of lager at the place opposite. Singh sat at the seat next to Browning, he gestured to Michael to take the third seat.

'Michael, I don't know if you've met Mister Browning.' Singh put his hand on Wayne's shoulder. Wayne smiled, looking for all the world like the village idiot, smiling, friendly, and not an intelligent thought in sight. 'A friendly chap, but I wouldn't shake his hand if I were you, could be bad for all of us.'

Of the three, Singh was the one Michael was the wariest of. In his youth, Michael had seen a fight start in a bar, a bar not unlike this one. Two drunken youths started trying to punch each other. Big lads, strong, but incompetent, neither landed a decent punch. Unfortunately one of them came close to punching another man at the bar. Michael had estimated the other man to be in his fifties if not older, wiry, thinning grey hair. The man took exception to being a target for the youths and hit back. With one fast and solid punch he knocked out the first youth, who dropped to the floor without a whimper. He stepped forward and jabbed at the second youth who dropped likewise. In all his years in the army and in Special Forces Michael had seen very few people who could punch that hard and fast. It was always the slim, quiet ones you had to worry about, they could be the most surprisingly violent.

'I don't suppose you invited me here to talk about old times,' said Michael. He ignored the pint of lager on the table.

'We could,' said Singh, 'but no. Thanks for the warning though, about the ambush at our friend's house.' He patted

Browning on the shoulder again, as though he was a pet. 'But it never was my intention to meet him at his own home, too obvious.'

'So why here?' asked Michael.

'I like the beer, but also because it's safe, no line of sight from outside, refreshingly few cameras, easy for our friend to reach by public transport.'

'So now what? You take him somewhere quiet and put him out of your misery?'

'Oh Michael, please,' said Singh, with mock indignation. 'Mister Browning has far more to contribute to our cause, he knows so much about so many systems, I really have no desire to do anything unpleasant to him.'

Michael never had liked Julian Singh's voice, it just grated. Born in Egypt, educated at Eton, and he exaggerated the accent.

'But I can't imagine you're going to contribute to Wayne's pension.'

'Ah, no, sorry. I'm afraid Mister Browning's longer-term prospects aren't particularly rosy.'

'So why bring me here?'

'Because there was too great a chance you would track down Mister Browning before I could pick him up and take him back. At least here you can't do anything.'

'Can't I?' said Michael, knowing full well he couldn't. The play had been well thought out. Michael was in a busy and public place, they couldn't start a fight, Michael certainly couldn't reveal his firearm. There was the ever-present threat of Bullock and his sniper rifle if he followed them outside.

'Michael,' said Singh, the accent grating again. 'Can't I implore you to leave us alone, just for a while? We'll be gone soon.'

'After what you did to Crossley? The police officers at the lockup? The young lad on the bike? The people in the lorry?'

'Ah yes, sorry about those. But you know how Marshall is, he does like to stick the boot in.' Michael had no doubt that Singh had been an active contributor in planning all those acts of violence.

'And Crossley? All that work to set him up simply as bait for us?'

Singh sighed a little. 'To be honest, Michael, we didn't need to do much to set up Crossley. You're all so keen to find terrorists that we didn't have to do much to pique your interest. We thought we needed the uranium to make you take the threat seriously, but as soon as you took notice of Gerald you didn't go digging much further.'

'What do you mean?' asked Michael, suspicious always of Singh, a man who lied as easily as he breathed.

'We did work setting up a history for Crossley that you never looked into,' said Singh, 'once you'd categorised him as a terrorist you were just like a dog with a bone, you'd have destroyed Crossley even if we didn't.'

Michael was quiet for a moment. 'You said you're coming for me,' he said, 'well I'm coming for you.'

'No you're not,' Singh's voice was suddenly harder. 'You have no idea where we are or what we're doing. Your forces are shattered and demoralised, political pressure will soon likely shut you down, and if the Head hasn't brought back her little hit squad then she soon will, and the only target they'll find is you.'

There was a silence between them. Years of animosity and thoughts of revenge hung in the air. Wayne just kept smiling.

'We're leaving now Michael, don't try to follow us.'

'Oh I will follow you, and if you want the quiet exit you planned, then you won't stop me.'

Slowly Michael and Singh stood up. He put his hand on Wayne Browning's shoulder who stood too, still clutching his bag. They made their way to the front of the pub and out through the door, Michael pulling the door closed behind them.

It was a short walk around the corner of the building to the car park. Michael was suddenly aware of how exposed he was. If Bullock and his rifle were anywhere close Michael wouldn't have a chance to reach cover in time.

'I'm afraid we have to leave you, Michael,' said Singh. 'I suggest you stay here, it's safer. We'll be in touch.' He gave a smile as he turned to walk away.

Michael heard the bullet hit Browning's chest before he heard the crack of the rifle firing. Wayne simply collapsed on the spot, a dark red stain already spreading across his chest. Without thinking Michael ducked behind the nearest car, his gun already in hand.

Michael heard Singh shouting. 'You bastard, Bullock, you stupid bastard.' Michael couldn't see Singh, and wasn't about to stick his head out and look, not with Bullock and his rifle lurking. He heard Singh's footsteps, running, fading, he had obviously decided to leave. No doubt there would be strong words between Singh and Bullock later, perhaps they might even kill each other, but Michael thought that was unlikely. How long would Bullock stick around? He leaned as far forwards as he dared and saw Browning's lifeless body lying on the asphalt of the car park. No-one had yet left the pub, but it could only be a matter of minutes before someone did.

Hoping that fortune was still on the side of the brave or the foolhardy, he sprinted out from behind the car and towards Browning's body. He grabbed Browning's jacket by the shoulders to pull him back behind the car. A blast of psychic energy hit him through his right hand and he staggered, almost falling backwards. In a moment he realised it was where Singh had kept touching Browning's shoulder and had left a psychic imprint. He doubted Singh had meant to, perhaps a moment's carelessness.

He focused on the jacket, still conscious that he was out in the open and still in Bullock's sights (literally) if Bullock was still there, but this was too good a chance to pass up. He let the glove of mental energy spread over his hand, and reached out to touch Browning's shoulder. He slowly let his psychic guard dissipate, and felt a connection to the imprint Singh had left. He could feel a rage, a torrent of anger. Singh had hidden his feelings well, but he was a master of that. Michael saw a flicker of an image, he saw Anna's face, he saw a shape with wheels, it must have been the surveillance vehicle. He saw another face, more clearly. He didn't recognise the man's face, but it was the clearest image.

He let go of the jacket and stood up, breaking into a sprint, running back to where Eric was waiting in the car, engine still running. He still didn't want to risk bringing the car into sight of any CCTV cameras, not with another dead body lying around. This was going to be difficult to explain to the Head. Michael didn't think she'd take the news well.

He reached the car and pulled open the door, shouting the order to drive to Eric as he climbed in.

The car accelerated hard, Eric turning it round in the road and left the pub behind. Michael turned to look over his shoulder and as the pub disappeared behind them Michael thought he saw people coming out of the front door.

Now he had to think how he was going to explain this.

THIRTY

Michael used his mobile phone to call the Head, he wanted this to be as private a call as he could. He'd had Eric pull over so he could have the call outside the car. He had no doubts about Eric's trustworthiness, but Eric was not privy to any details about the PsiClone project. The unknown face he had seen now worried Michael. It could be anyone, someone else in GCHQ, someone in MI5, someone else working for Marshall and gang, either willingly or through psychic coercion.

'Yes?' was all the Head said when she finally answered the call.

'Browning's dead,' he said. Perhaps being direct and to the point was the best way, under the circumstances.

There was silence from the Head. Michael was never sure if she was weighing up the implications of this, waiting for Michael to try to explain the situation, or had decided that the call was no longer of any value. He waited.

'The local police have already been called,' she said, obviously having had an analyst in the Command and Control room verify Michael's information. 'I want you back in The Office.'

'I've seen a face,' Michael said quickly, before she could end the call, 'it's someone else Singh has had contact with, I need to know who it was.'

'No Sanders, your role in this matter has ended. Return to The Office.'

'You've no other leads to work on, I have a face, I've seen someone involved in what they're planning.'

Again there was silence, but at least she hadn't ended the call.

'Come back to The Office, we'll identify whoever you saw,' said the Head.

'I need to do it here, if it's someone from GCHQ I can find them within half an hour.'

'I'll find you an analyst who can help,' said the Head, who added 'but there aren't many of them.' The call ended.

Michael went back to the car.

'Where now?' asked Eric.

'We wait for a moment,' said Michael. He pulled the laptop off the back seat and opened the lid. 'I need to identify someone before we leave.'

It was several moments before an instant messenger window opened on the laptop's screen. Michael had never considered the idea that anyone in GCHQ would bear him ill will over Anna's apparent death. He had imagined that they would all want to help him find whoever was responsible, not hold him accountable for it. The analyst who had made contact identified themselves only by their personnel number, no name was given.

> what do you need?

It was a stark message, not exactly overflowing with warmth. Michael typed his reply, slowly, typing never had been his strong suit.

> i need pictures of people anna hendrickson had contact with in previous week

It was a few moments before the reply came back.

> can access her diary and list contacts

Michael typed as quickly as he could, clarifying his request.

> need pictures, must see people contacted

The reply was not reassuring.

> wait

Michael waited. He wasn't sure if he should ask how it was going, and risk annoying whoever he was communicating with, or just let them get on with it. After nearly ten minutes, the next message appeared.

> sending names + pictures

The instant messenger window closed itself, the analyst had ended the conversation, obviously having no desire to engage in any more contact with Michael than was necessary. Michael noted the icon which had appeared at the bottom of the screen, indicating that a file had been delivered over the secure network connection. He clicked the icon and a document opened.

In the document was a list of pictures, under each picture a name and some basic contact information. Michael recognised the first one, Wayne Browning. He thought how little support he was going to receive once news of Browning's fate reached his former colleagues. He scrolled down. He didn't recognise many, most were people inside GCHQ.

The eighth picture made him stop. Staring out of the screen were the eyes of someone he'd seen, someone he'd only ever seen in the haze and energy of a telepathic connection. The face wasn't familiar, but he knew it was the face he'd seen. He looked at the name and contact details under the picture.

He turned to Eric. 'London, please, and quickly.'

As Eric set off, switching on the lights and siren, Michael used the phone to call the Head. This time he didn't have to wait long for her to answer.

'I know who they've contacted,' he said as soon as she

answered. He didn't wait for her to ask who, knowing she wouldn't. 'It's Jason Mason, IT Manager at the Bank of England.'

'That fits,' said the Head, 'he was part of the working group who set up the security protocols for the bullion delivery.'

'I'm sure he does more,' said Michael, 'the convoy was not their target.'

'This doesn't indicate any other viable target, report back to The Office as ordered.' She ended the call.

Michael had a strong urge to punch something, but since Eric was driving and doing some considerable speed and he needed the car and phone and laptop he decided not to damage anything in reach.

'Back to The Office?' Eric asked.

'Yes,' said Michael, 'but we need to take a small detour.'

THE ROUTE through London to Canary Wharf was as visually stunning as the drive through the Cotswolds, and Michael paid it as little attention. He focused his efforts on finding the whereabouts of Jason Mason and getting official sanction for a meeting. He had no doubt that if he turned up unannounced Mason would refuse to see him, and might even have some way of psychically alerting Singh or one of the others. If Michael's visit was arranged as part of the ongoing security operation he was hoping that Mason would simply take it as part of his working day.

It was late afternoon as the grey Audi threaded its way through the congestion of the A100, turning off before Tower Bridge and onto the A1203, heading finally for the Limehouse Link road and Canary Wharf. Michael ignored the Tower of London as he finally found someone in the Bank of England IT department who would verify his security clearance and agree to put a meeting in Jason Mason's calendar, and alert Mason as to the urgency of the meeting.

Eric finally delivered Michael to the front door of the office block, and Michael dashed into the entrance lobby, official ID badge slung around his neck. He announced himself at the front desk and was asked to wait. Michael couldn't help looking at his watch as he waited, and despite himself he found he was becoming more frustrated as the minutes slipped by. It was fast approaching six o'clock and it was only by luck that Mason was working late that day.

Finally, a young woman appeared from the other side of the turnstiles and invited him to accompany her. She used her badge to open the turnstile and she guided him to the bank of lifts which whisked them up to one of the higher floors, Michael was too busy planning ahead to notice which floor. He was shown to a small office and asked to wait. It was as featureless and bland as every other modern office he had seen, a place with no soul and no character. After another wait and waste of time the door opened and Jason Mason entered. He looked at Michael for a moment.

'Mr "Smith" is it?' Mason asked, obviously doubting that Smith was his guest's genuine name.

'It is, Mr Mason I assume?' Michael replied, standing and offering his hand to shake. Mason shook his hand half-heartedly and gestured for Michael to sit.

'I'm sorry I can't spare much time, I've a lot to do before I leave and I'm late already,' said Mason, making no attempt at introductory small talk.

'Then I'll get to the point,' said Michael, deciding that he really didn't like this man. 'I'm following up the attacks in London recently, and I need to know what you and Anna Hendrickson were working on.'

Mason didn't hesitate before answering. 'I can't tell you that.

If you needed to know then you'd already have been briefed, so I'm sorry, if you've not been updated about GCHQ's support for the Bank's security planning then I can't help you.'

Michael leaned a little closer, not to threaten Mason but to let him know that this was a serious matter. 'Mr Mason, I can't stress enough how imperative it is that we catch the people behind these attacks, and I have every reason to believe that Miss Hendrickson was inadvertently caught up in it, so I need to know...' But Mason cut him off.

'I said I can't help, now if there's nothing else...' Mason stood, and as a feeble attempt at politeness offered his hand to shake.

Michael looked at Mason and considered his options, which were becoming fewer by the minute. He decided what he needed to do. He smiled at Mason and stood, and accepted the handshake.

He needed to do this with care and with caution. Slowly but firmly he extended his mind out through the handshake, and projected a warming and inviting blanket of comforting thought-energy around Mason. He saw Mason exhale and his posture softened. Michael held a gentle idea in mind of sitting, and Mason duly complied. Michael sat opposite him, keeping hold of the man's hand. Michael opened his mind, becoming aware of whatever Mason was thinking/feeling/experiencing. He had images of people sitting around a table in a meeting room, of screens of emails, pages of word-processed documents, crowds of commuters packed into a Tube train, a sense of frustration, the smells of an office environment all artificial and manufactured, a sense of methodical focus and control.

That last sense was out of sorts with the others, and it felt familiar to Michael, like hearing a familiar voice above the noise of a room filled with conversation. There was a tone he knew, a tone he knew very well; this was the work of Julian Singh. There was no doubt; Marshall and friends had exerted their psychic control over the hapless Jason Mason. Michael listened with this mind, trying to leave as little impression as possible of his own presence. Michael simply held a sense of wandering, and allowed Mason's mind to wander, listening to whatever Mason happened upon, thoughts of a conversation with Anna, about a test, anger at GCHQ breaching his security arrangements, boredom at attending meetings, disinterest in the financial operations being planned, distance from conversations about arrangements for the gold bullion convoy. There was something else; Mason's thoughts weren't wandering aimlessly. He was mentally hopping from thought to thought, but always moving away from something. It was ever so subtle, but there was something that Mason was avoiding thinking about, something buried beneath his immediate awareness, but a something that was very big and powerful. Michael felt like he was handling something very fragile, like cradling a priceless glass antique, knowing that excess pressure could cause damage and loss.

The thought crept into Michael's mind that he should stop, that to press further would be to risk harm to Mason. But would it? He'd backed off before, a decision which had led to disaster. Perhaps he might cause harm to Mason, but Marshall and the others were planning something that would no doubt include visiting harm and destruction on a great many people. He'd heard soldiers who'd served in Northern Ireland say that when you played big boys' games you had to play by big boys' rules: soldiers are not diplomats, the rule is simple, kill or be killed, and enough had died already. It was time, Michael decided, it was time to take the initiative.

Michael pushed his mind against the resistance in Mason's thoughts. He felt the resistance, and the harder he pushed the more resistance he felt, but Mason's resistance was simply an instruction by his psychic masters, Michael's pushing was from his own intense psychic energy, and he could push harder than Mason could resist. It was as though someone had turned out all the lights; in an instant it all went still and quiet. Mason had stopped resisting. Almost as a reflex Michael stopped pushing. He kept his mind silent, waiting, listening.

A few thoughts came into Mason's mind, clear and simple thoughts. Thoughts that had the psychic scent of Julian Singh. This was their plan. Michael smiled to himself, and had to stop himself from laughing out loud. As plans go, it was audacious. It was certainly ambitious. It was definitely unexpected, and Michael had the uneasy feeling that it was unstoppable.

THIRTY ONE

The Head sat alone in her own office. It was small, sparsely furnished, devoid of any personal artefacts. The afternoon had seen little progress made by the MI5 and GCHQ analysts. The only significant development had been the confirmed killing of Wayne Browning. The press hadn't yet picked up on the significance of Browning's death or its possible link with events in London, but that was only a matter of time. Explaining things to the Director General of MI5 and to a succession of government ministers had not been easy. With the exception of the DG they had all expected quick and easy answers and solutions. Their fear of criticism in the press was palpable. The Head had no time for any of them, spineless cowards was the least offensive description she had for them. They were, however, right about one thing; a speedy solution was needed. Whatever the graduates of the PsiClone project had planned they had to be stopped.

The ringing of the mobile phone jerked her out of her contemplations. Her heart sank a little when she saw who was calling. Sanders had been nothing but bad luck on this project. He was supposed to be the one person who could stop Marshall and the others, but so far had achieved little, while the body count continued to rise.

She answered the call but said nothing, waiting for Sanders to speak first.

'I've had a quiet word with Mason,' said Sanders. Still the Head said nothing. Sanders had said nothing of value, she had no comment to make.

'The bullion delivery, the idea of the dirty bomb, they're all a distraction from the real aim,' Sanders continued. The Head knew that having had a "quiet word" was code for a psychic interrogation, but she was still unsure as to how reliable that was.

'I have to report to the Joint Intelligence Committee,' said the Head, a distinct lack of enthusiasm in her voice. 'I need to explain what we're doing to combat the threat of further armed attacks on the streets of London. What evidence do you have that I can present to them?'

There was silence, Sanders was no doubt trying to think how to answer the question. Eventually he said, 'I have no physical evidence, but you know that I know for certain what Mason is being ordered to do.'

'Sanders, I am not going to argue in front of the Director General and the others that one of my agents is psychic and has read the mind of a Bank of England manager and now knows for certain that we should stop our current investigations. Can you tell me where Marshall and the others are currently and what they are going to do next?'

'No, but...' there was a rising note of anger in Sander's voice.

'Then we will continue our efforts to locate them and to stop them. I repeat my previous order to you, return to The Office immediately. I want you off the streets of London, I think it's safer for everyone.'

She ended the call.

With the combined electronic surveillance of GCHQ and the intelligence gathering of MI5 it was only a matter of time before Marshall or one of the others was spotted, and from there the location of the rest of them would be established and then they could all be exterminated. There would be no involving the police, no messing around with warrants for arrest. The four soldiers on stand-by would be deployed the moment the target location was established. The thought occurred to the Head that Sanders could claim psychic knowledge of almost anything, she had no way of independently verifying his information, or his motives.

Her desk phone rang. She picked up the handset. 'Yes?'

The man's voice was instantly familiar. 'Are we on track for a speedy resolution of our problem?'

'They can't move without being seen. As soon as we see them we'll find them, then you'll have a target,' said the Head.

'Will all targets be at the same location?'

'Possibly not. Sanders is likely to be separate, and if he's not with them then he's not a target.'

A short pause. 'I can't guarantee that,' said the man, 'it would be better if all loose ends are tied up.' The line went dead.

THIRTY TWO

Singh opened his eyes. The light from the monitors in the control room made him blink. Marshall and Bullock watched him, waiting for him to speak. The bank of computer monitors continued to show images from the security cameras in and around the building, including the three Serbian soldiers still playing their video games.

'It seems Michael just won't leave things alone,' said Singh.

'Does he know anything?' asked Bullock.

'No, he asked Mason about the girl, but he doesn't know what their connection is.'

'Does he know the girl's alive?' asked Marshall.

'He's given no sign that he does,' Singh replied.

Marshall got up and started pacing up and down the room.

He stopped pacing and looked at the other two. 'Sanders concerns me,' he said.

'If he doesn't know anything, he can't cause problems,' said Bullock.

'No, but he's resourceful enough, he might find a way to cause problems,' said Marshall.

'Then I think we should cause a problem for him,' said Singh.

'Any suggestions?' asked Marshall.

'Yes,' said Singh, he looked around at the monitors. 'If we still had the help of Mr Browning we could leave traces of a message from Michael that would look suspicious.' The annoyance in his voice was obvious, deliberately so.

'He was too much of a liability,' said Bullock, 'we agreed that if he became a problem we'd get rid of him.'

Singh sighed. 'And now we've lost a key resource, too early.'

'Okay,' said Marshall, sounding like a parent intervening in an argument between quarrelsome children. 'We can't plant an incriminating message, so what can we do?'

'It's time we started to lead them down the garden path,' said Singh.

'Is Dulic ready?' Marshall asked.

Singh looked at the monitor showing the Serbians now arguing over their shoot-to-kill video game. 'Oh yes, he's ready.'

'Right, so we start the distraction operation, we also need to make life uncomfortable for Sanders. Ideas?' said Marshall.

'From the chink Mr Browning left in their comm's security I've been able to eavesdrop on some conversations,' said Singh, 'and it seems Michael is not flavour-of-the-month around GCHQ.'

'He never was flavour-of-the-month,' said Bullock.

'No, but our friends in Cheltenham, and therefore probably in London, hold him partly to blame for the reported deaths of their two analysts, and I'm not sure they trust him very much at the moment.'

'So how do we exploit that?' asked Marshall.

'I think once our Mr Dulic is in position he could make a quick telephone call and mention how valuable Michael's information was,' said Singh with a smile.

'Will that be enough?' said Bullock.

'It will be enough to make them more suspicious, and the more suspicious they are of him, the more they'll follow our lead, not his,' said Marshall.

'We need Dulic back,' said Bullock, 'I hope this won't compromise him.'

'Shouldn't,' said Singh, 'their surveillance is good but not perfect, once they've taken the bait we can make sure Dulic makes it back here.'

'Good,' said Marshall, clapping his hands together, grinning from ear to ear. He turned to Bullock. 'Go and set our Mr Dulic on his merry way, and bring our guest in, I think it's time Miss Hendrickson started to earn her keep.'

ANNA SAT at the table in the control room. She seemed oblivious to the banks of monitors behind her, to the video feed hijacked from GCHQ, the faces of Marshall and Bullock and Singh standing looking at her. She looked completely at peace.

Marshall looked at Singh. 'Go on then,' he said, 'she's all yours, make her work your magic.'

Singh sat down in the chair across the table from her, and not with a great deal of enthusiasm. He held out his hand, and she held out hers, taking his hand in a light hold. Singh closed his eyes to concentrate.

'Right,' said Marshall, turning away. 'I'm going for a coffee, this is as much fun to watch as tennis.' Bullock turned to follow him, but they were stopped in their tracks when Singh took a sharp intake of breath. They turned and stared. This had not happened before. They walked back to the table, slowly, as though not to wake a sleeping baby.

They could see Singh's face tensed, his eyes narrowed even

though closed, his jaw moving as if he were talking to himself, which he was.

'She's resisting,' said Singh, almost under his breath.

'She can't,' said Bullock, 'she's just a girl.' Marshall shot him a glance, Singh looked as though he had through closed eyes.

'She's able to pull her mind away from my contact,' said Singh.

'Well push harder, break through,' said Marshall.

'She's prancing around like a naughty schoolgirl,' Singh said, obviously not amused by Anna's mental antics. 'She's playing games.'

'For Christ's sake,' said Marshall coldly, 'get a grip and get control.'

Singh moved his head slightly from side to side, mimicking looking for something. 'If I push too hard I'll lose the connection with the information we need,' he said. He took a deep and slow inhalation, and as he exhaled Anna jerked suddenly, and then relaxed, the smile fading from her face and her eyes closing.

'Got her,' said Singh.

After a few minutes, during which Marshall and Bullock didn't take their eyes off him, Singh opened his eyes and let go of Anna's hand. She opened her eyes and blinked.

'Hello Anna,' said Singh.

'Hello Julian,' she said.

As though carrying on a previous conversation with hardly a pause, Singh continued. 'Anna, I need you to call Jason and get things ready.' He gestured to the long table in front of the monitors. Without hesitation Anna got up and took her seat at one of the workstations, keyboard and mouse to hand. Without further instruction she slipped on the Bluetooth ear-piece and picked up the mobile phone resting on the desk. She selected a contact from the phone's address book and dialled. Singh stood behind her, eyes half-closed, concentrating on the psychic connection. Anna immediately began typing at the keyboard, windows opening on the screens showing the status of various systems.

The phone call was answered after a single ring, the person answering was obviously expecting the call.

'Have you installed the package?' Anna asked, she nodded at the reply. 'And is the package open to port ninety?' Again she nodded at the reply. 'Now we need to configure the transfer protocols.'

Marshall and Bullock sat down and watched as Anna continued her conversation with Jason Mason, typing and clicking as she went. They didn't try to keep up with the technical jargon, confident that Julian Singh was the puppet master and his two puppets were busy configuring the Bank of England's computers to their design. Eventually their work was done and Anna ended the call, taking off the ear-piece. Singh opened his eyes fully and rubbed his temples. Exercising psychic control was not something he enjoyed.

'So this is all going to work then is it?' asked Bullock, with just a hint of sarcasm.

'Yes,' said Singh with a confident smile.

They were all shocked when Anna said 'no, it won't,' also with a smile.

'Organ grinder, your monkey's getting ideas,' said Bullock, leaning further back in his chair, enjoying the moment of someone else's problem.

Marshall was standing, slowly. 'What do you mean Anna? Why won't it work?' he asked.

'The plan is for Jason to send an encrypted message to Wayne's server in GCHQ to start the cascade,' Anna said, explaining their own plan to them. 'But GCHQ will soon close the open socket he left in the outer network layer.'

'No they won't,' said Singh in indignation, 'they don't know it's there.'

'After our successful penetration test of the Bank's outer firewall GCHQ implemented a rotating redundant socket scan on their own system, to stop anyone using my attack against them. Your open socket will soon be discovered and closed.'

'Fuck,' said Bullock, grinning even more, 'it's a good job we invited her to the party.'

'Now what do we do, Julian?' asked Marshall, anger starting to rise in his voice. 'We're kind of screwed if we can't trigger that cascade.'

'Maybe we could get Mister Mason to manually take down the firewall,' Singh suggested.

'No,' said Anna, 'he doesn't have the access to the systems to do that, the firewall has to be brought down by the cascade.'

'So how do we trigger the cascade Anna, if our access to the server has been blocked?' asked Marshall, trying ever so hard to sound friendly.

'If I go back to the Doughnut I can open another socket,' she suggested.

Marshall threw his hands up in despair. 'Of course, just mosey on in there, no-one will notice.'

'Am I being thick?' asked Bullock, and before anyone could answer said 'why don't we just do the cascade thing from here?'

Singh looked at him like a parent looking at a child who's just asked why water is wet.

'The cascade takes down the Bank's firewall, but it has to come from a trusted source, from GCHQ, otherwise it will set off their alarms, so we can't do the cascade from here,' Singh explained. Bullock just grinned and nodded, Singh suspect Bullock actually understood only too well.

'Anna?' Marshall said, still trying to sound friendly. 'Is there any other way of opening up a socket in the GCHQ network?'

'Wayne would do it, if I asked him,' she said, smiling again. Singh shot a fierce glance at Bullock, the malice was not feigned.

Marshall stopped the argument before it began. 'Browning was useless to us as soon as they were on to him.'

'Is there any way you can open up a socket for us?' Singh asked, stressing the "you".

Anna frowned a little. 'The redundant socket scan will only close sockets that are redundant, if Wayne's socket is active it won't be closed.'

'So how do we keep it active?' said Singh, the mock-friendliness sounding strained.

'Have Jason start the server's cascade program running, but set to send just a single packet every minute. The activity won't trigger the alarms and the socket will stay active. Jason can still signal the server to start the full-scale cascade whenever it is needed.' Anna beamed a big smile, looking really pleased with herself.

Julian Singh also smiled a little, the proud teacher whose star pupil just aced the exam. Marshall burst his bubble. 'Well get her to do it then.'

Singh prompted Anna to call Mason again and have him carry out her plan. It was a few minutes before Anna reported that the plan was working, that the hidden server in the GCHQ network was sending a single packet of information out through the network every minute and that the communications path, the socket, in the GCHQ outer network was remaining open and active. Marshall and Bullock sat back down, both looking pensive. Singh sat in a seat at the desk next to Anna. The three men considered how dependent their plan was on psychically controlled puppets and on those puppets manipulating secure and protected computer networks. Their plan was complicated and delicate, and audacious. But it had to be audacious, it wasn't every day anyone came along with a workable way to steal tens of billions of pounds straight out of the Bank of England.

THE ROUGH AND grassy ground was an island of dark in the night surrounded by areas of floodlight. Being this close to Heathrow airport was noisy, there were always aircraft in the air and on the taxi-ways, roaring in to land or taking off. The warehouses and hangers were surrounded by high fences, bathed in light, watched by numerous cameras and the occasional patrolling watchman.

The surveillance cameras would see everything in the areas covered by the floodlights, but would be blind to the unlit areas beyond the fences. Dulic lay flat in the grass. He was between the service road and fence, hidden in the dark. He watched, and waited. The plan was a simple one, as diversionary tactics went it was not challenging. His preference would be to throw a grenade or two, that would get people's attention. But he had his orders, and he felt a compulsion to follow them.

Ahead of him he could see where the service road curved to the left, passing under a pool of light, which also happened to be in view of a camera. It would be a mistake to creep through that area of illumination, a mistake he fully intended to make. Look up, he had to remember to look up at the right moment. He crawled forwards, almost to the edge of the light. He reached into his jacket pocket and pulled out the mobile phone and its battery. He flicked open the back of the device and clicked the battery into place. The screen lit up as the phone initialised, he waited until the device was ready. He selected the number from the list of contacts and dialled. When the call was answered, he gave the prearranged message and ended the call. He took the battery out and put it and the phone back in his pocket and zipped it up.

He looked behind him, he looked ahead of him. No vehicles. Rising into a crouching position he scurried forwards, keeping as low as he could, and hurried across the road towards the darkness beyond. As he was halfway across the road he looked up, just for a moment, looking straight at the surveillance camera. And then he was back into darkness. He waited again, making sure that no-one nearby had noticed him. His vehicle was half a mile away, it would take nearly an hour to reach it, keeping out of sight of all other cameras, but that would be easy.

THE HEAD WAS READING through a brief memo on her screen when a window popped up, alerting her to a development. It was a short walk back to the Command and Control room. It had been staffed continually, a non-stop analysis of all the surveillance and intercept intelligence they could acquire, looking for any clue as to the location of Singh, Bullock or Marshall, or any clue to their intentions.

As she entered one of the analysts, a woman perhaps in her thirties, caught her eye immediately 'Ma'am, we think we have something.' The analyst turned to one of the screens, on it was a frozen image, slightly blurred and grainy, typical of a medium resolution CCTV surveillance camera. The image showed a floodlit stretch of road, at the edge of the road, just in the light, was a crouching figure, dressed in dark clothing, caught in the act of glancing up at the camera.

'Who, where and when?' the Head asked. Sometimes, she'd found, the analysts could be a little shy and waited too long to be asked for basic information. She didn't have time to wait.

'Confirmed as Ilija Dulic, thirty minutes ago outside the

perimeter of the high-security warehouse at Heathrow,' said the analyst. Good summary.

The significance of the location was not lost on the Head. The high-security warehouse was where the gold bullion convoy had started. The gold had been flown in from its overseas seller and stored at the warehouse until it could be transferred to the Bank's vaults. It was also where the next delivery would be stored until it too could be transferred by road. Dulic's presence at the warehouse was an interesting development.

'We intercepted a call as well,' said the analyst. 'Confirmed to be made by Dulic from that location, the phone is the one Petric used in London. He said "Sanders was right, minimal extra security."'

The Head considered the information. She was aware that most in the room were making a very poor effort of not looking at her.

'Focus all efforts on mapping possible attacks on the next bullion convoy. Liaise with the Bank's security planners,' said the Head. 'Has Sanders checked in yet?'

The analysts exchanged glances. 'No, not yet,' said the analyst who'd briefed the Head.

'From now on if Sanders makes contact with anyone he's to be referred to me, no-one is to release any information to him or provide him with any support or assistance.' The Head looked at the faces around the room just long enough to know that the message had been received and understood. She left and returned to her office.

It hadn't escaped her thinking that it could be a diversion, a deliberate attempt by Marshall to implicate Sanders when in fact Sanders had no involvement with Marshall. Unfortunately, to an outsider, all the evidence pointed to Marshall and gang planning another attempt to hijack a bullion delivery and with a possibility that Sanders could not be trusted. She doubted

Sanders would be working with Marshall, but she had to admit that she found herself less and less willing to trust him. It would be regrettable if the kill squad which had been mobilised disposed of Sanders as well, but that would make a convenient end to the whole messy problem.

THIRTY THREE

Michael had used the bed & breakfast a few times in the past. He knew the owner would happily take cash, it was one small gesture in maintaining their anonymity. Situated on a residential road, it looked a little too familiar this time. The road bore a distinct resemblance to the road down which Michael had pursued Gerald Crossley, although here they were South of the river, in sight of Crystal Palace. Michael knew that there was no real point in trying to stay undercover; GCHQ, MI5 and the Head would know exactly where he and Eric were, the Audi was still plugged into the communications network.

Michael felt the need to stay out in the city tonight and not return home. He didn't feel home would be secure, he needed to feel more mobile. Curiously no-one had ordered Eric to return to base, not to return the car, so for the moment Michael still had one tangible resource left to work with. Perhaps the Head was trying to help him by not trying to hinder him. He never could tell with her.

Eric was inside finishing his dinner, the landlady cooked an excellent beef stew. Michael was sitting outside on one of the patio chairs. His laptop was open on the garden table in front of him, the glow of the screen shining brightly in the otherwise dark garden. Michael stared in frustration at the screen. Every attempt to access files relating to the convoy, Crossley, the ongoing surveillance, all were blocked. He had been locked out.

He had to make one last attempt to convince the Head that he had something tangible to offer. He rang her mobile phone, half expecting that she'd ignore his call. To his surprise, she answered.

'You're still not back,' she said.

'No, sorry, things to do,' he said.

'Like what?'

'Have they analysed the remains of the surveillance vehicle?' Michael asked. There were still several things about the attack he couldn't explain.

'Little left to analyse. The rocket launcher fired a high-intensity incendiary warhead, the vehicle was reduced to ashes.'

Michael thought that explained the intense heat he'd felt. He had wondered why there had been less of a blast wave than expected from the explosion.

'Why?' he asked. 'Why incinerate the vehicle?' Before she could answer, he voiced his theory. 'The only reason would be to obscure the fact that there was one body missing. If they hit the vehicle with armour-piercing shells there would have been enough bits of bodies to count, but this way there are no bodies, just ash.'

'So?'

'So no-one will notice that Anna Hendrickson is missing. All their targets have been IT and cyber-security specialists.'

'All have been connected with the bullion deliveries, and there is mounting evidence that they're planning to attack the next convoy.'

'A ruse, a hoax, a diversion. They are planning an attack, but not on the convoy, it's a distraction. They're aiming for a bigger prize, much bigger, I'm sure.'

'What are they planning, Michael?' she asked. It took Michael aback, she had almost never used his first name.

'Funnily enough, they haven't shared their detailed plans, and since you've locked me out I can't see what else you've found out.'

'I ordered you to return to The Office, you haven't, I don't want an unpredictable element in this operation.'

'I'm afraid you've already got three very unpredictable elements, so far you haven't predicted a single thing the Three are going to do, they've run rings around you from the beginning.' Michael realised his tone was sharper than he'd intended.

'And they've run rings around you,' she retorted. 'You're the ring they used to lead us by.' Touché. Michael couldn't argue with that. 'There's a trail of dead bodies across London, bombings, rocket attacks. We've just about kept a lid on it and prevented the whole story from coming out on the six o'clock news. But it has to end, it will end. The PsiClone project should have been terminated a long time ago, and now it will be. Your order still stands, Sanders. Return to The Office. And don't call them "the Three", it makes them sound like super-villains.'

'And what do you want me to call them? Marshall, Bullock and Singh? Sounds like a crap 60's folk trio.'

The line went dead. The message was clear. The Head had gone back to her original plan. Someone else's plan was also probably in operation: send in a kill squad to destroy the subjects from the PsiClone project, all of them, all four of them. Michael closed the lid of the laptop and sat in the near darkness. If the Head had sent the kill squad to find him that evening, then he would already be dead. Plans, half-plans, deceptions. Would the Head send the kill squad? Was there someone else who would do that? Was he seen as being valuable enough to be spared? His only hope was, and had always been, to find the Three before anyone else could.

What would have been most useful would be access to Anna Hendrickson and her skills at sifting through masses of surveillance data, plugging into all kinds of cameras and communications networks, putting together disparate clues and finding that one small needle in the middle of a city-sized haystack. But instead she had been kidnapped. Jason Mason had been "recruited" by Julian Singh's psychic control. Wayne Browning had been similarly recruited but then found to be surplus to requirements, and killed. Michael had learned a lot about their plans from his "meeting" with Jason Mason, but he had no doubt that they had not shared all their plans with Mason. Their plan was ambitious, but he had no concrete, physical evidence with which to convince the Head. He also had no way of stopping them, not yet. He did know that their plan would require intense psychic control, and for that Marshall and Singh and Bullock would need somewhere safe and quiet and secure, no doubt with Petric and friends standing guard. His primary objective had to be to find their location. No doubt the Head was working on that, but he suspected she and her team would not succeed.

Michael had only one thing left that he could rely on, apart from Eric and all the resources stashed away in the Audi. He had returned to MI5 promising to stop Marshall and the others, to be the one from the PsiClone project who could defeat the other three. The Three (perhaps that was what he would call them) had powers that set them far apart from "ordinary" criminals and terrorists. Perhaps Michael had to step up a gear, and use every psychic force he could summon.

The back door of the house opened and Eric stuck his head out.

'This apple sponge is brilliant,' he said. 'Better get in here if you want any.'

THE THREE SAT in their control room, most of the light coming from the computer monitors. Anna was asleep on a camp bed in one of the offices.

'Are you sure everything's ready?' Marshall asked, looking at Singh.

Singh gave him a withering look. 'You always ask that, and everything is always ready. Mason can set off the cascade, it will take down the Bank of England's firewall, that leaves us free to access their accounting system.'

'Best bit of online banking ever arranged,' said Bullock with a boyish grin.

'Have you got everything ready?' Singh asked, looking at Marshall with a "don't you question my abilities" kind of sneer.

'Our Serbian friends will keep guard, so I'm not worried about Michael trying to drop in. I've made arrangements that he won't get near the Bank's offices, and no-one in MI5 will talk to him,' said Marshall.

'Are they suitably distracted?' Bullock asked.

Singh looked around at the banks of monitors. 'Oh yes, they're quite convinced we want their gold, they're all over it like a rash.'

'They're not looking for the girl?'

'Only Sanders thinks she might be alive, he's not convinced anyone else, so no, they're not missing her.'

'Are you ready?' Marshall asked of Bullock, whose grin faded slightly.

'One of our Serbian friends will take care of Mason when

we're finished. The girl won't be a problem. Our exit strategy is all set to rock and roll,' said Bullock.

Marshall sat back in his chair, eyes narrowed slightly, his sign that he was thinking things through. 'No, I want you to deal with Mason,' he said.

'What?' said Bullock, the idea obviously coming as a surprise to him. 'That means being outside while we're trying to make this thing work.'

'Scared?' asked Singh, grinning again.

'Fuck off,' snapped Bullock. 'I don't like last-minute changes.'

'And I don't like leaving loose ends to the knuckle-heads next door,' said Marshall. 'Julian can get him out of the office and into a clear spot, you take him out with the rifle, from a distance.'

'This isn't planned,' said Bullock, 'I need to find a location, I need somewhere with a clear shot and a clear exit route.'

'Tomorrow, go first thing tomorrow, find somewhere,' said Marshall, 'don't worry, we won't leave without you.'

Bullock didn't answer, thinking through the options for himself. He had to admit that none of them liked the idea of leaving important jobs to any of the Serbian mercenaries. He equally didn't like last-minute changes to plans. Plans were what kept them safe, everything worked out in advance, all the risks identified and managed. Mason, though, would be too big a risk to have around, killing him had never been in doubt.

Bullock looked at Singh. 'Get me maps of the area, any live CCTV you can. I'll find somewhere tonight and go and scope it first thing tomorrow.' He paused. 'I've a mind to kill Sanders while I'm at it.'

'No,' said Marshall, sharply. 'We'll get to him soon enough.'

There was a moment of quiet as they looked at each other. Plans had been made, arrangements made, action taken. And now they were ready.

'We're set,' said Marshall, leaning back with his legs

outstretched and his hands clasped behind his head. 'Gentlemen, by this time tomorrow we'll be one hundred and fifty billion pounds richer.'

'Just a thought,' said Bullock, 'but what's that going to do to the British economy?'

Marshall let out a bark of a laugh. He thought for a moment, but Singh interjected.

'I expect news of their loss will leak out,' Singh smiled as he said it, 'and the Governor of the Bank of England will resign by the end of the day. They'll try to keep their loss a secret, but I'm sure the news will come out. By then the Chancellor of the Exchequer will be on his way out, and the Prime Minister and the rest of the Government won't be far behind. By then the country will be bankrupt.'

'And no worries about MI5 coming after us, they'll all be out of a job,' said Marshall.

THIRTY FOUR

FRIDAY MORNING

Michael sat at the dining room table in the bed & breakfast. It was like being in another, older world. The decor, the furnishing, was all "old fashioned", maybe from some collision of 1950s and 1960's styles. He liked it, the whole place was wonderfully devoid of technology. The kettle was boiled on the Aga in the kitchen, he could imagine the fireplace in winter would be filled with burning logs. The place had basic modern conveniences, like electricity, but no Wi-Fi or cable TV.

He stared at his mug of tea, perhaps hoping it would volunteer some ideas, or even inspiration. But the tea stayed silent. His thoughts were interrupted by Eric coming into the room, carrying a fresh mug of coffee. Eric sat at the table.

'It seems to me,' Eric began, 'that this whole operation is what we would refer to technically as "a complete fuck-up."'

Michael wasn't sure he was in the mood for sarcasm, or levity, but he couldn't disagree either.

'Yes, it's not exactly gone to plan,' he said.

'Oh it has,' said Eric, with an almost jovial tone, 'just not your plan.'

Michael could have sworn, but the landlady was within earshot and she was a lady of a certain age, it wouldn't be proper to swear in front of a lady. Michael mouthed "fuck off" to Eric.

'I'm rather hoping you're going to astound me with the cunning and brilliance of your plan,' Eric continued. Michael was never sure if he actually liked Eric. Certainly the man was a very capable field agent, and they'd worked together a number of times. Michael had no problem trusting Eric, or relying on him, he just wasn't a hundred per cent sure he liked him. Maybe he liked him a bit.

'I'm working on it,' was all Michael could manage.

'Couldn't work a bit quicker, could you? It's just I think the Head's not your biggest fan at the minute.'

'I'm well aware of the Head's view of me, but it's not the Head I'm worried about.'

'Maybe you should be, I can't think of anyone who fell out of her favour who's still around, anywhere,' said Eric.

'It's Marshall and his gang who worry me,' said Michael.

Eric leaned forward and looked at Michael. 'I know there's more to you and them and that it's probably secret and that the Head's probably privy to some of it or even more of it than you know, but somehow you need to get a leap ahead of all of them, before we all end up like Gerald Crossley.'

Michael sat back. Eric's words had prompted a thought, that annoying kind of thought that stayed just out of conscious awareness, but he knew it would come into view sooner or later, if he just let it.

'Crossley?' Michael mused. He sat back in his chair. What was it about Crossley?

Eric continued his own musing. 'I never understood why they shot Crossley the way they did. Why a long-range shot? Apparently no silencer. That's almost an execution, but he hadn't committed a crime.'

'No,' said Michael, 'they wanted to get a message to us, a message they knew we'd find irresistible and would have to follow up. The only way to make it dramatic enough to get our attention was to kill Crossley in the most dramatic way.'

'So one of them went to a great deal of trouble and effort to put that bullet in Crossley,' said Eric.

The thought came into Michael's consciousness, stepping out into the full glare of his awareness, a brilliant idea fully formed.

'Ahhhh,' Michael said slowly, as he realised the significance of what Eric had said. Eric just looked a touch confused.

Michael pulled out his phone and selected the number, the call was answered quickly.

'This is Mister Smith from Thames House, case number nine eight five one,' Michael said, his standard identification. The person receiving the call obviously said little, accepting Michael's identification.

Michael continued. 'I'm following up the Crossley killing, I need to see the bullet that was retrieved.' He listened to the reply, then went on. 'No, not images, I need to examine the bullet, physically. Where is it?'

There was obviously some resistance from the other person. Michael listened patiently. 'Commander Halbern,' Michael said, sounding less reasonable and more assertive. 'I appreciate the need to maintain the chain of evidence, but I need to stop more killings and so I need to examine that bullet. No, I'm not going to explain why. We need to end what's going on, and we need to end it very quickly.'

There was a pause, an answer from Halbern, and Michael ended the call.

He looked at Eric and grinned. 'We're off to New Scotland Yard, the game is afoot.'

Eric just looked nonplussed. 'Who are you now? Sherlock Holmes.'

'Just finish your coffee Watson and get the car ready.'

ERIC HAD GOT Michael to New Scotland Yard remarkably quickly, considering how dense the morning rush hour traffic had been. Eric had stayed with the car and Michael had been met in the foyer as arranged. An officer had signed Michael in as a visitor and escorted him downstairs to the basement and one of the dozen evidence rooms. Michael hadn't been surprised to be met by another officer, the two of them making it very clear that they would be with Michael the whole time and would observe everything he did. They explained, as if it had been necessary, that the bullet was evidence and the record of who had access to the evidence had to be maintained so that no defence lawyer could argue the case of tampering or contamination.

One of the officers retrieved the bullet from a box on a shelf. The bullet was in a clear plastic bag, a printed label stuck to the side detailing the case reference and the evidence item reference. Michael held it up and looked at it. The bullet misshapen, deformed no doubt by the initial impact with Gerald Crossley's skull. Michael pulled open the bag and immediately the two officers both took a sharp intake of breath and a half step forwards, no doubt in protest and about to explain that they had never agreed he could actually handle the item. Michael gave them the most severe stare he could. He really didn't want to have to try to exert any kind of psychic control over two people simultaneously, sometimes simple authority and bravado could work. It did. The two retreated half a step and allowed Michel to take the bullet out of the bag. The two officers both stared at the bullet, they'd obviously been given instructions that the bullet was not to leave their sight and they were going to take that order very literally. But Michael didn't need to do anything except hold it.

Mindful that the two officers were watching, but blissfully unaware of what they were watching, Michael let his mind settle on the bullet. This was a long shot, and Eric had made him aware of the pun, but he was hoping that when Bullock had made ready to kill Crossley, Bullock had held this bullet with his bare hands and loaded the rifle with focus and intention, and that he had therefore left a psychic imprint on the bullet. Michael had no idea if the imprint would have been affected by the heat and violence of the bullet being fired, but he had to try.

He let his mind open, settle on the bullet, and slowly he let in the impression given to him by the small piece of lead. He felt a wave of heat, he had the impression of a smell, an aftershave, he'd smelled it at Crossley's house, the bullet had picked up an impression from Crossley, even in the brief moment before Crossley's life force had left him. Then the smell was gone and he saw the sports field where Crossley had died, but from the other side, from Bullock's perspective. He saw the back of Crossley's head, as though through the scope of the rifle. He relaxed and let his mind connect to the images, to connect to Bullock, connect to Bullock where ever he was here and now, connect through the imprint left on the bullet. An image flashed into his mind and was gone almost as quickly, but it was an image of a large and well-lit space, and in the space were Marshall and Singh. He had another image, just as quick, but being inside a vehicle, a car of some sort, someone else driving. He recognised in that moment the face of Petric as the driver. He avoided the temptation of focusing on the image, he let it go, waiting for more, and soon enough more images came.

He had a flash of a street, a London street, but no landmarks.

He had the curious sensation of movement, even though he was standing still, he knew Bullock was moving. Michael had a sudden moment of disappointment, if Bullock was moving he wasn't with the others, he wasn't in whatever place they had made their base of operations. He let the feeling go. An image flickered in his mind, a park, somewhere similar to where Crossley had been killed, tennis courts and grass and trees, but somewhere different. The image was gone. Then another image, the entrance to a London underground station, he could see the logo, a word. The image was gone but the word remained: Saint.

He opened his eyes and looked at the two police officers, who were staring at him wide-eyed. He had no idea what he'd done or said while he been focused on the bullet, and he cared even less.

'London Underground station, Saint something?' he asked, hoping that one of the police officers would figure it out. They looked blankly at him.

'Saint Pancras,' said one of them.

Catching on the other said, 'Saint Paul's.'

Neither fitted the image in Michael's mind. 'Near a park, maybe tennis courts,' he tried.

Both frowned. One said, 'there's All Saints, but it's on the DLR, not the Underground.'

'Yeah,' said the other, 'but it's still got the Underground logo outside.'

Michael slipped the bullet back in the plastic wallet and tossed it back to one of the officers.

'I'm done,' he said emphatically, 'and there's somewhere I need to be.'

Bullock was out and about and on his way, and Michael knew where.

THIRTY FIVE

Eric was driving as fast as he could through the London traffic. Even with the lights and sirens it took nearly forty minutes to drive from New Scotland Yard to the Poplar area of London. Michael kept going over his reasoning, making sure he was drawing a real conclusion and not just leaping to one. All Saints was the station he had seen, Poplar Recreation Park was the area of grass and trees he'd seen. It was similar to the location where Crossley had been killed. It was a perfect spot to kill someone, especially if you could telepathically order them to walk into the park and stand conveniently still while you shot them from a safe distance with a sniper rifle. And who would it be convenient to kill in that way? Jason Mason. Because All Saints station was a stone's throw from Canary Wharf. If Bullock or either of the others wanted to kill Mason—and they surely would once they'd finished with him— they couldn't do it in or around Canary Wharf, the place was crammed with surveillance cameras. Why not instead have him take a short train ride, a short walk, and stand in a park?

Michael knew he faced a real problem. The area around Poplar Recreation Park was a big place, and Bullock could be almost anywhere in the area. He might have been on his way to the area, or from the area, or hidden somewhere. Michael didn't have enough information to drive right up to Bullock and have a conversation. What he needed was access to some heavy-duty surveillance of the area. But the Head was not answering his call, nor was anyone else he tried to call, nor could he get the laptop to connect to the MI5 network.

As a last resort, he tried Halbern. It was another long shot, and he couldn't give Halbern any reason to try to contact the Head and have steps taken to locate Bullock, nor could he say why he thought Poplar was an area to look at, nor could he say why any of this could be related to his earlier request to examine the bullet. He wouldn't have been surprised if Halbern had also put the phone down on him. But he didn't. He managed to get an 'I'll see what I can do' out of Halbern. That had been ten minutes ago. With every minute that passed the chances increased that Bullock would leave Canary Wharf, or would kill Mason, or would slip out of sight of surveillance. There was also the chance that Bullock could have sensed Michael's connection and changed his plans. This shot seemed to be getting longer and longer.

Eric had parked the car in a side road, close enough to the Poplar area but hopefully not too close to become visible to Bullock by mistake. Michael's phone rang, it was Halbern.

'Seems you don't have too many friends at the moment, Mr Smith,' said Halbern. 'And no-one's too keen to follow any leads that don't centre around Heathrow airport.'

'But do you have anything?' Michael asked, perhaps a little more sharply than he intended.

'One possible sighting, a traffic camera at the intersection of the A13 and the A102 caught an image, two occupants in the vehicle which might be the two you mentioned.'

'That's great, as they say, every little helps.' Michael put the phone away.

He consulted the maps on the laptop.

The location made sense. Bullock would follow Mason from the station, East along the East India Dock Road to the park, staying far enough behind that he wouldn't look suspicious, but close enough to maintain a strong psychic control. He could then carry on walking, double back and set up in a secluded part of the park. Even if anyone was watching they would never associate Bullock and Mason and Bullock was skilled enough to slip out of sight and set up for the shot.

Michael had Eric pull over at a bus stop on the A13, a few hundred yards before the All Saints station. The car had barely stopped as Michael got out and Eric set off again. Hopefully, even if Bullock was in the area, the Audi would be inconspicuous in the dense traffic. If Bullock was anywhere close then it had to mean that their plan was either in action or about to be, time was now getting short. Michael walked slowly towards the station. He hoped he was in time, that Bullock was still in the area and that Mason was still in the Bank of England's offices in Canary Wharf. Michael could get no sense of Bullock, not without direct contact with the bullet, obviously Bullock had completely disconnected the psychic link.

In theory there were only a few places Bullock could be. He would have to be able to watch the train station, have his rifle with him, probably in a guitar case or similar, and be somewhere that people would be expected to stand or sit and wait and so not attract attention.

At that instant Michael stopped, frozen to the spot. On the other side of the road, in the parade of shops, was a cafe, and sitting in the window sipping a cup of coffee (it had always been coffee) was Evan Bullock. He was staring in the direction of the train station and not looking at any of the passing pedestrians.

Michael crossed the road to be on the same side as the cafe, putting him out of Bullock's line of sight. Michael considered walking in through the front door, but quickly dismissed the idea. Bullock would see him coming and try to escape, or fight. He needed a way of getting close without being seen.

The cafe was the last in the series of old shop fronts, the next series of units along were modern retail premises and the first occupant was a betting shop, no use trying to get in there. The shop next to the cafe was a newsagent's, which looked like the owner had been there as long as the buildings. Michael walked in, ignoring the commuter standing browsing the newspapers.

The shopkeeper was indeed an old man, Far Eastern in descent, wispy hair and a bemused look. Michael pulled out his MI5 identification and waved it in the man's face.

'Back door?' Michael said in a stern voice. The old man looked over his shoulder to the back of the shop. Michael would have proceeded whatever the man's answer, the back door had to be in the back. Michael marched past the man, past the counter display of confectionary and the shelves of everything from alcohol to hairspray. He walked through the back room of the shop hardly noticing it. The back door was unlocked and Michael exited the shop and into the back yard.

A high wall separated the rear yard of each shop unit, but not so high that Michael couldn't jump and get his hands on top and heave himself up on to the top of the wall. He only then thought that often landlords put lines of broken glass on the tops of walls to deter burglars. He hoped his luck would continue to hold. He dropped down into the back yard of the cafe.

The back door of the cafe was open and Michael walked in, holding his ID badge out in front of him. The back room of the cafe was the kitchen and food preparation area, and a young woman was putting the finishing touches to a bacon sandwich.

She turned to see Michael, who put his finger to his lips, waved the ID badge and urged her to be quiet. He slid out into the serving area of the cafe, again bidding the two staff to be quiet and hoping that unless someone shouted, Bullock would remain focused on the world outside. Bullock was seated with his back to Michael, staring out of the window. There was no guitar case in sight, nothing large. Perhaps he was planning to kill Mason from close up? Perhaps a pistol, or a knife, or barehanded.

The two staff look bemused, but said nothing. As he stepped towards the opening out into the dining area Bullock promptly got up and headed for the door. Michael didn't move, and watched as Bullock kept his gaze on the world outside, and walked out of the door.

Now what? Stay? Follow? Bullock must have been just getting the lie of the land, and after leaving he'd turned right, towards the park. He was going to wait for Mason in the park. Mason would walk straight up to the man who was ready to kill him. Michael moved slowly between the tables and chairs. Some of the occupants gave him a quizzical look, most ignored him, not lifting their eyes from their mobile phones or tablets or morning papers. Michael reached the door and stepped outside. He looked to his right, and saw Bullock walking up the road, indistinguishable from any other pedestrian. Michael followed, matching his pace, staying far enough behind to avoid being obvious, he hoped.

A few hundred yards further up was a pedestrian crossing. Michael realised that Bullock would stop and use the crossing to get across the road. The A13 was a big and busy road, no point risking trying to cross through the traffic. But if Bullock waited, Michael would catch him up. If Michael stopped he would become obvious. Ahead of Michael, between him and Bullock was a group of men, they looked like construction workers. Orange overalls, hard hats, steel toe-capped boots. Newspapers underarm, cigarettes in fingers, they laughed and joked as they walked. Two of the group were big men, and Michael kept the group on his left and the shop-fronts on his right. His only chance was to keep on the other side of the group as they passed the waiting Bullock.

Sure enough, Bullock was waiting at the pedestrian crossing, and Michael kept his eyes down and his hands in his pockets as his guardian builders and he walked past Bullock. The group and Michael crossed the next side road and Michael was now ahead of Bullock. He couldn't look back, he'd have to keep walking until he reckoned Bullock would be in the park, and then cross the road and double back.

Out of the corner of his eye he could see he'd passed the park on the other side of the road, surely time enough for Bullock to have entered the park and now be out of sight. Keeping his head down as much as he could without looking obvious Michael waited for a break in the traffic so he could cross the road. Another pedestrian stopped beside him, and they crossed the main road at the same time. A stroke of luck, he would look less obvious. Michael reached the other side of the road not far beyond the entrance to the park.

The park was bounded on this side by a black metal railing on top of a low stone wall. Further ahead was the entrance to the park, an open pedestrian gateway between two white-painted gate posts. This would mean everyone going into the park was visible to anyone in the park watching the entrance, funnelled in through the one, narrow entrance. Bullock would need somewhere in the park that was secluded, but easy to reach. He'd need Mason to be able to get there quickly but then kill him with the minimum of risk of being seen. He would then also need to escape. Michael, unfortunately, was not familiar with the park. Between himself and the entrance was a side road, Hale Street. Michael looked down the street. The park was bounded on that side by a similar wall and railings, and no obvious access in sight. He would just have to hope that Bullock was somewhere inside the park finding a safe place, and not keeping an eye on the entrance. It was a risk, a big risk, but now was not the time to be overly cautious.

He walked down the main road, and through the gates into the park.

The green expanse of the park spread out before him, and without making it too obvious he looked around, and saw no sign of Bullock.

The park was lined with trees, and ahead was an ornamental fountain, and beyond that a small wooded area. There were few people in the park, too few to provide any effective cover. Michael pressed his finger into his ear and activated his earpiece.

'What's in this park?' he asked. He hoped Eric, sitting in the parked Audi somewhere close, would be able to access basic information from the laptop.

Eric took a few moments. 'Trees, ahead of you are tennis courts, beyond them the bowling green. Looks like sheds and stuff for the park keeper, two o'clock from the entrance.'

That felt like the right place for Bullock to meet Mason, beyond the trees, in the sheds, out of sight, except for the enormous towers of Canary Wharf, the larger tower of Canada Place and the not quite so enormous tower of the HSBC building towering (literally) over them. The park was surrounded by buildings, two and three stories, but only from the towers would someone have the elevation to see into the more secluded areas. But who in the towers would be looking, and even if they were what could they do? Michael set off towards the trees ahead of him. The footpath divided, the path ahead went into the wooded area (if you could call a few trees in the middle of London a "wood"), the tennis courts to the left, and the right fork in the path led to the wall and the "keep out" signs that heralded the domain of the park keeper.

'Stand still, keep your hands by your side and where I can see them,' said a voice from behind, unmistakably Bullock.

Michael cursed to himself. He'd been too focused on finding Bullock that he'd made the basic mistake of allowing Bullock to find him.

'Nice to see you again Evan,' said Michael, feigning a friendly tone.

'Piss off,' said Bullock, he'd always been full of charm. 'We keep trying to kill you, why don't you just do us all a favour and actually die?'

'Ah, sorry, not in my plans at the moment.'

'Well it's in mine, now walk forward,' ordered Bullock.

Michael began to walk. 'It's a clever plan you've got,' he said, 'pity it won't work.'

'Not interested,' said Bullock, sounding like he had no interest in any kind of conversation.

Michael walked as slowly as he dared, any slower and no doubt Bullock would order him to speed up. He needed time to think, to plan. If they got into the secluded area of the tool sheds things could get very ugly, he needed to change this situation quickly. His biggest problem was Bullock, a trained and experienced soldier who wasn't about to let Michael get within reach of a weapon or of anything that might provide cover.

His salvation came in a most unexpected form. From around a bend in the path a hundred yards ahead appeared two police officers, one male, one female. Michael guessed they were PCSOs, Police Community Support Officers, no doubt patrolling the park on the lookout for dog walkers not clearing up after their pets. He'd often thought that there's never a policeman around when you need one, and here come two at once. Yellow Hi-Viz vests, radio and mobile phone clipped to the jackets, all very pseudo-military, apart from the obvious age and swagger and being totally engrossed in their conversation. Michael guessed that Bullock would have to keep his gun inside his jacked, very usable but out of sight.

'Take the path to the right,' said Bullock, quietly enough not to be heard by the approaching officers.

'No, don't think I will,' said Michael, making an adjustment in direction so he was obviously headed straight for the police.

'Do as you're fucking told,' hissed Bullock.

'Piss off,' said Michael, 'if you're going to shoot me let's have a real firefight, right here.' He was gambling that Bullock hadn't planned on shooting police officers dead in broad daylight. There was no doubt he could do it, he had the skills and he certainly had the character, but it would be a huge risk. Shots would bring bystanders, the word would get out, and the police could seal off the whole area very quickly. Michael had at least succeeded in getting Bullock outside the parameters of his plan. The next move was what most people would call do-or-die.

As soon as he judged the police were close enough, Michael pulled out his own gun in a swift action pointing it straight at the police officers, shouting 'Don't Move!'. In a single action he stepped forward and to the side of them, turning, putting the officers almost between him and Bullock who, as planned, had been surprised by the move and had hesitated bringing his own weapon back out into view.

The police, to their credit, tried to remember their training and started trying to tell Michael to calm down and to take it easy. Michael had to bite his tongue and refrain from correcting the officer and telling him it should be "take it easily", now was not the time for a grammar lesson. He shouted at them to kneel and as they got to their knees he took another step and now they were fully between him and Bullock. Bullock was now caught in more than just a moment's indecision. With his hand still pushed inside his jacket he fumbled around, holstering his own weapon, and then brought out his hand.

'I don't know who you are,' said Bullock, feigning fear and surprise, 'just let me go.'

The police started agreeing saying he should let the other man go.

'Sorry, time to go,' said Michael, then apparently speaking to no-one in particular, 'I need the car, now.' He knew that at any moment Eric would be appearing, and as he had hoped, within moments there was a roar of a powerful engine, but the tone wasn't quite right. Michael looked between the trees at the fence bordering Hale Street. A big black SUV pulled up sharply, Bullock had somehow managed to summon his own support vehicle.

'Sorry, Michael, be seeing you later,' said Bullock starting to back away, fully confident that Michael wasn't about to start shooting people in broad daylight either. Bullock stuck his middle finger up at Michael and turned and ran. In a deft motion he vaulted the fence, boarded the vehicle, and was gone.

Michael shoved his pistol back in its holster inside his jacket. The police kneeling before him, facing away from him, were still trying to maintain the facade of control, probably trying to maintain self-control more than anything. He placed a hand on the back of the neck of each office. Now was not the time to be timid. He unleashed torrent of psychic energy into each of them. He felt them both shudder under the mental onslaught.

Amnesia was actually very difficult to achieve, memories couldn't be erased, not even telepathically, so all he could do was mess up their memories of the events. He poured into them visualisations of the confrontation, showing them Marshall in his own place, a clown in place of Bullock, he imagined (and had them imagine) that the firearms had been children's water pistols. He streamed the images through his hands and into their minds as fast and as powerfully as he could. And then he released them.

They both pitched forwards and collapsed, panting. He knew they'd have lots of problems to deal with from now on, he wasn't sure they'd ever recover from the experience, but he compartmentalised his guilt, he'd have to deal with that later. For the moment he had a bigger problem, Bullock was gone, leaving only a slim hope that one clue remained.

The grey Audi roared down the street and stopped in almost the exact same spot as the black SUV. Michael dashed to the fence, remembering where Bullock had grabbed it as he'd leapt over. Michael was hoping that as he'd made contact with the fence Bullock had a strong idea in mind to get back to wherever the others were based. With Eric watching with a quizzical look Michael took hold of the metal railing. He allowed himself to relax a moment, and opened his mind to the images and impressions that flashed through.

After a few moments he let go, climbed over the fence and got into the car.

'At some point you're going to have to tell me what's going on,' said Eric.

'I will, but first there's a building we need to find.'

THIRTY SIX

Finding a quiet side road was not easy, not as easy as Michael thought it should have been, not in the centre of London. He'd wanted to get far enough away from Poplar and Canary Wharf that neither Bullock nor the police were likely to happen upon them. Equally, he didn't want to head out towards Heathrow because that's where the police and MI5 were focusing their forces, nor did he want to be any closer to the city centre because that would be too close to Thames House. Eric had found a suitable place to stop, and now had the laptop balanced on his knees.

Michael, sitting in the passenger seat, closed his eyes.

'Okay,' he said, 'we need to find a building, I know it's some kind of big warehouse, on an estate of big warehouses.'

'Any clue as to where? London's a big place,' said Eric, always with the hint of sarcasm.

'I would have thought close to the centre, maybe somewhere close to Canary Wharf' said Michael. If their attack was on the Bank of England, then surely they would need to be close.

'Possibly,' said Eric, 'there are a few places, but I'd still need more.'

Michael let the images come back into his mind, images he'd sensed when he connected with the fence that Bullock had gripped. He saw the building, a dark grey block of a building, no windows, a high double fence surrounding it, a single road access, blocked by enormous yellow attack resistant barriers which rose up out of the road. This was a building with some serious security measures.

'Military, is there anywhere military?' asked Michael. 'Anywhere with military-level physical security? Fences? Barriers? Access control?'

Eric tapped a few keys, and Michael couldn't help thinking that Anna would have been faster, and more productive. Whatever Marshall was doing right now, no doubt he was quickly running out of uses for Anna.

'No, nowhere military,' said Eric.

An image flickered into Michael's mind, yellow arrows on a black background.

'Logo,' he said.

'Same to you,' quipped Eric. The humour was lost on Michael.

'No, someone's logo, yellow arrows on a black background.'

'Hermes Transport,' said Eric, without needing to consult the computer.

'Look for a warehouse owned by Hermes,' Michael said. Eric tapped and the laptop screen was filled with a map.

'They've got a place, a big warehouse, just off Stafford Road, Croydon.'

'Croydon?' mused Michael. Too far out of town, surely. Eric was tapping at the keys again.

'And look here,' said Eric, sounding a little triumphant. 'Just down the road, is a data centre, owned by Maxis Insurance, owned but not occupied.'

'Why not?' asked Michael.

More key tapping. 'Maxis Insurance had a profits warning, investment cut back, IT Director taken ill, data centre move postponed.'

With a few more keystrokes Eric had a photograph of the building on the screen and showed it to Michael. He stared at the building, just like he'd seen it.

Michael could feel pieces of a mental jigsaw falling into place. Croydon was geographically further from the City than he had been thinking, but an insurance company data centre would be plugged directly into the same network infrastructure as the rest of the Financial District. A data centre would be a large and secure building, no visitors. And how coincidental that the IT Director had suddenly been taken ill and the company's move into the centre had been delayed. It all fitted very neatly, the building would make an ideal base of operations for Marshall, Bullock and Singh. In fact, Croydon was South (in fact slightly South West) from Canary Wharf where the Bank of England was. It would be about an hour's drive, Bullock was probably halfway there by now.

'Drive,' said Michael. Eric had already sync'd the car's sat' nav' with the laptop. He snapped the lid of the laptop shut and tossed it onto the back seat. The flashing blue lights and the siren brought some curious looks from a few pedestrians, but it also helped them scythe a way through the traffic.

'You certain this is the place?' said Eric.

'Oh yes,' Michael replied. 'But if I'm wrong then Maxis Insurance is going to be very pissed off with what I'm planning to do to their data centre, and Marshall and the others will get away with it.'

'I don't know what all this stuff is with you and them, but if that analyst is still alive, it sounds like you're the only hope she's got.'

That fact had not been lost on Michael. It would be more

than just Anna. Even though he'd foiled this first attempt to kill Mason he didn't imagine that after they'd finished they would let him go. If Marshall and the others succeeded then Mason would be in desperate danger.

'At some point I might explain things,' said Michael, 'but for now I need somewhere close where I can suit up.'

'I'll find somewhere,' said Eric. Michael had no doubt that he would. 'If you start world war three down there, someone's going to call the police.'

'I'm counting on it,' said Michael, 'and I'll need you to get through to Commander Halbern and make him listen.'

'And say what?' asked Eric.

'You'll know,' said Michael.

As they tore down the A214, not far from the bed and breakfast they'd used the previous night, Michael retrieved the laptop from the back seat. Eric was still logged in to the laptop, and more importantly, still logged into the MI5 network. Michael didn't need access to highly classified files, but he did need any kind of floor plans or architectural diagrams of the data centre. Modern data centres were built to withstand terrorist attacks, they were difficult places to get into even with the correct access and permissions. An assault would be difficult. What he needed was a way in which avoided the security cameras, places like that always had security cameras, lots of them.

The financial services industry was vital to the economy and also reliant on its IT infrastructure, which meant the security of the infrastructure was of interest to MI5, so Michael soon had access to the plans for the building. As he'd suspected the building was secure against someone trying to drive a truck up to the front door and blowing it up, or even crashing a plane on it. The building could withstand a direct assault by a small army. But there was one weakness. The rear of the plot faced on to some undeveloped ground, accessible from further down the road. Inside the compound was the armour-plated fuel tanks and the emergency generators. The fence on the far side of the tanks was an area not covered by the CCTV cameras, which mainly focused on covering the access points into the building. Michael had a way into the compound, but once he attempted to break into the building itself he would be visible.

By the time they reached the outskirts of Croydon, Michael had a plan. Eric had found a disused shop unit with a secluded area to the rear, where they could prepare. It was only a few minutes' drive from there to the edge of the disused land from which Michael could approach the data centre. Michael looked at his watch. If Marshall hadn't started his plan by now, he soon would. It was now or never.

THIRTY SEVEN

FRIDAY - NOON

Marshall paced around the control room inside the data centre, Bullock slouched in one of the chairs. Anna sat at one of the workstations and Singh sat in another of the swivel chairs, to the side and slightly behind her. His eyes were half-closed.

'They're starting to get ready,' said Singh. 'Mason's in the room, the other IT managers are there. They're waiting for the Heads of Finance and Risk and some others.'

'Good,' said Marshall, 'how long before they start?'

Singh paused a moment. 'Hard to tell, the business people are taking their time.'

'And what do you propose to do about Mason when we've finished?' Marshall said, directing his stare at Bullock.

'We'll bring him here, well not here but closer to here, deal with him closer to home. We'll be long gone by the time anyone finds what's left.'

Marshall huffed, he didn't like the plan but then there wasn't much about this plan he did like. In fact, the size of the outcome was about the only thing he did like.

'I think it's time we had our Mister Mason start the proceedings,' said Singh. He closed his eyes for a moment.

After a minute or two, Anna tapped a few keys on her keyboard.

'The server in GCHQ has received Mister Mason's signal, it's started the cascade.' She tapped some more keys. 'So far the Bank's firewall is managing the attack.'

Singh leaned forward and looked at one of the monitors. 'It seems Mister Mason has been very good, the attack hasn't set off the alarms.'

'So, why do we need all this attack from GCHQ?' asked Bullock in a mock-bored voice, 'why not just get Mason to transfer the money to us?'

Singh looked at him. 'Because not even Mason can simply transfer one hundred and fifty billion pounds out of the Bank of England's finance systems, the security traps in the firewalls would stop him. But the data from GCHQ is seen as coming from a friendly source so it's let through, but there's so much that it finally cripples the firewalls, and then we have a clear channel through which he can send us the money.'

'Why can't Mason just switch it off?' asked Bullock.

'Because someone would notice,' said Singh, 'if the cascade attack causes the firewall to fail then the firewall will spend several minutes restarting itself.'

'Why don't you go and do something useful?' said Marshall.

'Like what?' snapped Bullock.

'Well thanks to you Michael-bloody-Sanders is still wandering around and I wouldn't put it past him to come and knock on the door. If you don't mind I'd rather he didn't.'

Bullock got up and marched out of the room in a manner more akin to a bad-tempered teenager than a soldier. Marshall half expected him to slam the door behind him, but he didn't.

Marshall reached for the gun in his shoulder holster, again, just to reassure himself.

'Do we still need her?' he asked, nodding his head at Anna.

'The firewall is holding, she may be able to help add to its problems,' said Singh. 'I'd rather we keep her a little longer.'

Marshall carried on pacing.

'Anna,' said Singh, back to trying to sound friendly, 'is there anything Jason can do to increase the stress on the firewall servers, without setting off the alarms.'

'Yes,' she said, 'he could switch on detailed network logging on the servers, they'll try to write a log-record of every hit. It's a normal process for the servers but it adds to the disk traffic.'

Singh closed his eyes and sent his psychic instructions to Mason.

'Everyone's in the room with Mason, they should be starting soon,' said Singh.

Marshall grinned, they were getting close, very close.

MICHAEL GOT BACK in the car, sitting in the passenger seat. He looked every bit the theatrical version of the SAS counter-terrorist soldier; black coveralls, grenades clipped to the black webbing he wore, sidearm, submachine gun, black balaclava in hand. The only thing he was missing was the black gas mask, but you can't have everything.

'Do you want to stop for a burger first?' asked Eric, 'there's a drive-thru just around the corner.'

'After this, you and I are going to have words,' said Michael.

Eric drove quickly to the point in the road where they were level with the end of the disused stretch of land. It was bounded by a cross-wire fence. Michael, now wearing the balaclava, opened the door and stepped out, keeping in a crouched position he used wire cutters to cut away a section of fence. There was a reasonable amount of traffic and Eric could see the looks from drivers, trying to see what Michael was doing. Soon enough Michael had finished, he slipped through the fence and shuffled along the outside wall of the first warehouse. Eric reached across and pulled the car door closed and set off.

Michael kept crouched, but it was broad daylight and he had no doubt that he had been seen by several people. Sooner or later someone would call the police to report his suspicious behaviour, he just hoped he had time before that to start some suspicious gunfire and suspicious grenade throwing. He quickly reached the fencing separating him from the emergency generator compound of the data centre. The wire cutters made short work of the fence and he slipped through. The compound was a secured area. The generators were in a secure building of their own, the fuel tanks in another building, another fence and fortified gate now separated him from the car parking area which surrounded the outside of the data centre. Whilst the gate was fortified and locked, the bolt which slipped from the lock into the recess was just visible.

He reached into a pocket and pulled out a roll of black dental-floss like wire. He stepped forward and slipped one end of the wire into the space above the bolt. With a bit of work he wounded three lengths of the wire around the bolt and pulled it tight.

He heard voices and stepped back, pressing himself into the space between the building and the fence. The voices were speaking in an Eastern European language, he recognised at least one of the voices. Petric and one of the other Serbians were obviously patrolling around the outside of the building. He leaned forward as far as he dared to peek round the edge of the building. He saw the two men walk down the side of the main building, turn the corner and along the next side, walking away from him. It took a couple of minutes for them to reach the far side of the building and turn the corner and disappear out of sight. Michael estimated it gave him no more than four minutes before they'd be back, providing they didn't at any point turn round and walk back the same way. He looked across the car park. Just as the schematics had shown, facing him, almost at the corner of the building was a door. Solid, grey, with a reader for security access cards. No convenient locks to pick.

He pushed his finger in his ear to activate the earpiece. 'Go,' he said.

Michael pulled his goggles out of another pocket and slipped them on. He stepped up to the gate, twisted the black tag on the end of the black wire and stepped back. There was intense light and hissing and smoke as the chemical impregnated wire ignited and burned at a high enough temperature to cut through the bolt. Molten metal dripped to the ground. As soon as the light dimmed Michael shoved the gate with his shoulder and the still soft remains of the bolt gave way, the gate swung open and Michael stepped through into the car park and jogged quickly to the end of the building furthest from the road.

He pulled back his sleeve at looked at his watch, any moment now.

He couldn't hear the sound of the car, the road being on the far side of the building from him, but he heard the enormous bang of the grenade that Eric had thrown into the pedestrian turnstile. He heard the crack-crack-crack of small arms fire from the two Serbians, no doubt shooting at the disappearing rear aspect of the Audi. Michael marched back around the corner to the door, lifted his sub-machine gun and fired two bursts into the lock. Debris and fragments of wood and metal exploded outwards as the bullets tore through the locking mechanism. It was all he needed. He pulled the door open and stepped inside just as the two Serbians came into view and started firing. Now he had only minutes before an armed police response unit would appear.

Despite being on one of the upper floors of the tower, there were no scenic views out over Canary Wharf or across to the city. The room was an internal room with no windows. Smart, modern office furniture, plush carpet, designer lighting all spoke of the money controlled from this room. The circular conference table dominated the room, each place at the table was equipped with video and audio conference facilities, and several with recessed keyboards and flat-panel screens. Jason Mason sat at one such station. He watched closely the three windows he had open on his screen. One showed the activities of the firewall servers, the small graphs showing the servers running at maximum capacity handling the onslaught of Internet traffic being thrown at it by the cascade attack. As planned, because the attack came in through the ports he'd left open the system did not trigger any alarms. The Bank of England's Internet defences were dying, and only he knew about it.

Most of the places at the table were now occupied. Conversation was now muted and the room was quiet. Mason looked around. He recognised some of the people—almost all men—some only from their media appearances. Senior officials of the Bank of England. He knew that the Governor of the Bank was on the conference call line from his office in Threadneedle Street.

He looked at one of the other windows open on his screen, a summary of part of the Bank's financial management system. Jason had never really understood much of the detail of the Bank's operations, the financial activities were extremely complex. He'd once asked one of the senior finance analysts to explain some of it, a smart young lady with a PhD in something finance-related, and he hadn't understood a word of it. He knew the basics of today's operation: Quantitative Easing. The Bank simply created money by entering a number into what was essentially a spreadsheet, and there at a stroke another one hundred and fifty billion pounds would have been created. The money would be moved to secure holding accounts in the Bank's finance systems, before being filtered out into the economy via the London financial markets to help boost activity in the economy. He looked at the three key lines, one was the creation account where the money would appear, the second was the secure holding account, and the third was an account that only Mason and his new-found friends knew about.

'Are you okay Mason?' someone asked. 'You look a little weary.' It was one of the senior finance managers, a man whose name he didn't know.

'I'm fine thank you sir, just focusing on the systems.'

He did feel a little spacey. It was a strange sensation. It was almost as if someone was sitting just behind him whispering instructions to him. He looked at the leather diary sitting on the desk in front of him. Looking at it gave him a sense of comfort. He didn't quite know why, but it did. And it was fine that he felt his friend close to him, he would do anything to help his friend, because he knew his friend would do anything to help him. He'd never thought of using another, secret account, but it was obvious that it was a sensible thing to do.

He looked at the account, in his slightly dazed state the numbers seemed to shimmer, if he squinted he could almost make a two become a five, or an eight become a nine.

A change in one of the graphs on his screen caught his eye. He felt a thrill of excitement, the firewall servers had failed. He knew they would now automatically go into their restart sequence, but that would take at least ten minutes for all the servers to restart, run their diagnostic routines, resynchronise and re-establish the firewall.

A voice cut through the quiet of the room. An older man called the meeting to order. He ran through the formal agenda, confirming the names and roles of those present, he confirmed the authenticity of the order from the Governor to complete this exercise in Quantitative Easing, he then went into detail about the various financial instruments the Bank would purchase with the newly created money and that the exercise was in part backed by the previous purchase of additional gold reserves to be held in the Bank's vaults.

'I have to say,' said one of the other finance managers, 'I'm very uncomfortable with recent events.' There was a murmur of agreement from some at the table. 'There was a violent act to try to steal some of the gold, the remainder of the gold has not yet been delivered and I'm not convinced that we can be entirely confident that it will be.'

The Governor's voice came over the secluded loudspeakers around the room, making him sound like he was everywhere in the room. 'I can assure you that the police, MI5 and other services have ensured the safety of the first consignment and will ensure the safety of the remaining consignments. The Chancellor of the Exchequer and the Minister of Defence have given me their assurances that the physical safety of the gold is their highest priority and that they support the completion of today's exercise.'

'And what of the threat of cyber-attack?' the finance manager asked. Mason felt his throat tighten, no-one had expressed any concerns before about that. 'Only recently MI5 hacked our systems.'

Mason felt himself getting very warm as all eyes in the room turned to him. He breathed in, slowly and deeply, forcing himself to take his time replying. Rushing would be a

A Mind To Kill

sign of nervousness, and this was his moment to show his confidence.

'Gentleman,' he said, in his most reassuring voice. 'We had a scheduled exercise with analysts from GCHQ and they did identify a weakness in one of our public facing systems, a weakness which has since been addressed. They are also supporting today's exercise and all our systems are ready and secured.'

He stopped talking. He wanted to add more, he wanted to explain all about the firewalls and the port scanners, but sometimes less is more. There was a silence in the room. He looked from man to man in the room, meeting their stare, not breaking eye contact.

'Very well,' said the finance manager, 'we should proceed.'

Mason had to stop himself letting out an audible sigh. He let his eyes drop to his monitor, the accounts were still as they should be and the firewall servers were still down. He tapped a couple of keys. At his command a pre-programmed signal was sent from one of the Bank's systems, routed through to GCHQ. The Doughnut's firewall recognised the digital signature of the Bank and let the message through. The message was routed deep into the Doughnut's network and found its way to Browning's server. On receipt of the message the server stopped the cascade, and started to delete its own files, removing all evidence of the programs it had been running.

The man chairing the meeting asked each of the senior finance managers for their approval, which they gave, and for them to enter their passwords to the finance system, and each tapped at the keypad in front of them. There was a pause, and Mason saw the creation account now had a balance, he had to count the zeroes carefully, one hundred and fifty billion pounds, one hundred and fifty thousand million pounds. He entered some more commands at his keyboard, and another program became active on another server, somewhere else in the Bank's network. The numbers changed, the creation account became zero and the value moved to the holding account, and the same amount showed also in his own special account. It was a very special account, only he could see that the money existed in the holding account where everyone expected it to be and also in his own special account. Very soon, leaving enough time for the various people present to log out and begin going back to their offices, his special program would transfer the money out of his special account and out of the Bank. He looked at the firewall monitor, the defences were still down, nothing would stop the money being transferred out of the Bank.

THIRTY EIGHT

'That's it,' said Singh, leaning close to look at one of the monitors, 'the firewall's down.'

'How long?' Marshall asked, pacing more quickly round the room.

Singh paused, closed his eyes for a moment. 'They've started the exercise, minutes at the most.'

Marshall let his attention turn to Bullock, he felt his words reach out. 'Secure?' was the question he asked.

'Quiet,' was the sense that came back. Marshall couldn't relax, he didn't trust anything going well, he always expected the worst, and was rarely disappointed, but at least he was ready.

His pacing brought him to behind Singh and Anna, he looked at the monitors showing the feed from the external surveillance cameras. He saw two of the Serbs walking along the side of the building, heading towards the front gate. He was about to continue pacing when he noticed the camera covering the pedestrian turnstile. A car pulled up on the road outside, the driver got out and walked up to the turnstile. Marshall had no concerns about the man getting through, the turnstile would stop an armoured lorry at full speed, but the man seemed to reach out and put something on top of the keycode pad, then calmly turned around, got in the car and drove away.

Anna tapped at the keyboard and one of the screens refreshed, showing the same display as Mason had been viewing.

'They've done it,' said Singh, 'they created the money and it's on its way to our account.'

The screen covering the turnstile went blank as the explosion tore through the turnstile and shrapnel ripped into the front of the building. They heard the explosion as a muffled bang, Marshall and Singh looked at each other and without telepathy shared a single thought: Sanders!

As MICHAEL STEPPED into the building, the Serb's bullets splintered part of the door frame behind him. As he recalled from the plans, he was faced with a door in front of him and a corridor stretching away to his left. He used another burst of machine-gun fire to blast the lock of the door in front. He pulled another grenade from his webbing with his left hand, pulled out the pin with a free finger on his right hand and dropped it back through the door behind him. He pulled open the door in front and stepped through, pulling it closed moments before the grenade exploded. He couldn't be sure if the two Serbs had rushed forwards and had been caught by the grenade or had been more cautious and held back, in which case he may still have two hostiles following him.

He'd stepped into the power room. The room wasn't large and there were four telephone-box sized cabinets of power distribution equipment. The walls were lined with instruments showing the health of the power supply to the building, and large circuit breaker handles gave control over power to different parts of the building. Sometimes a sledgehammer really was the best tool for the job. Another grenade off the webbing, out came the pin, and he placed it on the floor.

Submachine gun at the ready he pushed open the door and stepped back into the corridor. It was filled with smoke, the remains of the outer door was hanging off its hinges. He dashed up the corridor to his right, the power room door swinging closed. The explosion was deafening in the confined space. The door exploded out into the corridor and the blast knocked Michael to the ground. The lights went out, as he'd hoped. It was only a moment before a series of dim white lights came on, the emergency lighting. Bells started ringing and he heard the distinct metallic clicking of the electronic locks being released. The fire alarm system had gone into full emergency mode, detecting multiple fires and loss of power it would use what little power there was to enable the occupants to evacuate.

Michael pushed through the door at the end of the corridor and into the open-plan office area. It was now lit with dim and ghostly lights. No windows, the modern office desks were set out ready for the expected occupants, but no chairs, no computers, just shrink-wrapped containers of ready-to-assemble wall-mounted frames for more monitors and computer equipment. Holding his gun up in front of him, sinking his weight down and creeping forward one slow step at a time, Michael made his way deeper into the office. The space was L shaped, the shorter leg turning right ahead of him. In that space was the door into the data centre's control room, no doubt where Marshall and the others were working. He expected an assault from that direction and another from behind when the Serbs finally caught up with him. This was where the fun would begin.

Marshall sent a thought out to Bullock: 'stop him!' No doubt Bullock would now have let their three Serbian puppets off the leash. Marshall, Bullock and Singh were all focusing the same thought on their three employees: find Sanders and kill him. Finding Sanders wasn't a problem, they could see him clearly on one of the monitors, approaching the external door at the rear of the building. They saw him lift his weapon and fire at the lock. They heard the muffled rattling sound from somewhere behind them as Sanders shot out the lock and they saw him step in.

'We're on him,' was the thought that came from Bullock. Marshall got the message that Bullock was in the loading area, watching the monitors in there. One of the Serbs was with him and was already approaching the door from the loading bay into the power room. Sanders was about to be pincered. They heard the gunfire, louder this time, as Sanders blew apart the lock of the door into the power room. Moments later came the explosion of the second grenade, much louder, even though it was outside it shook the building.

Marshall and Singh were on the move, reaching for the automatic pistols they'd lined up on the desk on the other side of the room. Anna had turned to face them, with the psychic control now ended she was blinking as her conscious awareness returned and she took stock of where she was.

'The money,' ordered Marshall, 'check the money.'

Ignoring Anna, Singh marched to one of the workstations and checked the monitor. 'The money's been moved into the shadow account.'

'Then transfer it out, we're leaving,' snapped Marshall.

Singh tapped again at the keyboard, he frowned and sat down, and tapped some more, checking the figures on the screen.

'What?' demanded Marshall.

'I can't get it, I can't get the money,' said Singh, almost in disbelief.

It was at that moment that Michael's grenade took out the power room, the lights went out and for a moment the control room was bathed in the glow from the monitors until they too flickered and were dark.

'Where is he?' was the psychic message Marshall sent out. He waited. He was distracted a moment later as the emergency lights came on.

'Get those fucking computers on,' he shouted at Singh, who was already checking the computers and cables and keyboards.

'Main office area, they're closing in,' came the silent reply from Bullock's mind.

'Why aren't those computers on?' Marshall demanded.

'Because he blew up the fucking power supply,' shouted Singh in an uncharacteristic burst of temper.

Marshall looked around. 'Where's the girl?'

Anna was not in sight.

One of the screens lit up, Singh worked quickly at the keyboard, Marshall looked around the room, but had to see what Singh was doing.

'I thought these things didn't have power failures?' Marshall said,

'They don't normally, but normally people don't throw grenades into the power room,' said Singh.

The computer came back to life and Singh restarted the program he'd been using.

'Where's that money?' demanded Marshall.

Singh was clicking with the mouse and stabbing hard at the keyboard, as if the computer responded more the harder he hit the keys.

'I can't get the money to move,' he said, desperation creeping into his voice.

'What did she do?' said Marshall, looking around the room again for Anna.

'Not her,' said Singh, 'it was Mason, he's put the money in a shadow account, but it's not our account, I can't access it.'

'Sanders, it has to be, he got to Mason,' hissed Marshall. He turned around and picked up one of the chairs and threw it across the room. As he turned and hurled the chair he saw the door at the far end of the control room gliding shut, the door through to the open-plan office. In the same movement he had his gun in his hand and fired two bursts of two shots. Without hesitating, as soon as Marshall fired Singh also had his gun in hand was firing in support.

MICHAEL CREPT FORWARD through the gloom of the office, edging past the desks and plastic-wrapped aluminium frames. He heard a door ahead of him, he heard the hinges as it swung open, then the slower sound of it closing slowly. The noise of the fire alarm bells was punctuated by gunfire, two bursts of two shots then more gunfire, all small arms. Michael ducked behind the nearest desk. The office furniture was good quality and solid wood, it might stop a round or two, but not a sustained burst. He looked out from behind his cover. He saw no movement so he crept out and shuffled forwards, crouching as low as he could.

Something moved behind a desk ahead of him. He stood up and marched forwards, gun held up and in front ready to fire. He rounded the corner of a desk and found his target, his finger squeezed the trigger.

He saw Anna cowering behind the desk, hands over her face, shaking.

Michael lowered the gun and held out his hand.

'Anna,' he hissed, 'Anna, it's me, Michael, we need to go.'

Michael flicked his eyes between her and the door. Frightened as she maybe, any moment they were likely to be joined by very unfriendly people. Anna looked out from behind her hands. She looked closely, trying to see past the goggles.

'Anna, quickly, we have to go,' he hissed again. She started to hold out her hand towards him. He took it and hauled her into a standing position.

'Are you hurt? Can you walk?' he asked.

'Yes, but...' He cut her off, there was no time for conversation.

'Stay down and stay behind me,' he said. He started to move them forwards, towards the door further along from where Anna had come in, to the door that led out into the entrance foyer. Michael was hoping the owners hadn't changed any of the interior layout since GCHQ had acquired the designs. He'd barely taken a step when the door ahead of them burst open. Michael pushed back against Anna's weight, forcing her to retreat. He fired quick bursts, straight ahead. As he'd hoped, Anna ducked to the floor as soon as the gunfire started. They now had no choice but to retreat back the way Michael had come in.

'This way,' he said to her, trying to keep his voice down but maintain a friendly tone. He turned to shuffle towards the door by which he'd entered, making sure that Anna was keeping up behind him, knowing that any minute whoever had been about to enter the room would try again and probably come in shooting.

Michael heard the door he'd shot out, now behind them, open and someone pushed in, past the desks. No sooner were they through than they started shooting, spraying machine-gun fire in a wide arc, no attempt to aim, simply to force everyone under cover. Michael pushed Anna behind the nearest stack of aluminium shelving and he crouched behind a desk, gun levelled on the desk pointing at the end of the office. He fired another few bursts, hopefully to keep whoever (one or more of the Serbs no doubt) hesitating and not rushing in.

He was about to turn to their route of escape when that door opened and the two Serbs pushed their way in, one behind the other. This was getting out of control; as if it had ever been under control. Michael had the briefest of thoughts about using a grenade, but in such a confined space it would probably kill all of them. He sprayed gun fire in the direction of the two then another spray of fire towards the other end of the office, then ducked down under cover. Any moment he'd need to replace the clip in the gun. The Heckler & Koch submachine gun had thirty rounds in each clip, Michael estimated he'd used maybe twenty-five, but right now he didn't want to be caught with the clip out. He waited, it now seemed just a little too long since someone had last fired. The Serbs were trained soldiers, they would have no problem, and no fear about storming into the room, and were quite capable of killing both he and Anna without killing each other.

He popped his head up to look. The doors were shut again, debris dust and wood splinters were all floating back to the ground and a haze of gun smoke hung in the air.

'Have they gone?' asked Anna, sounding like she was trying to keep quiet despite being half deafened by the gunfire in the enclosed space.

'Yes,' mused Michael, 'but why?'

'Why? Does it matter?' she said.

'Yes, it does, I don't want them to escape.'

'Well, can't you go and stop them?' she asked.

He looked at her. She got the message that the question wasn't the most sensible.

Michael had suspected the Three had vehicles here, at least two, and since there hadn't been any vehicles in the car park they must be inside the building, and the only space they could be was in the loading bay, on the other side of the building.

'Come on,' he said, taking Anna's hand before she could refuse, 'we're going to stop them.'

'What? I was joking,' she protested.

He walked carefully towards the door at the front of the office, gun in right hand, pulling Anna along by the left.

'Could you please tell me what's going on?' Anna demanded. 'What did they do to me?' She was obviously starting to think more about recent events and remembering that she'd helped them without knowing why.

'Sorry, no time, not just now,' Michael said. He moved more quickly, reaching the door. He let go of Anna's hand and reached out to pull the door open.

He peered around the corner of the door into the entrance foyer. No furniture, just the building's front door to the left and to the right another door leading to a corridor down to the loading bay. He pulled open the door to the corridor. He had a clear line of sight down to the door at the far end. There was no-one in the corridor.

Michael had considered the possibility of booby traps, but this was the one place Marshall and the others needed to be able to move around freely, it was not somewhere they had planned on having to defend. Michael thought it would have been sensible to proceed down the corridor inch by inch, checking for booby traps, but they didn't have time. He couldn't be sure that his creative additions to Jason Mason's mental programming had derailed Singh's plan to transfer the money out of the Bank of England. For that and many other reasons he was keen that he stop Marshall and friends from leaving.

Keeping the gun up in front of him Michael moved as quickly as he dared down the corridor, checking occasionally that Anna was still behind him. The loss of power should have jammed the roller shutters to the loading bay, but he had a feeling that Marshall or Bullock or Singh would have made sure that their escape route was guaranteed. His worst fears were confirmed as he pushed open the door into the loading bay just in time to see the tail end of the second Land Rover disappearing out of the door.

He looked across to the door, a heavy-duty lorry battery had been wired into the power circuit for the door motors. He pushed his finger into his ear again.

The BMW X5 remained. Michael pulled open the driver's door. No keys. He checked behind the sun-visor, no luck. There was no time to look around in case they'd been kind enough to leave the keys, which they probably hadn't.

'Eric, they're on the move, come and get us.' He turned to Anna, 'come on, we're leaving.' He pulled her by the hand and they ran out of the wide and high door of the loading bay. The sounds of multiple sirens could be heard approaching from a distance. At the end of the car park the Land Rovers had turned left towards the main road, and now the anti-attack barriers were rising up out of the road and heavy gates were sliding shut. Michael ran hard, dragging Anna, who managed to keep up with him. The barriers weren't a problem, they would stop vehicles not people, but the gates would seal them in if they didn't get through. As the gate slid shut they made it through and out onto the road.

Only moments later the grey Audi approached at speed from the right. Michael pulled open the door.

'You'll be safer here with the police,' he said. He got in and the car roared away in pursuit of the two black Land Rovers, leaving Anna staring after them.

THIRTY NINE

Eric put his foot down and the Audi took off, blue lights flashing from behind the front grill, sirens blaring. Michael could see in the wing mirror Anna standing by the side of the road, shaking a fist at him. They quickly reached the junction with the main road. The second Land Rover was to their left, just disappearing into a side road. Eric pulled straight out into the traffic, prompting a couple of drivers to blare their horns and flash their lights. A couple of hundred yards along Eric turned sharp right into the side road, cutting across more traffic and prompting more horns and lights and this time fists and raised middle fingers. London drivers, at least in Croydon, didn't seem to appreciate the urgency the blue lights and sirens were supposed to communicate.

As they swung into the side road Michael caught sight of more blue lights approaching from either direction along the main road, armed police units, tactical units, dog units, all heading for the data centre.

'Here comes the cavalry,' said Michael, 'always coming over the hill, late as usual.'

'Pity it's usually the wrong hill,' said Eric.

The two Land Rovers had a head start on them, but not by much, and they roared along the residential street at an increasing pace. Michael was only too well aware that at any moment a child could step out, not expecting vehicles at this speed, and he doubted Marshall or any of others would stop, or even swerve. Michael wondered of all the police units, where was the helicopter? The airborne unit was the one distinct advantage they had over the Three.

'I have no idea where they're heading,' said Eric, 'there's nothing strategic around here.'

Michael had wondered about this. 'I can only think they've got a helicopter standing by somewhere.' It was the only escape route he could think of that made sense. A helicopter to a local airfield, a light aircraft out of England and across to mainland Europe, and then disappear.

'You did tell Halbern what was happening, didn't you?' Michael asked, as if he needed to.

Eric gave him "a look". 'Of course, he said he'd try and alert the Head, but he didn't promise anything.'

Michael tried dialling Halbern from his mobile. It rang and rang, no answer, not even voicemail. He pressed the key hard to end the call, then tried the Head's number. Same, no answer.

Before they could speculate further the Land Rovers had reached the end of the housing estate, they dog-legged and set off along a straight road lined with small office and industrial units. Their speed increased, Eric kept pace.

Michael strained to listen, he heard another siren. He turned to Eric. 'They've got sirens on those vehicles,' he said.

Eric replied, 'that's cheating.'

Over the roar of the engine and the tyres and the sirens, Michael was sure he heard a helicopter. He looked up, through the windscreen then out of the side windows, he was sure he could hear it but he couldn't see it.

'This is very wrong,' said Eric, 'this road really goes nowhere special.' Michael knew that while he'd been in the data centre entertaining himself with the Serbs and with Marshall and friends, Eric would have taken some time to use the car's sat' nav' to familiarise himself with the local roads and major features. He looked at the animated map on the car's centre console, it showed them on Beddington Lane, a long straight road, which came to an end no more than a mile ahead.

'They have a plan, they always have a plan,' said Michael. He just wished he had a clue what that plan might be.

Ahead and to the left, Michael could see the low, circular shapes of the sewage treatment works, and beyond that a big concrete building. Plain, featureless, sand coloured, it seemed to be a concrete block dropped in the middle of undeveloped land.

'What's that?' Michael asked, he pointed towards the concrete building.

'Not sure,' said Eric, obviously not familiar with every feature in the area.

They flashed past a hand-painted sign advertising someone's quad-biking experience somewhere to the left. Brake lights flared ahead as the Land Rovers slowed suddenly, and then dived left down a dirt track, heading towards the concrete building. As they raced past the entrance, Michael caught a brief glimpse of a sign saying something about a new waste centre and incinerator. The building looked only half-finished, and there was no construction work, no builders, perhaps someone had run out of money. Whatever the place was, it was becoming obvious this was the destination of the two black vehicles ahead.

It took less than half a minute to reach the building. In what looked like the front where two gaping entrance ways, looking more like gigantic mouths. Kicking up a cloud of dust behind them the Land Rovers didn't slow as they raced straight into the mouth and were gone from sight.

Eric braked hard, dust billowing up around the car. They were barely a couple of hundred yards from the entrance to the building, out in the open with no cover. There was a blast of sound, the unmistakable sound of a helicopter, and the dust suddenly swirled around them, so much dust it obscured all vision.

As the dust settled, they could see the darkness inside the concrete structure. The helicopter couldn't be seen, but it could be heard, its sound muffled, obscured but obviously somewhere close. Eric switched off the sirens and the lights. The car's engine purred.

'That's not a police helicopter,' said Eric.

'No, it's not, and I'm worried that they just got reinforcements,' said Michael.

'Whichever way you cut it, this doesn't look good,' said Eric.

'I'm inclined to agree,' said Michael.

'That's disappointing.'

'Why?' asked Michael.

Eric half smiled at him, 'I was rather hoping you were going to disagree and say you had a cunning plan and actually the odds were very much in our favour.'

'Ah, sorry,' was all Michael could manage.

Michael opened the door and stepped out of car, holding his submachine gun in front of him. Eric stepped out, pistol in hand. It seemed woefully little compared to the fire-power the six professional soldiers were likely to have with them in their vehicles.

'Is fortune still favouring the bold?' asked Eric.

'Only one way to find out,' said Michael.

They started to move forward, step by step, weapons raised. There were no sounds of approaching sirens, no indication that support was coming. Halbern and the police had obviously decided that the data centre was where they needed to focus their efforts, and the Head had fallen hook, line and sinker for the yarn about the Heathrow gold shipment being the Three's next target.

As they moved closer Michael and Eric could start to make out features inside the building. Scaffolding towers inside suggested construction work inside was as incomplete as it was outside. There were no lights inside, and no sign yet of the two vehicles.

The sound of the gunfire was deafening, amplified by the cavernous space inside the building, Michael and Eric instinctively threw themselves to the ground, straining to keep their weapons aimed in front of them and their eyes trained on the building. Continuous volleys from multiple sub-machine guns echoed from inside the building. Whoever was firing was inside the building, and whoever they were firing at were also inside.

The firing stopped as suddenly as it had started, and the comparative quiet was unnerving, the only sound again the muffled beating of the helicopter, most likely landed on the far side of the building.

They waited. And waited. There was no movement from within the building.

The helicopter must have been low to the ground because from their vantage point, lying in the dust, they couldn't see the aircraft. The sound of its engine rose in tone and volume, the distinct sound of the aircraft taking off. The sound faded and was soon gone, and a troubling quiet fell over the landscape.

Michael and Eric both kept looking ahead at the opening of the building, not sure what they should expect. Almost in unison they got up, weapons still held out ahead of them.

If Marshall and the others were to come out shooting then Michael and Eric would have no protection, no cover to hide behind. Step by slow step they moved forwards until they could just see the two Land Rovers, stationary, deep inside the building. Michael could start to make out some of the building's internal structure. A high concrete wall separated the internal space in two. The vehicles were in the space to the left, parked between the left wall of the building and piles of construction materials. No sound came, the engines were switched off. Each vehicle's front doors were open. There was no movement.

Eric exchanged a quick glance with Michael. They'd come this far, they had to see this through. Picking up speed a little they walked forwards into the vast space of the building. It was almost cathedral-like in its size and the way their footsteps echoed. The concrete floor was dusty, and their footsteps crunched loudly. The air around the vehicles was heavy with gun smoke and the floor was littered with spent casings.

As they approached the vehicles they saw the reason for the lack of movement. Each vehicle was riddled with dozens of bullet holes. Glass and metal fragments littered the floor around the vehicles. Whoever had been firing had poured hundreds of rounds of machine-gun fire into the two vehicles. As Michael's eyes adjusted to the gloomy light, he could start to make out wisps of smoke rising from the engine of each vehicle.

They each kept scanning the space around them, whoever had been shooting was almost certainly still here, and the building offered numerous hiding places; mezzanine levels of scaffolding, maintenance gangways suspended from the ceiling, workspaces in the walls. Michael and Eric approached to within a few feet of the vehicles. It was obvious there were bodies sitting in the vehicles.

Michael raised his left hand slightly, and made a sharp cutting action, gesturing forwards. At this signal they both strode forwards quickly, Michael approaching the vehicle on the left, Eric the vehicle on the right. They marched up to the driver's side door on each vehicle and looked inside.

The volley of gunfire had reduced the bodies in the car to an

A Mind To Kill

almost unrecognisable mess. Almost, but not quite. Michael stared at the driver and passenger in the vehicle, the bodies were unmistakably those of Dulic and Petric.

Michael leaned closer to look at the rear seats of the vehicle; empty.

'I've got two dead Serbs here,' said Michael.

'One here, a full set,' said Eric.

'Looks like Marshall and friends used these three as a decoy,' said Michael.

'But where did they go?' Eric asked. 'I assume you didn't leave them in the data centre.'

'Nope, but if they were hiding there the armed police would have them surrounded.'

Whatever had happened, it was plain that the three Serbs, three loose ends, had been taken care of. No doubt Marshall, Bullock and Singh had used their psychic control over the three men to direct them to drive to this location. That only left one rather troubling question.

Michael voiced the question. 'So who did all the shooting?'

Eric answered it. 'I think they did.'

Michael looked up. On the other side of the vehicle from Eric was a man dressed like Michael; black combat fatigues, black gloves, black balaclava obscuring his face, sub-machine gun raised and pointed at Eric. Michael had no doubt that there were similar soldiers somewhere behind him. The solider in front of Eric emerged from the darkness and approached slowly, moving round the front of the SUV, keeping both Eric and Michael in his clear line of sight.

'You,' said the soldier, gesturing to Eric, 'on the ground, now.'

Eric, on the other side of the vehicle from Michael, slowly lowered himself to the ground, disappearing from view.

'Put the weapon down and step back two paces,' came a voice from behind Michael.

Michael lay his firearm on the bonnet of the vehicle, let go of it, and took two slow steps backwards.

'Turn around,' came the voice behind.

Michael turned around. He was facing another man dressed in black, an automatic pistol in hand, pointed at Michael. The man was slightly to one side. The positioning was clear, the man and his colleague could shoot Michael and Eric without firing at each other.

The man raised his free hand to his head, and touched his ear, obviously activating his comm's ear-piece.

'We have Sanders,' the man said. There was a pause as he listened to the response.

'Confirmed, the three Serbians are dead,' said the man in black.

Another pause. 'Negative,' he said. Michael surmised he'd been asked if there was any information of the whereabouts of Marshall, Singh and Bullock.

'Shoot or release?' the man asked of whoever was on the other end of the comm' link. For a moment Michael wondered if it was the Head.

There was another pause, which seemed to Michael to stretch out almost without end. The face of the man in front of him showed no expression, no flicker of movement to indicate what response he had been given. Michael had the thought that death could be one word away.

Without a word Michael watched as the man in front of him started to move to the side, towards the front of the building. As he turned to watch him, he could see out of the corner of his eye the man covering Eric was also retreating. He became aware of another man emerging from the shadows, and then a fourth became apparent, probably from somewhere behind the tower of stacked scaffolding pieces.

A new noise intruded on the scene. The sound of the helicopter. It grew loud and fierce and the helicopter swung into view in front of the building. Instantly its down-draft kicked up a storm of sand. Michael had to shield his eyes from the dust and he could just make out the four shadowy figures backing into the swirling dust.

Moments later the engines of the helicopter rose in pitch as it lifted into the air. The aircraft turned and disappeared from view and it sound was soon gone.

Eric spoke, with a distinct note of anger in his voice. 'I know a lot of this shit is on a "need to know" basis, but I think some bastard sticking a gun in my face qualifies as a "need" to know.'

Michael looked at him. He knew Eric had earned the right to know what was going on, but that wasn't how things worked.

'Sorry,' Michael said, 'not my decision.' He was sure he heard Eric utter "bastard" under his breath.

FORTY

As they drove back to the data centre Eric approached the police cordon with the Audi's blue lights flashing, it sometimes helped establish some credibility. They had made time for Michael to change out of his combat fatigues, he was dressed again like any other civilian. He wasn't sure how much challenge they'd face from the police. Eric stayed with the car, content to let Michael deal with the more difficult conversations.

Michael showed his ID badge to the uniform standing behind the line of blue and white "crime scene" tape, he flashed the badge just long enough for the young woman to see it was official-looking, but not long enough to actually read the name.

'Mister Smith from Thames House, I need to speak to Commander Halbern,' Michael said.

Without hesitating, or making any attempt to record Michael's name on the register of persons entering the crime scene, she lifted up the tape to allow Michael in.

'I think he's expecting you,' she said. Michael wasn't sure that was a good thing.

There was a fleet of various police and other emergency

service vehicles parked at angles in the road outside the data centre. White suited forensics teams mingled with black combat-ready armed response officers with automatic sub-machine guns slung across their chests. He could see Anna sitting in the back of an ambulance, cradling a cup, probably very sweet tea to counteract the shock she was no doubt experiencing.

Michael became aware of a man marching towards him. It was Halbern, with a look of anger on his face.

'I very much hope you can report that all this was worth it,' demanded Halbern, 'did you get them? Are they all "taken care of?"'

Michael made an effort to keep his cool. This wasn't the time to pick a fight. 'I can tell you that three Serbian mercenaries were killed by persons as yet unidentified.'

Halbern hadn't expected this, and wasn't sure how to respond.

Michael nodded towards the data centre. 'Any sign of Marshall and the others?'

'You must have run right over them,' said Halbern.

Michael frowned. 'I don't follow,' he said.

Halbern obviously took some pleasure in pointing out Michael's oversight.

'They'd tunnelled down from the loading bay into a service tunnel, they ran away like rats down a sewer.'

Michael realised the opening to their shaft must have been under the BMW. They must have had a vehicle waiting close to wherever the service tunnel emerged, and from there they would have controlled their three pet mercenaries. Had they known there were armed soldiers waiting at the incinerator? Or had their plan been to have the Serbians kill Michael and Eric in a firefight?

'We will still need a statement from you,' Halbern said, 'a

much longer statement now, there's a lot of damage that needs accounting for.'

Halbern walked away. Michael was about to go and see Anna when his ear was caught by the ringtone of his mobile phone. He pulled it out of his pocket and answered. It was the Head.

'So you decided not to have me shot?' said Michael, straining to keep the anger out of his voice.

'I did wonder if you'd think it was me that sent them after you,' said the Head. Michael had to admit, to himself, he'd never been sure.

'Then who did call them off?'

'There are some at a very senior level who have always held the view that the graduates of the PsiClone project should be got rid of.' At least the Head never used those lame euphemisms, like "retired" or "cancelled". 'I can't stop them issuing their own orders, I could make the case that you are still a valuable asset and as long as there's no suspicion you're with them then you're still a useful weapon against them.'

'And if it had been Marshall and the others in those vehicles?'

'I'm just glad it wasn't, Sanders.'

Michael said nothing, he let the silence linger.

'You came close,' she finally said, 'you did at least stop them getting the money. The Governor of the Bank has confirmed that one of his IT managers has been taken into custody for attempted fraud and theft.'

'He wasn't responsible,' said Michael. Mason had been a puppet, like so many, just used and discarded, but at least he was still alive.

'I don't think either of us can go to the police and plead psychic control as a mitigating factor,' said the Head.

Again Michael said nothing. The thought of Jason Mason

being prosecuted for aiding an attempted theft of over one hundred billion pounds left a bad taste.

'I argued that we should take you back because you were our only realistic prospect of finding and stopping Marshall and the others,' said the Head, 'I still believe that is the case.'

'I can't do it alone,' said Michael, 'this time we didn't find them, they found us, and we came too close to not stopping them, with too many casualties.'

'What do you suggest?'

'I need a team and I need dedicated resources,' said Michael.

'No team, we can't share the detail of the PsiClone project,' said the Head, in her usual firm manner, calculated to close the discussion.

Michael turned around and saw Eric standing, chatting to the uniformed officer at the tape barrier. He turned back to look at Anna sitting in the ambulance.

'I think the Three have already caused some detail to be shared. I can't do this alone, not one against Three. I need some specialist support for this.'

He thought he heard the Head take an intake of breath.

'Very well. Keep your team as small as possible, I'll arrange for specialist resources to be made available. Any idea who you'll recruit?'

'Not yet, but I'm sure I'll think of someone,' said Michael, smiling.

'Do it quickly,' said the Head, 'they'll be back and they'll be angry, you'll need to be ready.'

'I don't intend to wait for them, I'll be going after them.' Michael pressed the key to end the call.

IT TOOK Anna slightly by surprise when Michael sat down next to her in the ambulance. She'd been lost in thought and hadn't even been aware of him climbing in.

'I can imagine you have a lot of questions, and probably a lot of confusion,' he said.

'Yes,' was about all she could manage to say.

'Soon,' he said, 'you need to get over the shock first, but then we'll have a talk and I'll fill you in on certain facts.'

'They've offered me counselling,' she said, almost as though she was afraid of the idea.

'Standard procedure, but don't worry, they can't force you to have counselling.'

She breathed a little sigh of relief.

'A little word of wisdom, if you're up for it,' he said.

'Sure,' she said, managing a weak smile.

'The counselling will help. Take it. I will.'

Anna gave no reply. Michael thought he actually had no idea how he'd explain the psychic control she'd been under, or what he would need to do to make sure the link was broken and she was under no further risk of being influenced. However he'd explain it, it wasn't a job for today.

He stepped out of the ambulance.

'Did they get away?' Anna said.

Michael turned back to face her. 'Yes,' he said, 'they did, but they got away empty-handed.'

'Will they come back?' she asked, and the fear in her voice was unmistakable.

'Yes, almost certainly.' Michael had thought for a moment about saying something reassuring, like "no, of course not, don't worry." But it would be a lie, a cruel lie.

'Can you stop them?'

'Yes,' he said with more confidence than he felt. 'But there are things I need to do first.'

'What do you need to do?'

'I need to go and see Gerald Crossley's widow. I need to explain to her that her husband was a good man, that he wasn't a terrorist, that he was victimised and murdered and that he hadn't done anything to deserve it.'

'And then?' Anna sounded like she wanted to hear an action plan, something that would convince her that steps were being taken to keep her safe.

'After that, I need to sit down with you and with Eric, and I need to tell you a story.'

To be continued in ...

Force Of Mind

FORCE OF MIND

The second book in the Psiclone series. The Three have escaped, and their anger at Michael Sanders for thwarting their plans is colossal. Now, they have to find a new way to get what they really came back for. Murder and kidnap are the tools of their trade, and the body count rises.

Sanders must find them, quickly, but he must also maintain the secret of the Psiclone project. Racing against the clock and battling those in MI5 who would isolate him, he follows leads into the shadowy world of the forces behind the Psiclone project. But time is running out to defeat the Three before they can become too powerful ever to be stopped.

To find out more, go to:

www.simonstanton.com

A NOTE FROM THE AUTHOR

Can I ask a favour?

Recommendations and reviews are gold-dust for authors, it's how new readers get to hear of our work. If you've enjoyed this book it would be great if you recommend it to friends and family, or just tell them about it. Even if they don't read this kind of story the more people know about an author the more the word spreads.

Similarly, if you can leave a review on sites such as Amazon this will help new readers decide if this is a book for them.

Michael Sanders' journey is far from over. You can find out more about the Psiclone series, and about my short stories and future novels on my website.

Thank you,

Simon Stanton

ABOUT SIMON STANTON

Simon Stanton

Simon Stanton fell in love with stories at an early age, reading and writing science fiction. Despite the best efforts of parents and teachers to broaden his horizons, Simon remained obsessed with sci-fi. Teaching himself to touch-type so he could get his thoughts on paper quicker, Simon wrote shorts stories, ideas for bigger works, and finally his first novel length work - a piece which remains safely locked away. Then he stopped writing, and after a thirty year hiatus (which not even he can adequately explain) he began writing again, first short stories and then his first novel, A Mind To Kill. The first book in The Psiclone Series was followed by Force Of Mind, then The Psiclone Project, Power In Mind, and finally Final Mind.

Simon lives in West Yorkshire, UK, and balances his writing with home life, a job in project management, and his practise of Aikido (a Japanese martial art).

To find out more about Simon and the Psiclone novels (but, to be fair, not much about Yorkshire), visit his website at:

About Simon Stanton

www.simonstanton.com

or on Facebook at:

www.facebook.com/simonstantonwriter

Printed in Great Britain
by Amazon